EMERALD COAST

Also by Anita Hughes

White Sand, Blue Sea
Christmas in Paris
Santorini Sunsets
Island in the Sea
Rome in Love
French Coast
Lake Como
Market Street
Monarch Beach

EMERALD
COAST

ANITA HUGHES

St. Martin's Griffin ❧ New York

EMERALD COAST. Copyright © 2017 by Anita Hughes. All rights reserved. Printed in the United States of America. For information, address St. Martin's Press, 175 Fifth Avenue, New York, N.Y. 10010.

www.stmartins.com

The Library of Congress Cataloging-in-Publication Data is available upon request.

ISBN 978-1-250-13087-7 (trade paperback)
ISBN 978-1-250-13088-4 (ebook)

Our books may be purchased in bulk for promotional, educational, or business use. Please contact your local bookseller or the Macmillan Corporate and Premium Sales Department at 1-800-221-7945, extension 5442, or by email at MacmillanSpecialMarkets@macmillan.com.

First Edition: August 2017

10 9 8 7 6 5 4 3 2 1

To my mother

EMERALD COAST

Chapter One

LILY PRESSED HER FACE AGAINST the glass and saw the white sand beach and azure Mediterranean, and La Maddalena Archipelago in the distance. The Porto Cervo marina was lined with gleaming yachts, and above her, Sardinia's green hills were dotted with myrtle bushes and juniper trees.

The taxi pulled up in front of Hotel Cervo, and Lily poked her head out the window. It was like an impossibly glamorous movie set, with men wearing dark sunglasses and pastel colored shirts and women draped in caftans and gold jewelry. She half expected James Bond to appear and ask her to climb into his sports car or take a ride on his Jet Ski.

The driver pointed to the fare box, and Lily opened her purse. She rummaged through her lipsticks and had a sinking feeling. She couldn't have misplaced her credit cards. They must be buried under the paperback book she bought for the plane or the extra pair of stockings rolled up in the side compartment.

The driver tapped impatiently on the dashboard, and Lily's stomach turned. Perhaps she'd left the credit cards on the metal counter when she went through customs. The customs officer had been so intimidating, tossing her underwear in the air. Lily had been tempted to leave her ivory slip behind and rush to the exit.

She picked up the phone to call Oliver and then put it down. Oliver had moved out of their restored Connecticut farmhouse six months ago. She could hardly ask his advice as if she were wondering if he could refill the espresso maker or see if they were out of chocolate croissants.

Anyway, she was a successful thirty-two-year-old business-woman with home furnishing stores on three continents. She didn't need her ex-husband to help her pay the taxi driver. She fiddled with her leather pump, the way she did when she was nervous. The sole was lumpy, and she peeled it back curiously. She felt a sharp edge, and a smile crossed her face. A Visa card was taped inside!

She hadn't worn the pumps in months; Oliver must have taped it inside her shoe. She was notoriously absentminded when she traveled. Oliver insisted the only way to guarantee she didn't get stranded at Heathrow Airport or the train station in Paris was to hide a credit card where she couldn't forget it.

Now she peered at the hotel's stucco walls and Moorish patio and wondered if she should be in Sardinia at all. She had only signed the divorce papers a week ago. All the magazines said she should be tucked under a down comforter with a stack of novels and a box of tissues.

And how could she leave Louisa? Louisa was six years old; surely she needed her mother. But Louisa was used to Lily being away. Lily often went on buying trips to discover a set of Chinese end tables or one perfect French armoire.

Lily's parents were staying on the farm for a week, and Louisa adored being with her grandparents. Lily pictured them picking apples and baking sugar cookies and had to smile. Louisa was in heaven and wouldn't miss her at all.

And she had been looking forward to this trip for months! In six days, her newest store, Lily Bristol Sardinia, was having its grand opening, and she had to be there. A silver cocktail dress was carefully folded in her suitcase, and she'd bought a new sequined evening bag.

The valet opened the car door, and Lily stepped onto the pavement. The breeze lifted her skirt, and a man whistled. Lily opened her mouth and then closed it. Why shouldn't a man whistle? She had to start thinking differently; she was a young divorcée on one of the sexiest coastlines in the world. She shot him a brilliant smile and strode into the lobby.

"Oh, it is gorgeous," Lily breathed, setting her purse on the ground.

The white marble floors were scattered with blue love seats. Floor-to-ceiling windows looked out on the harbor, and it was as if she had entered an underwater cave. The wood shutters were blue, and the tiles behind the concierge desk were blue, and the abstract paintings on the walls were splashed with turquoise and gold. And the people! Women with metallic sandals and dangling earrings, and arms and legs the color of pennies. The men had cheekbones you only saw in magazines, and skin like honey.

"Hello, I'm Lily Bristol." Lily approached the front desk. "I have a reservation."

"Of course, Mrs. Bristol," a man in a gold uniform greeted her. "Welcome to Sardinia's Emerald Coast. I trust you had a pleasant trip?"

Lily flashed on her credit cards that were probably sitting in a bin at Olbia Airport and reminded herself to cancel them and order new ones.

"Yes, thank you. It was an eleven-hour flight, and I'm terribly thirsty." She nodded. "I would do anything for a bath and a glass of orange juice."

"Enzo, your butler, will escort you to your suite. He just started his shift, he'll be here in a minute." He consulted his computer. "You have the finest accommodation, with a private terrace and a view of the marina."

"I don't need a butler." Lily shook her head. "I have a daughter and I'm used to putting things away. All I want is a soft bed and perhaps a piece of fruit."

"Enzo will only do what you ask." The man rang a silver bell and smiled. "You are our guest. We want everything about your stay to be perfect."

Enzo opened the door of the suite and Lily walked straight to the terrace. The lush grounds were filled with lime trees and beds of daisies. Fishing boats bobbed in the harbor, and speedboats scudded over the waves. And the air! It was balmy and sweet and smelled like the most exotic perfume.

She turned back inside and glanced at the rounded walls and sea foam sofa and window seat scattered with silk cushions. There was a coffee table set with a ceramic fruit bowl and a pitcher of iced water.

"My daughter would love this suite. She would line all her dolls on that sofa and serve them lemonade and cookies," she said to Enzo. "Do you have children?"

"Two girls." Enzo nodded, setting her suitcase on the tile floor. "Maria is five and Gia is seven."

"Louisa is six. It's a wonderful age." Lily slipped off her pumps. "One minute they're curled up in your lap, reading *Anne of Green Gables*, the next they're commenting on your shade of lipstick." She paused. "That's the thing you don't realize you'll miss in a divorce. It's not the romantic dinners or the fact that there's someone else who knows your health insurance information, it's not having someone to talk to about your child.

"But we both tried to make it work. I've never tried so hard at anything since I played water polo in high school. No matter how much I practiced, every time I spiked the ball I felt like I might drown." She peered into the bedroom.

"We're going to have one of those terribly civilized divorces, where you spend holidays together and comment 'how well you look' and 'being single must agree with you,'" she continued. "Louisa is going to have the undivided attention of each parent, and we're both free to be happy. It is important to be happy, isn't it? I mean, that's what we teach our children. How can they learn from us, if we don't show them how to do it?"

"I'm sure your daughter will be very happy," Enzo offered.

"I'm behaving like a guest on an afternoon talk show." Lily laughed. "It must be the dark coffee I drank at the airport. I've never tasted anything so strong. No wonder Sardinians swim in the ocean all day and dance at clubs at night.

"I'm not going to talk about my divorce anymore. You'll help me, won't you? If I mention divorce, you can give me a terse look; like when I was sixteen and borrowed my mother's Mercedes without asking her."

"That's not exactly my place." Enzo fiddled with is bow tie. "I make sure the water pitchers are full and you have fresh flowers and warm towels."

"It would be so helpful," Lily urged. "I'm not even going to think about divorce. I'm going to watch the yacht races at the Yacht Club and listen to music in the *piazzetta* and eat suckling pig and fish stew." She paused. "God, I'm starving! I haven't eaten anything since somewhere over Greenland. I'd give anything for some bread and cheese."

"Of course." Enzo beamed. "I will bring it right away."

"I'm going to take a shower and put on something cool and pretty." She stopped, and a smile lit up her face. "Thank you, Enzo. Having a private butler might be just what I need after all. I feel better already."

Lily turned on the faucet and stepped under the hot water. The bathroom was gorgeous, with a mosaic ceiling and a tile counter lined with luxurious lotions. She rinsed her hair and noticed a man's razor near the sink. She looked more closely and saw a jar of shaving cream and a leather case.

Perhaps the previous guest had forgotten his toiletries. It was so easy to leave things behind when you traveled. She had lost so many things: a bottle opener in a field in Tuscany where she and Oliver had a picnic, a raincoat in Brussels because the sun finally came out and she was so thrilled she tossed it on a bench and forgot it.

But Hotel Cervo was a five-star hotel. Surely the maids would have given the items to the front desk. She noticed a navy robe flung over the towel rack and pair of men's slippers nestled on the bath mat.

What if she was in the wrong suite, and a German banker burst in while she was shampooing her hair? She turned off the shower and pulled on a cotton robe. She padded into the hallway to search for Enzo, and the door closed behind her. She turned the doorknob and gasped. She had locked herself out and would have to go down to the lobby with bare feet and a towel wrapped around her head.

"Mrs. Bristol," the front desk manager said when she approached the desk. "Did something happen to your luggage? I'll send Enzo to the gift shop to pick out a blouse and skirt."

"I'm afraid I'm in the wrong suite," she explained, pulling the robe around her waist. "There was a man's shaving kit on the sink, and a silk robe hanging on the towel rack."

"How strange, Mr. Bristol didn't mention anything was amiss. He checked in three hours ago. He specifically requested a suite with a private terrace." He showed her a registration card. "If it is not to your satisfaction, Enzo can bring extra pillows for the bed or replace the lotions in the bathroom."

"What did you say?" Lily gasped.

She leaned forward and glanced at Oliver's wavy signature on the ivory card. The lobby started spinning, and she clutched the marble counter,

"Are you all right?" he inquired. "Perhaps you should sit down."

"It must be the jet lag," Lily replied. "If I could have a glass of water, I'll be fine."

Lily's heart raced, and she tried to think. Oliver had made the reservation months ago when they still thought their marriage could be saved by romantic dinners and trips to exotic destinations. And the dates were perfect! Lily's new store was opening in Sardinia the first week of August, and Oliver had been asked to review the grand opening of Nero's, Porto Cervo's hottest new restaurant.

They had imagined lounging beside the infinity pool and swimming at the private beach and lingering over plates of scallops and tiramisu. They would rent a car and drive along the coast, and their tension would drift away like bark at high tide.

How could she not have known Oliver planned on using the reservation? But that was the thing about divorce. You went from being two people who stayed awake all night shelling pistachios and discussing the latest episode of *Homeland*, to strangers who stood silently on the front porch while Louisa tied her tennis shoes.

Lily had been in the attorney's office the week before. She was flipping through a copy of *Architectural Digest*, when she looked up and noticed a man with dark curly hair and freshly shaved cheeks. He wore jeans and a blue blazer.

"Oliver!" she exclaimed. "What are you doing here?"

Thank goodness she always dressed up when she took the train into Manhattan. Her white linen dress was paired with a navy tote. Her dark hair fell smoothly to her shoulders, and she wore Tory Burch sandals.

"You look well," he said. "That color agrees with you."

"It's white." She glanced down at her skirt. "It looks good on anyone."

"I suppose you're right." He nodded, as if remembering where he was. "I'm doing the same thing you're doing. I'm signing our divorce papers."

Lily flushed and recalled when they had separated and agreed to use the same attorney. Why should they fund two attorneys' tastes in Italian shoes and French wines, when they agreed on everything? Lily would buy Oliver out of the farmhouse, and Oliver would get Louisa on the weekends and every other Wednesday.

"Oh," Lily said and tried to laugh. "This is awkward, isn't it?"

"Getting a divorce is supposed to be painful. It's like going to the dentist," Oliver answered. "If the drill didn't hurt, you wouldn't be reminded that if you avoided M&M'S and Milk Duds, you wouldn't be there in the first place."

"Oliver, please." Lily's eyes darted around the reception area. "We promised we wouldn't do this."

"Do you remember our wedding day? You were so nervous you couldn't eat a bite. I said you had to swallow something or you'd faint during the first dance. We went to a café in Big Sur, and I fed you cream of potato soup and French bread."

Lily's parents had wanted to hold the ceremony at Saints Peter and Paul Church in San Francisco, followed by a sit-down dinner at the Bohemian Club. But she and Oliver spent a weekend in Carmel and fell in love with a chapel on Ocean Avenue. It had a stone floor and stained-glass windows, and when you stepped outside you could smell the ocean.

"What's your point?" Lily asked.

"It was so spectacular, with the waves crashing on the sand, we said maybe we should stay for dessert and get married another day," Oliver continued. "I'm supposed to review a new tapas bar in Chelsea. Why don't we go out to lunch and get divorced tomorrow?"

"Louisa's summer camp has a field trip tomorrow. We're going crabbing."

"You do know we pay the camp counselors almost the price of their college tuition to go to the beach? You don't need to accompany them."

Lily noticed Oliver was wearing a pair of loafers she had never seen before, and he was using a different aftershave. She opened her mouth to say something and then changed her mind.

"I have to go to my appointment." She approached the reception desk. "I'll see you later."

Now Lily glanced at the vases filled with calla lilies and thought she and Oliver couldn't possibly stay at the same hotel. But she had been looking forward to playing tennis at the tennis club and shopping in the hotel's boutiques and drinking Mirto at the Cervo Bar.

"I'm afraid there has been a misunderstanding," she said to the manager when he returned with a glass of water. "I must find another hotel."

"It's high season, all the hotels are booked." He studied Lily's slender cheekbones and gold necklace. "There isn't a room available on the entire Emerald Coast."

"I suppose you're right." Lily sighed, thinking she was being silly.

The Hotel Cervo had dozens of suites and rooms scattered over the grounds. She wouldn't have to see Oliver at all. And there were so many ways to keep busy. She wanted to see the ancient stone towers and take the ferry to La Maddalena and visit the town of Arzachena high in the hills.

"Do you have a room in another wing? It doesn't have to be a suite, anything will do. You see, my husband and I just got divorced. We can't possibly share the same suite," she said and gulped. "I'll even give up Enzo."

"My apologies." He shook his head. "We are fully booked."

She leaned forward, and her brown eyes glistened. "There must be something. All I need is a bed and a shower."

"We had one cancellation." He glanced at the screen. "It's a one-bedroom suite with a view of the harbor."

"Oh, that's wonderful!" Lily beamed. "If I could have the key, I'll go there right now."

"It will be Enzo's pleasure to escort you." He handed her a metallic key. "Suite 233."

"But I was in 231." Lily wavered.

"That is correct, Mrs. Bristol." He nodded. "233 is the adjoining suite."

Lily sat on the cotton bedspread and thought everything had gone wrong. First she'd arrived without her credit cards and now she was practically sharing a wall with Oliver. She wished she were in the farmhouse's sunny kitchen, preparing waffles with blueberries for Louisa.

But she couldn't live her life avoiding Oliver. They were going to have to attend sports days and piano recitals and graduations. And really, there was nowhere she wanted to be right now more than Sardinia. When she gazed at the turquoise ocean, she felt excited and alive.

"Is the new suite to your liking?" Enzo asked, opening the door to the balcony and rearranging the vase of yellow tulips on the side table.

"It's lovely. I just wish it was on a different side of the hotel." She paused. "I'm not complaining, I'm grateful the concierge could accommodate me. But the last person I want to see on my first trip abroad as a divorced woman is Oliver, my ex-husband."

"Don't think of yourself as a divorced woman," Enzo offered, filling a pewter bowl with pistachios.

"How should I think of myself?" she wondered aloud.

Enzo noticed her dark hair and large brown eyes. "Think of yourself as a beautiful young American divorcée," he suggested. "Arriving on the Emerald Coast to have a great adventure."

"A beautiful young American divorcée," Lily said and laughed. "I like that. Thank you, Enzo. I feel much better."

Enzo left, and she slipped a caftan over her bathing suit and entered the hallway. The door closed, and she realized she'd forgotten her paperback book. She rummaged through her purse and thought that was the problem with hotel card keys: they were so thin, they were almost invisible.

She emptied her purse onto the wool rug and crouched on the floor. A door opened, and she heard footsteps.

"Can I help you?" a male voice asked.

"I lost my key," she said, sifting through tubes of mascara. "I miss the days when hotels gave you keys the size of small tennis racquets. They were bulky to carry but impossible to misplace."

"I'll help you look." The man kneeled beside her.

"You don't need to do that," she replied and thought his voice sounded familiar. She looked up and saw Oliver's curly hair and blue eyes. Her cheeks flushed, and she waved the key. "You see, I found it."

"Lily!" he exclaimed. "What on earth are you doing here?"

Her heart pounded, and she was tempted to run back into her room. She'd send him a text explaining what had happened, suggesting they invent a code for when the hallway was clear and either one could dash to the elevator.

"I'm doing the same thing you're doing," she said finally, taking off her sunglasses. "I'm using our reservation at Hotel Cervo on the Emerald Coast."

Oliver's cheeks were pale, and he rubbed his chin. Suddenly his face broke into a smile, and he laughed.

"I didn't tell you I was coming to Sardinia, did I?" he asked.

"And I never mentioned I was going away, because my parents were coming to take care of Louisa."

His eyes flickered, and he gasped. "We're not staying in the same suite?"

"Don't worry, I discovered a shaving kit on the sink and realized the mistake. I asked for a room on a different floor, but this was all they had." She sighed. "You're in 231 and I'm in 233."

"Aren't we a couple of geniuses." He grinned. "We both travel nine thousand miles to forget those papers in their brown manila folder and end up in the same place. We could have saved ourselves an eleven-hour flight and a taxi ride with a driver who shouldn't be allowed to steer a tricycle, and met at Per Se for lunch."

"I didn't come to Sardinia to forget the divorce." She straightened her shoulders. "I came for the opening of Lily Bristol. The Emerald Coast has miles of beaches. I'm sure we can both go Jet

Skiing without interfering with each other's fun. If you'll excuse me, I'm going to the pool."

"Lily, wait." He touched her arm. "We shared a closet for ten years, we can be in the same hallway." His blue eyes sparkled. "I'll tap on the wall when it's safe for you to walk to the elevator."

"I was thinking we could do the same thing. I don't want to have to slink along the balcony like a cat burglar." She laughed. "And I am excited to be here. Did you see the view on the drive from the airport? Rugged cliffs and cobalt blue inlets like on Louisa's DVD of *Finding Nemo*."

A door opened, and a woman who appeared to be in her late twenties entered the hallway. She had coppery hair and wore a knit dress and silver sandals.

"The gift shop didn't have any Tylenol. I got some brand of Italian aspirin," she said to Oliver. She carried an orange purse, and her mouth was the color of cherries.

Oliver jumped back and ran his hands through his hair. He glanced at the door as if he were planning an escape route.

"Lily, this is Angela," he said stiffly. "She's a floral designer in New York."

"It's nice to meet you. I got the most terrible headache on the plane," Angela explained. "I might have to spend my first day in Porto Cervo under cotton sheets."

"Floral designer?" Lily stammered.

"I do weddings, mostly." Angela nodded. "It's lovely to be part of the most important day of two people's lives."

"I'm sure it is." Lily's hands were cold, and she thought she might faint. "Is Oliver one of your clients?"

"Of course not. He just got divorced." Angela laughed. "Have we met? I could swear I've seen your face somewhere."

Oliver turned to Angela and looked like a small boy caught taking a Tootsie Pop from the corner market. His eyes watered, and his cheeks were the color of putty.

"This is Lily." He wiped his brow. "She's my ex-wife."

Lily slid her key into the lock and stumbled into her suite. She had wanted to race to the pool, but her knees buckled and she could hardly breathe. Now she sank onto the sofa and slipped off her sandals.

She glanced at the marble bar and wondered if it was too early for a shot of vodka. What was Oliver doing with a woman in Sardinia? In the six months they'd been separated, he'd never mentioned having a girlfriend. She remembered when they'd run into each other at a wedding in East Hampton in June, and thought they were the only two single people left in New York. . . .

Summer weddings in the Hamptons were three days of sailing and shucking oysters and swimming in pools so big they belonged at the Olympics. Lily had skipped the rehearsal dinner and arrived mid-afternoon. She played croquet and drank gin fizzes and admired the bride's sapphire-and-diamond ring.

Now the ceremony was over and guests gathered in the gazebo for cocktails. There were handcrafted martinis and an ice sculpture of the bride and groom. Lily nibbled canapés and was suddenly tired of listening to couples discuss their upcoming trips to Cancún and the benefits of couples massages. She slipped off her pumps and ran down to the lawn.

"You're missing out on some delicious hors d'oeuvres," a male voice said behind her. "The duck confit is perfect, and the smoked soft eggs are superb."

"Oliver, what are you doing here!" Lily exclaimed.

Why hadn't she realized Oliver would be at the wedding? They had known the bride and groom for years. But she promised herself she wouldn't be one of those ex-wives who pored over the guest list. She glanced up at the huge house, with its gabled roof and wide porch, and wondered how they had ended up on the lawn alone.

"I suppose we should divide up this sort of thing." Oliver stood beside her. It was early evening, and the sky was a muted purple. "You attend the weddings where the groom's last name starts with A through K, and I'll take the last half of the alphabet."

"Why is everyone getting married all of a sudden?" Lily asked. "I can't open the mailbox without an invitation the size of a novel falling out. And they want so much information: do you request the braised eggplant and are you bringing a plus one?" she continued. "We're the only unattached people at the whole affair. The mother of the bride keeps giving me dirty looks, as if I'm going to jinx the bride and groom."

"Tell her divorce isn't contagious," he said and then stopped. "Do you remember how smug our single friends were when we were married? They were all signing up for Mexican cooking classes while we took turns feeding Louisa SpaghettiOs. Now they're registering at Barneys and jetting off to St. Croix for their honeymoon. What if we got it wrong?"

"We did get it wrong." Lily clutched her glass. "That's why we're getting divorced."

"What if we started the whole thing too soon? Sort of like that movie *Back to the Future*," he urged. "Instead of giving up and getting a divorce, we should fast-forward to the present and try again."

Lily studied his tan cheeks, and her heart beat a little faster.

"We pressed the restart button on our marriage more often than the ones on our iPhones," she answered. "And it wasn't the SpaghettiOs. We enjoyed feeding Louisa, she waved her spoon like an orchestra conductor."

Oliver stared at Lily for so long, she was afraid the wedding party would come out to find them.

"Are you sure?" he asked.

"Quite sure." She gulped her martini.

"Then we better go in to dinner," he sighed. "The only reason I came was for the stuffed pigeon with chanterelle mushrooms. The groom's cousin is a Cordon Bleu–trained chef, and it's supposed to be as good as at the Ritz in Paris."

Now Lily walked to the minibar of her suite and poured a glass of orange juice. That had been only two months ago, and Oliver was at the wedding alone. Surely he wouldn't bring a woman he hardly knew to Sardinia.

She pictured Angela's coppery hair and curvy figure, and thought she wasn't going to assess Oliver's girlfriends like a bookie making odds on a horse race. They were both free to date whomever they liked.

Lily had had a crush on a single father in Louisa's art class just last week. It had only lasted a day because the next afternoon he'd smelled faintly of cigarettes and she could never date anyone who smoked. But it had been lovely to feel that frisson of excitement while they examined their daughters' papier mâché.

It didn't bother her to imagine Oliver entertaining women in his new apartment in the West Village. She had only been there once to pick up Louisa and had barely poked her head inside the entry. It did seem quite modern, and the chintz sofa Oliver took from the farmhouse looked out of place with the sleek bookshelves and chrome furniture.

But it was different to inhale the other woman's perfume when they passed in the hallway. And what if she heard things through the walls?

She noticed her purse on the tile coffee table and remembered her credit cards. How could she call the credit card company when the phone number was on the card that was missing? Oliver would know, but she had to figure out how to do these kinds of things herself.

It couldn't be that difficult. People lost their credit cards when they traveled all the time. It was so easy to do when you were juggling documents like a circus performer. She would ask Enzo! Guests must forget their credit cards at the pool or while paying the bill at the bar. She picked up the phone and pressed the buzzer. She waited, and there was a knock at the door.

"Enzo, you came!" She opened the door.

Enzo carried a silver tray with a glass of pineapple juice, and Lily felt a flash of joy. She wasn't all alone in Sardinia; there was someone she could count on. "I wasn't sure the buzzer would call you directly. It's like the bat phone on those *Batman* reruns on classic TV."

"I am always at your service." Enzo noticed the fresh flowers on the coffee table and the sideboard set with fruits and cheeses. "It looks like the maids have completely done the room. Is there something they missed?"

"I have a problem. I lost my credit cards, and Oliver used to handle ordering new ones," she explained. "How are you supposed to call to get a new card if you don't have the number?"

"I'm sure we have a card on file from when you made the initial reservation," he suggested. "I'll ask the concierge to call and put you through to the right department."

"Aren't you clever!" Lily beamed. "I wouldn't have thought of that."

Enzo walked to the door, and she realized she didn't want to be alone.

"Can I ask you something else?" she stopped him. "Does your wife work? I mean, besides taking care of Maria and Gia. I'm sure they keep her busy. I can spend all day cleaning Louisa's closet and listening to her tell me about the snails she found in the garden."

"Carmella takes in sewing," Enzo said. "Before we were married, she wanted to be a dress designer."

"She must be talented. I'll pick up some fabric and pay her to make a dress for Louisa." She paused thoughtfully. "What if suddenly she had the chance to work for a designer in Paris or Milan? Do you think it would be right for her to leave you and the girls for weeks at a time?"

"I don't understand the question." He frowned.

"I mean, if she found something that made her so happy but

took her away from the family . . ." She leaned forward. "Should she do it? Or should she stay in Porto Cervo to make sure Maria and Gia don't wear dresses to school with tears in the hem?"

Enzo stopped to think. "Of course she should go. Maria and Gia would be proud to have a mother who designed dresses for important clients. And think of all the things she could tell them about the cities she visited."

Lily took a sip of juice and asked the question that pressed on her chest like a cold compress. "And would you trust her completely when she was away? Even if something odd happened and you couldn't reach her?"

"We've been together since we were seventeen." He shrugged. "Trust is the most important ingredient in a marriage."

"Thank you, Enzo." Lily sank back onto the silk cushions. "I knew you would agree."

"I still don't understand the question, but I'm glad I helped," he offered. "Is there anything else I can do?"

She suddenly pictured Angela standing next to Oliver in the hallway and felt a pang of loneliness.

"I enjoy our conversations and I'd like us to be friends." She looked up. "Perhaps you can call me Lily."

"I'm afraid that's against hotel protocol." He shook his head.

"Think about it, Enzo," Lily said and smiled. "You did say you'd do anything I ask."

Enzo walked out and Lily stood at the window. The sea was a brilliant azure, and yachts lined the port like a fantastic string of pearls. If things had turned out differently, she and Oliver would be sharing a bottle of champagne and a plate of mangoes and peaches.

But what was the point of thinking about that now? The divorce papers were signed, and Oliver was here with another woman.

The sun touched her shoulders, and she remembered when she and Oliver had met, ten years ago. It was the end of July, and the sun was so hot, she could have been in the Sahara Desert instead of Southern Italy. She'd gazed up at the train station's revolving board with names like Roma and Venezia and wondered how she'd ended up at the train station in Naples. . . .

Lily gazed around the train station and bit her lip. Posters advertised fizzy sodas, and kiosks sold buffalo mozzarella and lemon gelato. She set her suitcase on the pavement and was so hungry she longed for a spinach calzone or orange sorbet.

She still couldn't understand how she ended up on the wrong train. The taxi ride to Roma Termini train station took forever, and when she arrived, the platforms were as confusing as some elaborate labyrinth. She asked the ticket-taker for directions, but he spoke so quickly she only caught the first word.

That was the problem with Italians. You couldn't understand a thing they said, and when you asked them to repeat themselves, they just talked faster. Finally she gave up and maneuvered through the terminal herself.

Now she had to get to Florence by the day after tomorrow or she would miss her flight to San Francisco. But she wasn't going anywhere without money, and her wallet with her credit cards had disappeared.

She remembered entering the restaurant compartment of the train and trying to decide between the pizza Napolitana and the Tuscan bread roll with prosciutto and *formaggio*. She should have ordered the pizza. The bread roll was soggy, the prosciutto fell on the floor, and the *formaggio* was one slice of white cheese.

She must have left her wallet on the counter when she paid for her sandwich. A pit formed in her stomach and she tried not to panic. The station was full of people, and someone would help her.

She noticed a young man in his early twenties leaning against the wall. He had dark hair and ate a ripe peach.

"Scusami," she began, wishing she had memorized her Italian phrase book. *"Dove uno telefono pagamento, per favore?"*

"Your Italian is worse than mine." The man grinned. "I've learned one is much better off speaking English and flashing a wad of euros."

"Oh, you're American," Lily said, and her shoulders relaxed.

That was the wonderful thing about traveling. A complete stranger seemed like an old friend because your passports had an eagle on the cover and you both watched *American Idol*.

"Oliver Bristol." He nodded. "I'd shake your hand, but I'd get peach juice all over it."

"That looks delicious." Lily sighed. "I haven't eaten a thing since a hard-boiled egg in Rome. I was supposed to be on the train to Florence, but I was late getting to the station. When I did arrive, I ended up on the wrong platform. If I don't catch a train to Florence, I'll miss my flight home."

"There are plenty of trains to Florence." Oliver waved at the ticket booth. "Just purchase a new ticket."

"That's the thing. I lost my credit card." She flushed. "I must have left it on the counter when I paid for my sandwich. The sandwich fell on the floor, and the whole day has been a disaster. Do you know if there's a pay phone nearby? I need to call my parents and ask them to wire money."

"I'm afraid you're out of luck. It's Sunday, and the banks are closed." Oliver shook his head. "And in Naples, you have to allow an extra day for any transaction. No one is in a hurry, and the locals enjoy saying 'no' more than eating spaghetti *alle vongole*."

Lily's eyes filled with tears, and she turned away. How could she have forgotten it was Sunday? But she wasn't going to fall apart in front of a curly-haired stranger.

"Are you all right?" he asked.

"I always get emotional when I'm hungry." She wiped her eyes. "I'll figure something out. I'm sure there's an American Express office or American consulate nearby."

"Here." He reached into a paper sack and took out a peach. He handed it to Lily and picked up her suitcase. "I'm from Michigan, and we were taught never to abandon a woman in distress. Come with me."

"Where are we going?" Lily asked.

"You'll see." Oliver smiled, and she noticed his eyes were blue as the summer sky. "I promise it will be more pleasant than the Naples train station."

They crossed a piazza with stone fountains and crumbling statues. Teenage boys on Vespas swerved between wrought-iron tables, and it was like a scene in an Italian movie.

Oliver turned onto a cobblestone lane with brightly colored window boxes. They passed a pasticceria with trays of orange sponge cake and vanilla custard.

"Follow me." He led her to the back of a stucco building. He took a key from under the flowerpot and opened the door into a kitchen.

"What are we doing here?" Lily glanced at the huge pots and industrial-sized stove. There was a set of carving knives and a pantry filled with spices.

"We're going to eat the best meal you've had in Italy." Oliver walked through a hallway.

Round tables were set with checkered tablecloths and ceramic vases. The walls were lined with abstract paintings and wine casks hung from the ceiling.

"We can't just break into a restaurant and help ourselves to whatever is in the kitchen," Lily protested.

"We can when I work here." He pulled out her chair. "Umberto's has been in the same family for a century, and the owner treats the employees like family. Giuseppe would be furious if I didn't feed a pretty young tourist."

Oliver disappeared into the kitchen, and Lily bit her lip. She was alone with a man in an empty restaurant. But Oliver had a bright smile, and the smells wafting from the kitchen were intoxicating.

He reappeared with plates of eggplant parmigiana and mussels cooked in their own broth. There were bowls of minestrone and a green salad.

"You couldn't have cooked all this so quickly," Lily said, eating a forkful of eggplant.

"I didn't cook any of it." Oliver dipped a focaccia in olive oil. "The chef always leaves plates for the waiters to eat before their shifts. You can't serve spaghetti *alla puttanesca* and ravioli *caprese* when you're starving."

"Are you a waiter?" Lily asked.

"It's not what I got my degree for, but it will do for now." Oliver nodded. "I love to travel but I don't like moving through cities so fast, all you remember is where to find the cheapest coffee. I've been in Naples for a month and visited the Catacombs and Castel dell'Ovo and Vesuvius."

"I know what you mean. I visited five countries in three weeks," Lily agreed. "It seemed I always carried the wrong currency and just when I learned to say 'good night,' I had to speak a new language. But I saw wonderful things: poppy fields near Amsterdam and Lipizzaner horses in Vienna and medieval castles in Prague."

"What do you do when you aren't getting stranded in train stations?" Oliver asked.

"I want to collect furnishings from all over the world and open my own store. It won't be a jumble of items like someone's attic. It will have different areas: leather armchairs and walnut bookshelves, so you think you're in an English library, and silk ottomans scattered with gold cushions like an Indian palace."

"That's quite ambitious," Oliver said and smiled. "I thought you were a just a girl who couldn't find the right train."

"I'm perfectly capable of taking care of myself." Lily flushed. "Though there was the time I left my straw hat on top of the canopy on a gondola in Venice, and it fell into the canal. The gondolier fished it out and said he wouldn't have had a hook if it didn't happen all the time."

"I'm glad you took the wrong train," Oliver said.

"You are?" Lily looked up.

"If you hadn't, I'd be haggling with my landlady over how much she owed me for the peaches I bought at the market." Oliver's blue eyes sparkled. "Instead, I'm eating eggplant parmigiana and drinking Chianti with a beautiful American."

They ate lemon sponge cake for dessert, and Lily used the phone in the kitchen. She returned to the table and pulled out her chair.

"You've been very kind. I feel much better." She sipped a cup of inky coffee. "If you tell me how to get to the train station, I'll wait there until the money arrives."

"You can't sleep at the train station," Oliver spluttered.

"I once spent twenty-four hours at Oslo Airport because the plane needed a part and was stuck in Iceland." Lily shrugged. "I'll use my suitcase as a pillow and cover myself with my sweater."

"You'll get arrested, and someone will have to bribe the police to release you." He shook his head. "The Italian police can practically smell money—even if it belongs to your parents in another country."

"I don't have a choice," she explained.

"You can have my room at the hostel, and I'll sleep in the pantry at the restaurant."

"I can't kick you out of your hostel," she protested.

"Giuseppe sleeps in the pantry whenever his wife is angry with him for flirting with the hostess." He grinned. "There's an air mattress and blanket."

"Are you sure?" she asked.

"Perfectly sure." He nodded "But there's somewhere I want to take you first."

"I'm terribly tired." She hesitated. "Can it wait until tomorrow?"

"You just drank Italian espresso." He stood up and smiled. "You won't sleep for hours."

They took the metro to Mergellina and climbed a winding road flanked by fir trees. Villas stood behind iron gates, and the air smelled of hibiscus and hyacinths.

"Tour buses take tourists to Castel Sant'Elmo to see the sunset, but it's so crowded, you worry about being elbowed in the stomach," Oliver said when they reached the top. "Posillipo is a residential neighborhood, so it's completely private. And it has the best views in Naples."

Lily turned around and gasped. Mount Vesuvius rose in the distance, and the Bay of Naples was a turquoise horseshoe. White sailboats bobbed in the harbor, and she felt like she had stepped into an Impressionist painting.

"Oh, it's gorgeous," she breathed.

"Naples doesn't have ornate fountains like Rome or palaces like Venice, or museums filled with Renaissance paintings like Florence." Oliver waved his hand. "But when you stand up here, you feel like a god on Mount Olympus."

Lily glanced at the buildings bathed in a golden light and felt warm and happy. Oliver's hand brushed her arm, and a shiver ran down her spine.

"You didn't tell me why you were at the train station," she said.

"I was seeing off a friend." He shrugged.

"A male friend or female friend?" she asked.

"It doesn't matter," Oliver said and looked at Lily. "Whoever it was is gone."

Lily stood on the balcony of her suite at Hotel Cervo and tipped her face to the sun. She remembered bumping into Oliver in the hallway and shuddered. That was one of the perils of divorce. You romanticized everything about your marriage: the early years when you'd rather have eaten takeout than attended a glamorous cocktail party, the Sundays you spent in bed and never got dressed at all.

She and Oliver were twenty-two when they met. Of course, they fell in love! You fell in love with everything at that age: Michelangelo's *David* or a pair of Italian loafers. It was the later years that were impossible. The silly mistakes and betrayals and pain that wouldn't go away. Toward the end, she felt like she was buried under ash in Pompeii.

But all that was over. She entered the suite and slipped on her sandals. She scooped up her book and took a deep breath. She was a single woman on the Emerald Coast, and nothing was going to stop her from enjoying herself.

Chapter Two

OLIVER SIPPED A *SPREMUTA* MADE with blood oranges and sugar and adjusted his sunglasses. Angela lathered lotion on her shoulders, and he felt like a boy discovering his teenage neighbor sunbathing in the garden. She really was lovely, with her wavy hair and full breasts and toned thighs.

That was the funny thing about divorce. All of a sudden, you were allowed to look at other women. Not that he'd had much desire when he was married to Lily. She was perfect, with her glossy brown hair and white smile. But now when he walked down Fifth Avenue, there were blondes with shapely calves and brunettes with curvy waists and the occasional redhead with alabaster skin.

He pictured bumping into Lily in the hallway and shuddered. Angela had brushed it off with a flick of her coppery hair, but he could tell she was unsettled. And he couldn't blame her. Who would have thought they would be practically sharing a terrace with his ex-wife?

He should have checked with Lily before he used the reservation, but they were like two fencers who forgot to wear their protective padding. They had to keep a distance from each other for fear of getting hurt.

And he knew exactly what Lily was thinking. She was as easy to read as the side of a cereal box. They had only signed the divorce papers a week ago; what was he doing with another woman in Sardinia?

He'd only met Angela two months ago, at the opening of a fusion restaurant in SoHo. She was arranging flowers in a crystal vase, and her lips were the color of plums. He squinted into the sun and remembered how he couldn't take his eyes off her.

Oliver sipped a lemon-berry martini and glanced at his watch. He almost never arrived at restaurant openings early. He usually had to squeeze them in between picking up pumpkin soup for Lily at Zabar's and running to the train. But that was one of the things about divorce; suddenly, he had so much free time.

At first, he loved being alone in Manhattan on summer evenings. He visited the Guggenheim and listened to concerts in Central Park. But lately, time seemed to hang on him like an oversized suit.

Sometimes, rather than taking a cab, he walked from his office at the *New York Times* to his apartment in the West Village just so he didn't arrive home while it was still light. He hadn't had time to buy window coverings, and the late afternoon sun kept his living room like a sauna.

Now he nibbled rice balls and noticed a young woman arranging tulips. Her reddish hair cascaded down her back, and she wore shimmering lipstick.

"You're staring at me." She looked up. She wore an orange dress and beige pumps.

"I was admiring your lipstick." Oliver flushed. "My daughter is six and she's obsessed with lip gloss. She would love that color."

"Tell your wife it's called Estée Lauder crimson rose," she replied.

"I'm not married," Oliver said, shaking his head.

"You're wearing a wedding ring." She pointed to his finger.

"I mean, we're separated, but we're trying to ease our daughter into the idea," he continued. "Like when you start talking to her about the dentist weeks before her appointment. We thought we'd take off our wedding rings when the divorce is final."

"That probably puts a cramp in your dating style." She laughed, fiddling with a stem.

"I haven't dated in ten years. I don't know where to start." Oliver sighed. "These days, the whole thing happens on smartphones. And I was used to ordering for Lily at a restaurant. If I do that on a date, I'll offend someone."

"Most women are capable of choosing between cream of asparagus soup and a spinach salad."

"I'm a restaurant critic for the *New York Times*. I'm paid to choose the best thing on the menu," he explained. "And I know what Lily likes. She adores soufflé and won't eat any fish with bones."

"Would you like dating advice?" The woman placed the vase on a pink tablecloth. "You have lovely eyes and you look handsome in that sports coat, but you should stop mentioning your ex-wife."

She drifted away, and Oliver wanted to stuff the cocktail napkin in his mouth. When he and Lily had been together, he had no trouble talking to women. But now when he met an attractive woman, he behaved like a schoolboy with a crush on his teacher.

He sampled prawn dumplings and sticky rice in lettuce leaves and thought he would leave early, catch the latest James Bond movie or pick up hair ribbons for Louisa at Duane Reade. He turned, and the woman with coppery hair walked toward him. She took her lipstick out of her purse and grabbed his hand.

"You can't give me your lipstick," he protested.

"I'm not. I'm giving you something much better." She scribbled her name and phone number on his palm in purple lipstick. "I dare you to use it."

It took Oliver a week to gather the courage to call her and another two days to choose the restaurant. He changed his blazer three times and threw out the bouquet of lilacs he bought at Scott's Flowers. What was he thinking? She was a floral designer; giving her flowers would be like bringing truffles to a French chef.

Now they sat across from each other at a Korean restaurant in Midtown, and Oliver looked miserably at the menu. Going to Danfi's had seemed like a good idea when he made the reservation. The owners were friendly, the prices were reasonable, and the food was superb.

But he and Lily loved ordering the spiciest dishes: scallion pancakes with chili peppers and spicy yellow sashimi. He could hardly sit across from a complete stranger with tears pricking his eyes. He finally settled on the eggs over rice and sweet potato noodles.

"It's a little warm in here," Angela said, sipping a guava margarita.

"It's the kitchen vents," Oliver explained. "They open into the dining room. It's clever because the room always smells of delicious spices, but in the summer, it gets quite hot." He paused. "If you don't like it, we can go somewhere else."

"It's fine," she said, removing her jacket. "I've never had Korean food before. You'll have to tell me what to order."

Oliver looked up and saw her low-cut dress and full breasts. Those breasts! They were like tender peaches, round and pink and covered with the slightest fuzz.

Suddenly he felt like a scientist who had been stationed in Antarctica and hadn't seen the sun in months. The pinpoint lighting danced before his eyes, and his forehead was covered in sweat.

"I've changed my mind," he said to the waiter, and his shoulders relaxed. "We'll have the spicy pork belly and Korean fire chicken wings, and black cod with spicy daikon."

Oliver walked the last block to Angela's apartment and stuffed his hands into his pockets. Dinner had been surprisingly pleasant. They talked about Angela's work and how Manhattan in the summer was as stifling as her hometown in Ohio.

Oliver listened to her describe the poodle she left in Toledo and imagined caressing those breasts. But now that they were bouncing beside him instead of safely on the other side of the table, he felt suddenly clammy. He wasn't ready to go up to a woman's apartment, and he could hardly stroke them on her front steps.

And he wasn't that kind of guy. He'd never hidden girly magazines under his bed as a teenager or spent hours surfing the Internet in college.

"Thank you for a lovely dinner," she said when they reached her building. "Would you like to come up for a cup of coffee?"

"I'm afraid I can't." He shifted on the sidewalk. "My daughter's coming tomorrow, and I have to stop at Whole Foods. She refuses to eat Honey Nut Cheerios or Frosted Mini-Wheats."

"Perhaps another time." Angela fiddled with her key. "You know, you have real dating potential. You make good conversation and have the sexiest smile. But you forgot one thing."

"I did?" Oliver wondered if he'd neglected to leave the waiter a tip.

She leaned forward and kissed him. Her mouth was warm, and her breath smelled sweet, and her hair brushed his cheek.

"You forgot to kiss me good night."

Now Oliver studied a drop of lotion on Angela's thigh and wondered why he felt slightly guilty. That was the point of divorce; he and Lily could do whatever they liked. For all he knew, Lily was dating a brain surgeon from Connecticut or a hedge-fund manager on the Upper East Side.

Angela dove into the pool, and he thought of everything he had planned for the week: lying on the private beach and sailing in the ocean and dancing at the Billionaire Club in Porto Cervo. So what if every activity entailed Angela wearing a swimsuit or a sheer dress and high heels? They were on the Emerald Coast; they were hardly going to spend their time in museums.

He remembered when he'd met Lily in Naples all those years ago, and felt a sudden pang in his chest. The first time he saw her in a swimsuit, he almost passed out. It wasn't that she was stunning. Her breasts were high but small, and her hips belonged on a boy. But he took one look at her in her blue bikini with her hair dripping wet and never wanted to look at another woman in his life.

_____

Oliver climbed the steps of the hostel and fumbled with his key. His back hurt from sleeping on the mattress at the restaurant, and he needed a shave and shower. He pictured Lily in her cotton dress and sandals and wondered if he was crazy to let a complete stranger stay in his room.

But there was nothing to steal besides a collection of Kurt Vonnegut books, and she had nowhere else to go. And there was something about the way her mouth trembled when she was upset that made him want to act like a modern-day Lancelot.

He entered the hallway and heard someone singing in the shower. He listened more closely and realized it was Lily.

"You do know there isn't a lock on the bathroom door," Oliver said, covering his eyes and entering the bathroom. "Signora Giannini is afraid the tenants will use up all the hot water."

"I'm glad you're here." Lily peered out from behind the shower curtain. "I slept so well, I could have stayed in bed for weeks. Then I came in to take a shower and realized I didn't bring a towel. I've been standing here for ages hoping someone would walk by. If you could get me a towel, I'll go back to the room and get dressed."

"Signora Giannini doesn't provide towels," he explained. "Everyone has to bring their own."

"I didn't pack a towel." She bit her lip. "Could I borrow yours?"

"I sent all my laundry to the Laundromat, it doesn't come back until this afternoon," Oliver said and smiled. "I'm afraid you're going to have stay in there all day, or run naked down the hall."

"I'm not going to streak in an Italian hostel," Lily spluttered. "There must be a blanket somewhere."

"Wait there," Oliver said and opened the door.

Oliver walked to his room and saw Lily's suitcase open on the bed. He fished out a blue bathing suit and walked back to the bathroom.

"This is the best I could find." He handed it to her. "At least you'll be decent."

The shower curtain opened, and Oliver gasped. Her arms and legs glistened and her hair clung to her head like a cap. Her eyes were as big as saucers, and her eyelashes were thicker than he remembered.

"That's much better." She stepped out of the shower. "How can I thank you?"

"For starters, by not getting water on my loafers." He glanced at the puddle on the tiles. "Then perhaps we can have breakfast before you leave."

"It will be my treat after we go to the American Express office." Lily shook out her hair. "I've never been one of these people who starts the day with a piece of toast. Breakfast should be eggs and fresh fruit and the darkest coffee possible."

They sat at an outdoor table at Caffè Spaccanapoli and ate poached eggs and fruit salad and Napolitano pastries.

"This is delicious." Lily tore apart a pastry stuffed with sweetened ricotta cheese. "You're looking at me as if I'm an animal in the zoo. Haven't you ever seen a girl eat a croissant? Or do you only date models who exist on celery sticks and the olives in their martinis?"

"It's hard to date when you're living on a waiter's salary." Oliver poured sugar into his coffee. "I've just never seen a girl eat like you. I could fit both hands around your waist, but you already polished off two eggs and half a melon."

"My mother thinks it's because I never sit still, I'm like a hummingbird paused mid-flight." She wiped her mouth with a napkin. "Sometimes I go all day without thinking about food. But when I sit at the table, I could eat for ages."

"Well, I'm glad you're paying for breakfast." He laughed. "I usually make do with a piece of fruit before I go into the restaurant."

"What do you want to do when you stop being a waiter?" Lily glanced around the piazza at women in summery dresses and men wearing leather jackets. "You can't stay in Naples forever."

"I have a journalism degree but I hate newspapers filled with wars and natural disasters," Oliver mused. "And I love food, but I'm a hopeless cook. I burn anything I put in the oven."

"You should be a food critic." Lily ate the last bite of *sfogliatella*. "I've always thought that it would be the most exciting career: you'd get paid to eat creamy pastas and exotic vegetables at new restaurants."

"That is a good idea." He beamed. "I don't know why I didn't think of it."

"Sometimes we're too close to something to see the solution," she replied. "That's why I love traveling. Everywhere you go, people have different problems. As long as you have a pillow to rest your head on and food in your stomach, life is wonderful."

"I hope you feel that way when you can't get to Florence." Oliver glanced at a newspaper on the neighboring table. "I'm afraid there's a train strike."

"That's impossible." Lily followed his gaze. "We were at the train station yesterday."

"In Italy, something is always on strike." He shrugged. "It will be days before the proper official's palm is greased. And you don't want to take the bus. It's more terrifying than a prison cell on Alcatraz."

"I can't stay in Naples! My flight leaves tomorrow, and I start work in San Francisco on Monday." Lily bit her lip. "I got a job at Gump's, San Francisco's oldest furnishings store. If I don't show up the first day, I'll be fired before I start."

"You could rent a car," he suggested.

"I don't have an international license." She shook her head. "And I've seen how Italians drive. Every time I took a taxi in Rome I was so afraid, I gripped the seat."

"I don't know what else you can do." Oliver drained his coffee cup.

"You can drive me!" Lily exclaimed. "I'll pay for gas and food and your time away from work."

"Drive you to Florence," he spluttered. "We hardly know each other."

"It's only six hours by car. Please, I don't have a choice."

Oliver looked at Lily, and his heart did a little flip. Her lips trembled, and her eyes belonged on a young deer.

"I suppose I could." He sighed, wishing he hadn't drunk a second espresso. Too much caffeine made him do things he later regretted. "Giuseppe's cousin has a restaurant in Florence. He serves the best veal parmigiana in Italy."

"I told you, there's always a solution. We'll rent one of those adorable little Fiats with a sunroof," Lily said and smiled. "We'll drink limoncello and stop in quaint villages, and it will be like the pages of a travel magazine."

"I'm so glad I didn't take the train." Lily clutched the guidebook. They stood in a piazza filled with geranium pots and red scooters and old men playing chess. Mount Subasio rose in the distance and the sun was an orange ball.

"We never would have discovered Spello. It's one of the most charming towns in Umbria," she continued, leading Oliver across the cobblestones. "Nothing has changed for centuries. The church of Santa Maria Maggiore has been here for a thousand years, and the bell tower was built in the 1300s."

Driving through Naples had been harrowing. Lily clutched the dashboard, and Oliver felt like he was steering a bumper car in an amusement park. But then the city fell away, and the fields were bright green, and they talked about art and books and movies.

Whenever he thought they had exhausted every possible subject, she went on to something else. Now and then, she pointed to a medieval ruin or vineyard tucked into the hills. Her cheeks glowed, and she smelled of some kind of floral perfume.

"I hope they've heard of refrigeration." Oliver wiped his brow. "I could use a cold beer or a glass of lemonade."

"The guidebook says there's a wonderful trattoria here in Spello that serves lamb medallions with artichokes," Lily suggested. "But first we have to see the Arch of Augustus. They were built in the fourteenth century to protect the village from intruders."

They walked down cobblestone alleys lined with lacquered window boxes. There were piazzas with quaint shops and fruit stands with baskets of plums and cherries. They reached the stone arches, and the valley spread out before them.

"I could live here someday," Lily sighed. "I'd open a furniture store filled with antiques and tapestries. On Sundays, I'd buy sausages and cheese at the outdoor market and ride a bicycle through the countryside."

"I've always wanted to live in a big city like New York or Chicago," Oliver offered. "Somewhere you can go to the theater and eat a burger at two AM."

"Have you ever thought what your ideal life would be?" Lily turned to him.

"The usual things," he mused. "Have a rewarding career and loving family and plenty of money."

"Those things are important, I suppose," she agreed reluctantly.

"Well, what is your ideal life?" Oliver asked.

Lily looked at Oliver, and a smile lit up her face. "I just want to be happy. Really, what else is there?"

They sat at an outdoor café and ate pesto linguini and braised asparagus. Lily flipped through the guidebook and they talked about her childhood in San Francisco and Oliver's summers on Lake Michigan.

Now they walked back to the car, and Oliver opened Lily's door. He stepped into the driver's seat and turned to Lily.

"Could I have the car key, please?"

"I don't have it." She shook her head.

"Of course you have it," he insisted. "You put it in your purse."

"I must have pulled it out at the restaurant or when I paid for the postcards." She rummaged through her lipsticks.

"We can't go anywhere without a car key." Oliver groaned. "And we're miles from the nearest rental car company."

"It must have fallen out. I'm terribly sorry," she apologized. "I'll go to the restaurant and look."

"I'll look. You stay here." Oliver tried to stop the queasy feeling in his stomach. "I don't want you to get lost too."

He searched the café, but their table had been cleared. He stopped at the fruit stand where they had bought pears and the boutique where Lily had admired a silk scarf. Finally, he reached the souvenir shop.

"My friend lost a car key," he said in stilted Italian. "Did you find it?"

"The pretty American wearing oval sunglasses?" the man asked in English.

"Yes, that's her." Oliver nodded.

"She left it next to the postcards." He fished it out of a drawer. "My wife was going to run after her, but I said she'd be back."

"Thank you." He clutched the key.

"If I were you, I'd tell her you couldn't find it." The man leaned forward.

"Why would I do that?" Oliver demanded.

"To be young and stranded with a beautiful woman in an Italian hill town." He sighed. "What more could a man want?"

Oliver ran down the alley and saw Lily leaning against the car. Her eyes were closed, and her face was tipped up to the sun.

"I found it," he called, waving the key.

"I heard your voice and thought I was dreaming." She opened her eyes and laughed. "I was worried we'd be stranded here for days."

Oliver suddenly had the urge to kiss her. But if she pulled away, they'd be stuck together in the car and it would be uncomfortable.

"We should get on the road." He shifted on the cobblestones. "We still have three hours to go. Traffic near Florence could be horrendous."

"Wait, you have tomato sauce on your cheek." Lily brushed his skin with her palm. She reached up and kissed him.

"What was that for?" he asked.

"First you bought me dinner and then you gave me a place to sleep. Now you found the car key." Her brown eyes sparkled. "I don't know how to thank you."

Oliver turned the key in the ignition and backed down the road. The fields were dotted with daisies, and the sun melted on the horizon, and he felt completely happy.

Oliver rubbed his shoulders with suntan lotion. The sun in Sardinia was fierce, and he didn't want to go back to New York with leathery skin.

What did it matter if he didn't have a deep connection with Angela, the feeling that he had known her all his life? The only thing it had done for him and Lily was make the later pain unbearable. And he couldn't ignore Angela's looks. She was a centerfold come to life.

He remembered wanting to help Lily find her hotel key in the hallway. That didn't mean he still had feelings for her. Wanting to help Lily was a Pavlovian response.

In the ten years they were together, he was always rescuing her from some kind of trouble. And it didn't matter anyway. They'd hurt each other so much, there was no way back.

"Oliver," Angela called from the shallow end. "Come join me, the water is perfect."

He was a thirty-three-year-old man on vacation with a woman with flaming hair and pouty lips. He unbuttoned his shirt and jumped into the pool.

Chapter Three

LILY SAT AT THE CERVO Bar and moved *fregola* pasta around her plate. She wasn't hungry, but the waiter had tapped his foot, and she'd pointed to the first thing she saw on the menu. Now she nibbled a piece of sausage, but it got stuck in her throat.

She had walked down to the swimming pool and seen Oliver and Angela cavorting in the shallow end. Angela's hair clung to her back and she looked like a mermaid in one of Louisa's story-books.

Lily gasped and wanted to hide under a chaise longue. She walked blindly to the bar and sank onto a leather stool. Now she sipped mineral water and wished she were choosing fabrics in her office.

It wasn't Oliver's fault. He could bring whomever he liked to the Emerald Coast. But Oliver had been her husband for ten years. She couldn't just hand him over to another woman like a DVD she'd already watched.

And there had been that moment when Oliver looked up. His hair was wet and his blue eyes sparkled and she thought his smile was for her.

A man studied her legs, and Lily flushed and rearranged her caftan. She was in Sardinia; she had to get used to men looking at her. Admiring women was almost a national sport. And it was nice to feel beautiful. It was like putting on a spring dress or dabbing your wrists with perfume. It made you feel vital and alive.

Suddenly she had an idea. She hurried through the lobby and approached the front desk.

"Mrs. Bristol, how nice to see you." The manager looked up. "I trust you have everything you need?"

"I was wondering where I could find Enzo."

"Would you like him to come to your suite?" he asked.

"I'll wait here," Lily replied. "It will only take a minute."

"This is highly unusual." Enzo stepped over a laundry basket. "I don't usually meet guests in housekeeping."

Lily didn't want Oliver and Angela deciding they needed a cocktail and seeing her in the bar. And if she went to her suite, she was in danger of meeting them in the hallway. She pulled Enzo into the laundry room and closed the door.

"You did say you would do anything I asked." Lily perched on a pile of pillowcases.

"This is quite extraordinary." He fiddled with his bow tie. "Our guests don't usually want to inspect the bedding."

"Enzo, we're friends. And you did say I could ask for anything. I'm hardly one of those hotel critics who doesn't reveal his true identity until he checks out." Lily laughed. "It's very important. I need you to find me an escort."

"Mrs. Bristol!" Enzo exclaimed. "Hotel Cervo is a respectable hotel."

"I asked you not to call me that, it sounds so formal. I don't mean that kind of escort," Lily protested. "I just want some company. A man to take me to dinner and explore the Emerald Coast."

"You are a beautiful young American divorcée and very capable," Enzo reminded her. "You don't need my help."

"This morning, after you left, I ran into Oliver, my ex-husband, in the hallway," she began. "It was a little embarrassing. I lost my key and was searching for it on the floor."

"I'm sure he realized what he was missing," Enzo offered. "Any man would wish he was still enjoying your company."

"That's very sweet. You and your wife must have a wonderful marriage, you know just what to say to make a woman feel good." She paused. "But the thing is, he wasn't alone in the hallway. He had someone with him."

"Someone?" Enzo repeated.

"A stunning redhead. He didn't know I was here, and I had no idea he was using the reservation. But every time I see them, I feel like I have a terrible flu. If I had someone to distract me, I'd feel better."

"You want to make your ex-husband jealous?" he asked.

"Not exactly. I want Oliver to be happy," Lily answered. "I just feel like a doll that Louisa outgrew and put back on the shelf. Is it wrong to want someone to bring you roses and ask if you prefer the grilled sea bass or baked salmon?"

"In Sardinia, love is even more important than wealth or fame." Enzo nodded.

"I'm not even talking about love. I just want to be happy." Lily sighed. "Could you please help? I promise I won't ask for anything else that's unconventional."

"My sister is dating a man whose cousin owns a boutique in the marina. Ricky was educated overseas and is very handsome."

"He sounds wonderful." She beamed. "When can I meet him?"

Enzo scribbled down a name and handed it to Lily.

"Here is the name of the boutique. If Ricky appeals to you, I'll have my sister make an introduction."

"I knew I could count on you. You're the best butler in all of Sardinia." Lily's face lit up in a smile. "Now, if you would just call me Lily, everything would be perfect."

Lily walked onto the marina and thought it was even more glamorous than in the brochure. Mannequins in the window at Chanel wore yellow tunics, jewelry cases in Harry Winston held dazzling pendants, and there were ostrich-skin purses and leather sandals at Gucci.

When she'd decided to open a Lily Bristol on the Emerald Coast, she expected to visit on a regular basis. She would stay in a boutique hotel in Porto Cervo and pick out pieces for the store: local pottery and hand-painted linens and silk cushions.

But then her marriage had crumbled, and she'd turned the project over to her top designer. Dolores had sent photos of the store: textured walls and terra-cotta floors and Lily's trademark gold sign in the window. But the pictures hadn't captured the local beauty: the water like a sheet of glass, fishing boats idling at the shore, and the scent of perfume and hibiscus.

Now Lily consulted the scrap of paper and stopped in front of a plate glass window. Ricky's had a red front door and striped awnings. A Bentley waited outside, and there was a pot of geraniums in the window box.

"Can I help you?" a man asked when she walked inside. He had dark curly hair and wore a white shirt and navy slacks.

"I'm just browsing." She looked up. "I've never been in Porto Cervo before. The harbor is stunning. It's like the French Riviera without the traffic and tourists."

"I'm glad you like it." He arranged blouses on a table. "Sardinia is a wonderful blend of the old and new. Farmers have been tending sheep in the hills for centuries, and the fishermen pass their boats on to their children. But in the summer, the yachts arrive, and the marina is filled with European royalty and American movie stars."

"I've never seen such glamorous people," Lily agreed. "I feel completely underdressed. I thought I'd be all right in cotton caftans and sandals, but everyone looks like they just came from the runway shows in Milan."

He studied Lily's dark hair and round sunglasses. He pulled a dress from the rack and handed it to her. "Try this on, it's from Pucci's summer collection."

Lily took the dress into the dressing room and slipped it over her shoulders. She stepped outside and studied herself in the mirror.

"You see, now you look like a native." The man beamed. "You just need a smart hat and you can have lunch at Cala di Volpe with all the fashionable people."

"I'm sure you say that to all your customers." Lily laughed. "I'm from New York. The summers are so humid you can't wear a dress without the fabric sticking to your thighs."

"In Sardinia, we are lucky." He nodded. "A cool breeze wafts in from the ocean, and the climate is perfect."

"I'm having a wonderful time," Lily agreed. "I wish I had

brought my daughter. She'd spend all day building sand castles and splashing in the waves."

"And your husband?" he asked. "Does he like the Emerald Coast?"

"I'm not married. Well, I was married, but I'm divorced." She flushed. "Louisa is only six, and I thought she might get bored. But I was wrong, the *piazzetta* is filled with quaint shops and the hills are covered with beds of flowers. We could have had picnics and made daisy chains."

The man walked to a display case and took out a straw purse. He wrapped it in tissue paper and handed it to Lily.

"What's that for?" she asked.

"It's for your daughter," he replied.

"I can't take this." She shook her head.

"In Sardinia, men are taught to give gifts to beautiful women, and women are taught to accept them." He smiled. "It makes for a civilized society."

"Thank you." Lily took the purse. "Louisa will love it."

"Here's my card." He reached into his shirt pocket. "Please call if I can make your stay more pleasant."

Lily slipped the card into her purse and held out her hand. "Lily Bristol."

He shook her hand, and she noticed his palms were smooth and he smelled of citrus cologne. "Ricky Pirelli. It's a pleasure to meet you."

Lily sat at an outdoor table at Cala di Volpe and thought Ricky was right; she had never seen such glamorous people. Women wore wraparound sunglasses and jeweled sandals. The men had their hair slicked back and fiddled with gold cigarette cases.

Lily ate steamed lobster salad and felt light and happy. Maybe she didn't need a man. She was perfectly content sitting with the sun warming her shoulders.

But it wouldn't hurt to ask Ricky to dinner. After all, he had given her his card. She wondered what would they talk about. She didn't know anything about him.

That was a funny thing about divorce. You had to learn everything about someone new. She knew Oliver loved peanut butter and was terrified of horror movies and refused to sleep with the window open.

Of course, there were things she wished she hadn't learned about Oliver. They had both betrayed each other, and no matter how they tried to forget, it didn't work. Marriage was like a coloring book filled in with Magic Marker. The only way to erase it was to rip out the pages.

It was like Enzo said, trust was the most important ingredient in a marriage. She wondered again if things would have turned out differently if she hadn't opened Lily Bristol stores on different continents. But that was silly. Distance had nothing to do with it. Astronauts spent half their time in space and had happy marriages. It was about telling the truth.

If Oliver hadn't lied to her about where he was that night, she never would have had let down her guard and done something she regretted. You couldn't lie in a marriage; it made the whole thing unravel like the hem of her new Pucci dress.

Or was she wrong? Had they started to drift apart because she was often on an airplane, and he spent almost every night reviewing restaurants in Manhattan? It was all so easy in the beginning. They were like barnacles on the ocean floor. They didn't need anything except each other, and all they wanted was to be together.

She nibbled flat bread and remembered the first evening they'd spent in Florence. They'd strolled along the Arno and talked about music and politics until their feet ached and she fell asleep on Oliver's shoulder.

The Fiat pulled into the Piazza del Duomo and Lily gazed up at the Cathedral of Santa Maria del Fiore. It was more dramatic than in the photos, with its pink marble panels and wide dome. The sun set over the clock tower, and the whole piazza was bathed in a golden light.

"I can't believe we're in Florence." She rolled down the window. "Dante used to walk down this very street, and Donatello and Brunelleschi met for coffee in the Piazza della Signoria."

"I should go." Oliver rubbed his forehead. "If I don't leave now, I won't reach Naples until midnight."

"You can't turn around and drive back to Naples," Lily protested. "That's like skipping the Sistine Chapel in Rome or leaving Paris without seeing the Eiffel Tower."

"I don't have a choice. The rental car needs to be returned, and I have to work in the morning."

"What's the point of being in Italy if you spend all your time in a restaurant kitchen?" she asked. "Giuseppe won't mind if you stay an extra day."

"I suppose I could drive back in the morning." He wavered. "But I don't have anywhere to sleep and I can't afford a hostel."

"Giuseppe's cousin said you were welcome to stay at his restaurant," she reminded him. "We'll visit the Pitti Palace and see the view from Piazzale Michelangelo. Tomorrow morning we'll have cappuccinos and *cornetto*s at Caffè Gilli. It opened in the eighteenth century and is the oldest café in Florence."

"Why not?" Oliver relented. "I hate driving at night. Italian drivers act as if they're practicing for the Grand Prix."

They marveled at Michelangelo's *David* at the Galleria dell'Accademia. They bought roasted chestnuts in the San Lorenzo market and soaked up the Titians and Bronzinos at the Uffizi Gallery. The guard tapped his watch and said if they stayed any longer, they'd be locked inside with the paintings.

Now they strolled along the Ponte Vecchio, and silver lights flickered on the Arno. The city was bathed in a warm glow, and Lily had never seen anything more beautiful.

"Tell me," Oliver said, licking a gelato cone. "What makes you happy?"

"Why do you ask?" Lily asked.

"You said you only wanted to be happy," he answered. "Most people don't even know what it means."

"I know exactly what makes me happy." She leaned against the railing. "Rereading the books I loved as a girl: *Little Women* and *To Kill a Mockingbird*. February in San Francisco, when the apple blossoms are in bloom. Discovering a piece of furniture at an estate sale that I can't live without."

"What about love?" Oliver asked.

"Love is wonderful in books and movies but it doesn't make you happy in real life." She shook her head.

"I thought young women went to sleep with visions of wedding dresses swirling in their heads." He laughed.

"That's the most sexist thing I've ever heard," Lily retorted.

"Whoever said marriage makes you happy? In my experience, it's the reverse."

"Let me guess: your father ran off with his secretary and left your mother the mansion with the view of the San Francisco Bay," Oliver replied. "He feels so guilty he sends you money, even when you don't ask for it, and your mother begs you not to move out, because what would she do with all that space?"

"You wouldn't make a good psychologist." She smiled. "My parents have been married for twenty-five years, but they rarely talk to each other. Of course, they are lovely in public; they host the most exclusive dinners and are invited to all the best parties."

"Why don't they talk to each other?" he asked.

"I tried to find out when I was younger, but getting either of them to open up was harder than opening a jar of pickles." She paused. "But if I get married, I'm going to marry my best friend. You can't get mad at your best friend; then you wouldn't have anyone at all."

Lily finished her cone and turned to Oliver.

"Enough about me, what makes you happy?"

"The usual things." He shrugged. "Pretty girls, a good book, delicious food."

"The usual things! Is that your best answer?" she demanded. "Surely some unusual things make you happy."

"I suppose you're right," he said slowly. "I know a very unusual girl. She has the figure of a bird but eats like a horse. She can be absentminded but says the cleverest things." He looked at Lily. "For some reason, when I'm with her, I feel happy."

A wooden *barchetto* drifted down the Arno and Lily suddenly felt unsteady.

"That is unusual," she whispered. "I've never heard anything like it."

They strolled to the Piazza Santa Croce and stopped in front of a brick building. Oliver peered at a sign in the window and ran his hands through his hair.

"I'm afraid the restaurant is closed. Giuseppe's cousin went to visit his sister in Pisa," he said. "We can't have dinner, and I don't have a place to stay. I'll have to drive to Naples after all."

"How can the restaurant be closed?" Lily asked. "Surely he has a staff."

"All the employees are family, and it's his sister's fiftieth birthday."

"He can't turn people away!" she exclaimed. "He'll go out of business."

"In Italy, family is more important than work." He shrugged. "His sister would be furious if he missed her birthday. But the customers will return."

"There are dozens of cafés close by." Lily consulted her guidebook. "We'll find a trattoria along the Via Andrea del Verrocchio."

"I can't afford to eat anywhere else."

"It will be my treat," she offered. "I may as well spend my euros, they won't do me any good in America. And you can share my room at the Hotel degli Orafi. It was built in the sixteenth century and has a view of Giotto's Campanile."

"Share a room?" Oliver raised his eyebrow.

"You can sleep on the roll-out, and I'll take the bed," she said and smiled. "Don't tell me you've never had a coed sleepover?"

"Not since I was in seventh grade." Oliver shifted his feet. "I was so nervous. I drank warm milk with honey and fell asleep when my head hit the pillow."

Lily opened the door of the hotel room and took a deep breath. What was she thinking, inviting Oliver to share her room? But he was warm and sincere, and there was something about him that made her feel like she had known him forever.

Was the real reason she'd asked him to stay that she didn't want him to drive back to Naples? The thought of never seeing him again made her slightly dizzy.

"This is certainly not Signora Giannini's hostel." Oliver whistled, picking an apple from the fruit bowl.

Lily put down her suitcase and noticed the green carpet and chintz sofa. There was a double bed with a floral bedspread and wooden headboard.

"Oh, look at the view." She ran to the balcony. The sky was black velvet and the Duomo was lit up with pink and yellow lights.

"The view is stunning. But if I don't get some sleep, I won't wake up and leave early," Oliver said. "Where should I change? I told the concierge I lost my bag, and he lent me pajamas."

"In the bathroom." Lily pointed at the door and laughed. "We're young Americans in Italy. We are supposed to be going to nightclubs and drinking Campari. And you want to be in bed by midnight."

"I was never one of those college students who thought a good time was one you couldn't remember." Oliver disappeared into the bathroom.

Lily scooped up a handful of cashew nuts and turned around.

Oliver's pajama top was too small and the pants barely reached his calves. His hair was rumpled and she had the urge to kiss him.

"If you kissed me, people would think you were taking advantage of a young woman in a hotel room," she said, dusting her hands on her skirt.

"Absolutely." Oliver nodded. "I wouldn't dream of it."

"But if I kissed you, it would just be a girl kissing a boy. No one would say anything at all."

She walked over to Oliver and kissed him. He kissed her back and tasted of *caramello* gelato.

"I knew you were clever," he whispered, tucking her hair behind her ear.

Lily closed her eyes and kissed him again.

Lily ate the last bite of lobster salad and fiddled with her sunglasses. So what if she had to learn new things about Ricky? Enzo said he was well educated and traveled. For all she knew, they both loved modern art and cheese soufflé and romantic movies.

That was the thing about divorce; you had to be courageous. And she was on one of the most exciting coasts in the world. Why shouldn't she have fun?

She fished his card out of her purse and picked up her phone. The sun glinted on the screen, and she found Ricky's number. She typed out a quick text inviting him to dinner and pressed send.

Chapter Four

OLIVER WRAPPED A TOWEL AROUND his waist and entered the suite's bedroom. The wood table held a basket of fruit, and the air smelled of orchids and berries.

He and Angela had spent hours at the pool, lying on chaise longues and nibbling ceviche. On their way back, she stopped in the hotel's gift shop to buy a magazine, and he went up to the suite to take a shower.

Now he picked up a paperback book and thought it would be nice to take an afternoon nap. Perhaps he could suggest they make love before dinner. He pictured Angela in her bandeau bikini and decided bringing her to Sardinia was a good idea.

The bedspread was neatly folded, and he froze. What if Angela liked the right side of the bed? He could never sleep facing the window.

They had slept together, of course. On the third date, he accepted her invitation to come upstairs, and they made love like teenagers. God! The joy of sex with someone new and fresh and inventive. He got dizzy thinking about it.

Her lotions had been arranged on her bedside table, so he naturally slid into the other side of the bed. And he rarely spent the night. He didn't want to go to work smelling of Ivory soap and potpourri.

But sharing a hotel bed was a different experience. How did they pick sides, and what if he chose the wrong one? He didn't want Angela harboring a grudge because she had to sleep on the left.

Of course, he could just ask her. But that seemed too serious, like asking if she would empty out a drawer for his socks. That was the thing about dating postdivorce: just when you thought things were progressing at the correct pace, you felt like you were tossed into a high-speed dryer.

He sank onto the bed and rubbed his forehead. During the first weeks they were dating, everything about being together was new and thrilling and confusing.

Oliver sat at a table at Totto Ramen and ate chicken *paitan* with kikurage mushroom. He glanced at his phone and wondered if he should call Angela. Did one call during work hours or should he send a text? There were so many ways to communicate these days. He didn't want to give the wrong signal about their relationship.

He thought about making love on Angela's satin sheets and felt a rush of desire. Married sex had been constrained by train schedules and Louisa's bedtime stories and taking out the garbage. With Angela, their only concern was whether her downstairs neighbor heard them through the floorboards.

Were they exclusive, and should he know her birthday and the name of her first pet? And what kind of a term was exclusive, anyway? He felt like a teenager wondering if a prom kiss meant they were going steady.

He skewered noodles with his fork and realized he had no clue what he wanted. All he knew was that for the first time since he'd moved out of the farmhouse, he had jogged five miles without getting winded and devoured a six-egg omelet for breakfast.

"Oliver!" a female voice called. "There you are, I've been looking for you everywhere."

"Angela! What are you doing here?" Oliver asked. "Did I leave my wallet at your apartment? I swore I grabbed it from the dresser."

"I stopped by to see you, and the receptionist said you often eat here." She sat across from him. Her hair coiled down her back, and she wore an orange dress and cork sandals. "I thought I'd join you for lunch."

"You want to have lunch?" Oliver repeated, wondering if he had sauce on his chin.

"It's a gorgeous day." She took off her sunglasses. "It would be nice to spend time together."

Oliver's gaze traveled down her legs, and he adjusted his collar. Their dinners had been extended versions of some delicious foreplay. They'd sat across from each other at a Thai restaurant in Midtown or a trattoria in Chelsea, and Oliver tried to concentrate on his bean sprouts or spaghetti Bolognese. But all he was conscious of was Angela's mouth wrapped around her pasta or the small mole on her neck.

"I don't really have time to go to your apartment." He hesitated. "I have a deadline and I'm having trouble saying something new about Kobe sliders."

"Why would we go to my apartment? We can eat here." Angela picked up the menu. "The *char siu* pork sounds perfect."

"Of course we can eat here." He paused. "I just thought . . ."

"Thought what, Oliver?" she prompted. "That every meal has to end with sex?"

Oliver looked up and noticed Angela's thick mascara and shimmering lipstick.

"Well, yes," he admitted.

"Do you really think I like you just for sex?"

"Of course not." He fumbled. "Though we are good together. I'm really enjoying it."

"So am I. But there's more to a relationship." She crossed her legs. "We can walk in Central Park or see a movie."

Oliver coughed and thought a noodle had gone down the wrong way. He hadn't seen a movie with anyone but Lily and Louisa in a decade, and if they went for a walk, would they have enough to talk about?

"Never mind. When we met at the restaurant opening, I thought you were one of the good ones: a divorced guy who opens the door for a woman and doesn't bound up the stairs on a first date," she began. "But you're just like the rest; all you want is sex. You're like a cast member of *Survivor* left alone with a carton of Häagen-Dazs."

"You invited me up to your apartment, and I said no," Oliver reminded her.

"It was a test." She sighed. "I'm tired of men wanting to feel me up before they ask for my phone number. You passed with flying colors. But you didn't send flowers on my birthday and you hardly ever text during the day. I'm afraid this isn't going anywhere."

"I can't send you flowers, you're a florist!" he exclaimed. "And I haven't dated in a decade. Back then, we had flip phones. There was none of this sending sexy pictures or cute emojis. What if I send a smiley face instead of a heart? I don't want to offend you."

"Do you want a relationship?" she asked.

Oliver remembered looking in the mirror when he was shaving and seeing a guy with a glint in his eye and broad shoulders. He thought about the way Angela's hair was tousled after they made love and of her lipstick on his collar.

"Yes." He nodded. "I think about you all the time."

"That's good." She handed him the menu and smiled. "Would you order for me, Mr. New York Times Food Critic? I'm starving."

It was the end of the week, and Oliver climbed the steps to Angela's apartment. He checked his blazer pocket to make sure he had the tickets. He rang Angela's doorbell and took a deep breath.

All week, he had tried to think of something special to do with Angela. If they dined at a trendy restaurant, someone was bound to recognize him and ask if he was writing a review. It was hard to be romantic when the maître d' hovered nearby, wondering if the fish was sautéed properly or the tenderloin steak was medium rare.

Angela wasn't keen on museums, and it was too muggy to take a horse-and-buggy ride through Central Park. He finally decided on a dinner cruise. They would sip Bloody Marys and sail under the lights of the Brooklyn Bridge.

"Oliver!" Angela opened the door. "I didn't know how to dress. You haven't told me where we're going."

"You look stunning." Oliver studied her patterned teal dress and narrow stilettos. Suddenly, he wished they could skip dinner and fall into her bed.

"We should go." He took her hand. "If we're late, they'll leave without us."

"Oh, Oliver," Angela breathed. "This is the most exciting thing I've done in New York."

Oliver sipped a glass of champagne and felt quite pleased with himself. The boat resembled a French bateau, with hardwood floors and benches scattered with pastel-colored cushions. Waiters passed around trays of canapés, and light jazz played over the speakers.

And the view! The Chrysler Building was lit up like a Christmas tree, and the Statue of Liberty resembled a Greek goddess. The Freedom Tower loomed in the distance, and the river was bathed in a pink and purple glow.

"I can't imagine a better surprise." Angela beamed. "My mother and grandmother watched *Breakfast at Tiffany's* every Sunday, and I dreamed of living in New York." She turned to Oliver. "Now I have a job and my own apartment. I look up at the Empire State Building and feel I belong."

Oliver remembered the first time he and Lily had visited New York. They ate dim sum in Chinatown and spent hours at the Frick and the Guggenheim. At night, they collapsed in their room at the Hilton and watched romantic movies on television. They were so happy! Oliver was going to be a restaurant critic at the *New York Times*, and Lily would open a Lily Bristol store.

He thought of the years since then, when he rarely got home to Connecticut for dinner, and Lily was constantly flying to San Francisco. Their dreams and goals were replaced by constant biting, like puppies nipping at each other's paws.

"I know exactly what you mean," Oliver said and felt a twinge in his chest. "It's the greatest city in the world."

Couples in elegant evening wear drifted inside, and Oliver inhaled the smell of butter and herbs. The brochure promised a three-course meal with goat cheese salad and filet of sole, and warm butter cake for dessert.

"I get seasick if I eat on a boat," Angela said. "I'm afraid we'll have to skip dinner."

"It's a dinner cruise!" Oliver exclaimed. "Three hours of nibbling glazed duck and sipping French wine and floating under the Williamsburg Bridge. And the barge is hardly built like a row-boat. If you close your eyes, you can't tell we're on the river at all."

"I can't eat with my eyes closed. And just the sight of water when I'm eating makes me seasick." She shook her head. "I'm sorry, Oliver. We'll have to eat when we disembark."

They wouldn't dock until midnight, and all the good restaurants would be closed. And he was starving! He pictured plates of blackened sea bass and braised brussels sprouts, and his stomach ached.

It wasn't Angela's fault; he hadn't told her they were taking a dinner cruise. But who got seasick on a barge on the Hudson River? It was like being afraid of heights when you were standing on the second floor at Macy's.

"I suppose we'll find a burger somewhere." Oliver slumped on a bench. He discovered a mint in his pocket and popped it into his mouth.

"I'm terribly sorry. It was so thoughtful." She sat beside him. "Why don't we pick up a chicken and a carton of pecan ice cream and go back to my apartment? There's nothing more fun than eating ice cream in bed. I always feel like a little girl who can eat anything she likes because she got her tonsils removed."

Her hair glinted in the moonlight, and Oliver let out his breath. Wasn't being hungry for a few hours worth it, to be entangled between Angela's sheets?

"I get tired of fancy sauces and rich desserts," he agreed. "I'd much rather have baked chicken and a bowl of ice cream."

Oliver rearranged the striped bedspread and suddenly had an idea. He would pretend he was shaving and let Angela climb into bed first. After all, he wanted her to be happy. If she picked the left side, he could ask the butler for a sleeping mask.

Just because he didn't know what side of the bed Angela slept on, it didn't mean their relationship wasn't progressing. He had learned dozens of things about her: she split her loyalties between the New York Yankees and the Cleveland Indians, and wore heels even when they walked in Central Park. She was voted Most Photogenic in high school and spent a month after graduation as an extra in commercials for an amusement park. He pictured her in denim shorts and white sneakers and got hard underneath his towel.

Now Angela stepped out of the bathroom and unwrapped the towel from her hair. She wore a man's white T-shirt and slippers. Oliver sat on the edge of the bed and grabbed his book. If she thought he was reading, she would pick a side of the bed first.

Angela walked to the minibar. She examined the bottles, and Oliver couldn't concentrate on his book. How could a size-L Hanes T-shirt look so sexy, and was she wearing panties?

"You're staring at me, Oliver." Angela looked up. "Haven't you ever seen a woman wearing a man's T-shirt?"

"Of course I have," he bristled. "In college, I spent a spring break in Miami. They had wet T-shirt contests every night. I started to feel sorry for the women. Wet cotton must get uncomfortable against bare skin. But they seemed to enjoy it, and they never had to pay for drinks."

"That's a deplorable practice," Angela responded. "They should have wet board-short contests, where men have to sit in a bucket filled with ice cubes."

"I hadn't thought of that." He shifted under his towel. "Why don't you pour us a couple of glasses of pineapple juice, and I'll find some coasters. The bedside tables are solid teak, I wouldn't want to get water marks on them."

He opened the oyster shell armoire and sifted through the television remote and shoe shine kit. If Angela put her glass on the bedside table first, he would know which side of the bed she slept on.

But when he turned around, she was standing near the closet. Her lips were pursed together, and she drummed her fingernails on the glass.

"Is something wrong?" he asked.

"I left my ChapStick next to the pool," she replied. "I'll have to go buy a new one."

"Now?" Oliver asked, more loudly than he intended. "I mean, I thought we might take a nap. It's nice to have a rest in the afternoon. Then we'll have more energy to go dancing."

"A nap?" She arched her eyebrows. "That's why you're wearing aftershave."

He rubbed his cheeks and wondered if he'd applied too much aftershave after his shower.

"A nap, among other things," he murmured.

"I like making love during the day." She nodded. "It's so refreshing, and afterwards I sleep like a baby. But first I need Chap-Stick, my lips will be raw without it." She opened the closet. "I'll put on a pair of slacks and be right back."

There was a flash of silk panties when she reached up, and Oliver gulped. If Angela went to the gift shop, she might be distracted by a magazine or a pretty blouse. She wouldn't come back for ages, and the mood would be ruined.

"I'll go for you," he announced.

"I'm perfectly capable of picking out my own ChapStick, Oliver."

"Of course you are." He pulled on a pair of shorts. "But your hair is wet, and the air-conditioning might be on high in the gift shop. I'll get it for you."

"My hair is wet." She ran her fingers through it. "Are you sure you don't mind?"

"Perfectly sure." Oliver hurried to the door.

"Oliver, wait," she called after him.

"Yes?" he asked hopefully. Maybe she didn't need the Chap-Stick after all and just wanted to make love.

"If they have it, get cherry ChapStick. It's my favorite."

Oliver strode down the hallway and pressed the button on the elevator. A woman wearing a floral dress walked toward him. She wore oversized sunglasses and carried a leather clutch.

"Oliver," a female voice said. "I thought that was you."

"Lily!" Oliver jumped. "What are you doing?"

"Obviously our plan of tapping a secret code on the wall when we entered the hallway didn't work." She laughed. "Here we are together."

"You look very nice, aren't you a little dressed up?"

"The dress is Pucci, I bought it at a boutique in the marina."

She smoothed the skirt. "I thought it might be a little fancy for the daytime. But Ricky, the owner of the boutique, said it was perfect for Porto Cervo."

Oliver pulled at his collar and wondered if you were supposed to compliment your ex-wife's attire while you were running an errand for your girlfriend. There were so many scenarios they didn't cover in books about divorce. Maybe he'd pitch a monthly column for the *New York Times*.

"It suits you," he said finally. "You should always wear Pucci."

"I feel quite fashionable," Lily said, and her smile was bright. "I'm going to do a little last minute buying for the store. Enzo said there's a gorgeous little town called Tempio Pausania that sells wonderful cork products. I'm sure he would have gone with me if I had asked. He's very accommodating."

"Who's Enzo?" he asked.

"My personal butler, you must have one too." She paused. "At first I thought I didn't need one, but he's been so helpful, and we've had some interesting talks. It's nice to have a friend."

"You seem to have made friends quickly," Oliver muttered. "A boutique owner who tells you what to wear, and a butler who suggests excursions to picturesque towns."

"Enzo says I'm supposed to make new friends. After all, I am a young American divorcée on the Emerald Coast," Lily said when they reached the lobby. "Have a nice afternoon. Next time, I'll tap on your wall and let you know when I use the elevator."

Oliver sat on the balcony and sipped his glass of pineapple juice. When he returned from the gift shop with the ChapStick, Angela was asleep. He thought about waking her, but somehow he wasn't in the mood.

Lily could make as many male friends as she liked. He didn't know anything about her life, and she wasn't part of his. That was the whole point of divorce. But she had looked so radiant in her bright dress and straw hat. There was a lightness about her she hadn't had in months.

He suddenly remembered the early days of their courtship. Lily was different from anyone he'd ever met. Her enthusiasm was infectious, and when she got excited, she bubbled over like a glass of champagne.

The August heat drifted through the window, and Giuseppe's kitchen was a furnace. Oliver wiped his hands on his apron and unfolded the envelope.

He and Lily had exchanged addresses before he left Florence, but he hadn't expected to hear from her. They had barely exchanged a kiss, and they lived on different continents. What was the point of writing when they would never see each other again?

But her first letter arrived a week after she returned to San Francisco. And it was so descriptive! He felt like he was riding the cable car with her down Lombard Street and eating clam chowder at Fisherman's Wharf.

"Oliver." Giuseppe appeared in the doorway. "Can I see you in my office?"

Oliver swallowed and wondered if he was going to be fired. Ever since he'd returned from Florence, he couldn't concentrate.

He'd suggested the linguini pesto with pine nuts to a regular customer who was allergic to nuts, and served beef lasagna to a diner who was a vegetarian.

"I have bad news." Giuseppe sat at his desk.

"I could have sworn the chef said the plate on the right was the meatless lasagna," Oliver explained. "I'll never make the mistake again."

"What are you talking about?" Giuseppe asked.

Oliver wished he could stuff his mouth with pastry dough. "I thought you were going to let me go."

"I'm closing the restaurant for August. We will reopen the first of September."

"You can't close the restaurant for a month!" Oliver urged him. "I'll lose my work permit and have to go home. Michigan in August is so humid, it makes Naples seem like a seaside resort."

"The air-conditioning bill is too high, and my regular customers go on package tours of Ibiza." Giuseppe shrugged. "My niece and her husband invited me to their farm in Tuscany. Three weeks of drinking Chianti and eating gnocchi and summer vegetables."

"That's what you do here! Let me run the restaurant. I'll make sure the butcher doesn't short you on the ground beef and there are a dozen eggs in every carton."

"I already canceled the deliveries," Giuseppe continued. "I have a cousin with an Italian restaurant in San Francisco. Guido serves the best veal *piccata* with fresh oregano." He scribbled on a piece of paper. "He'd be happy to give you a job."

"San Francisco?" Oliver suddenly thought of Lily.

"It's a beautiful city, like Europe but with better drivers. You're a bright young man. You shouldn't be stuck in a second-rate restaurant in Naples."

"You know about Lily?" Oliver looked up.

"My wife read the mail. They were addressed to you, care of the restaurant. She thought that was subterfuge and I was getting love letters," Giuseppe admitted. "You have to go. When you're young, women send you letters because of your curly hair and thick chest. When you're my age, they want you to fix the vacuum cleaner and share your Bolognese recipe."

"Thank you. I'll consider it." Oliver took the paper. "You really won't give your wife your recipe?"

"What if she gets angry with me and starts her own restaurant?" Giuseppe asked. "Every man must have his secrets."

Oliver walked back to the hostel and opened the door. Could he really go to San Francisco to see Lily? They had only spent two days together, and part of that had been navigating Italian traffic. He pictured her sipping limoncello at the café in Spello and sighed. God, she was lovely, with her dark hair and sparkling eyes.

What if Lily didn't want a serious relationship? Maybe she just liked writing letters, like when his little sister had a Swedish pen pal.

But Giuseppe was right; he had to take a chance. And San Francisco was filled with wonderful restaurants; it was the perfect place to become a food critic.

He bounded up the steps of the hostel and entered his room. He opened a shoebox and stuffed the euros into his pocket. He was going to go down to the American Airlines office and book the next flight to San Francisco.

———

Oliver gazed at the stone mansion and took a deep breath. He had assumed Lily's parents were wealthy but he hadn't expected three stories and a circular driveway and marble fountain. And the view! Whitewashed houses fell down to the bay, and the Golden Gate Bridge shimmered in the distance.

What if Lily was used to dating someone who drove a sports car and dined at three-star restaurants? He should look up her number at a pay phone and call her. Then she could let him down easily.

"Oliver!" a female voice called. "What are you doing here?"

Oliver looked up, and his heart did a flip. Her brown hair was tucked behind her ears, and she wore a floral dress and oval sunglasses.

"You said in your last letter that I should look you up if I'm ever in San Francisco," he stammered. "But if you're going out, I can come back another time."

"What are you doing in town?" Lily demanded. "You never told me you were coming."

"Giuseppe closed the restaurant for August. His cousin, Guido, offered me a job in San Francisco."

"Giuseppe has a lot of cousins." Lily laughed. "Are you sure that's why you came?"

"There is another reason." Oliver shifted his feet. "I want to ask you on a date."

"You rescued me from the train station in Naples and we spent the night at a hotel in Florence," Lily answered. "Aren't we past going on a first date?"

"We haven't been on a proper date," Oliver insisted. "I want to take you to dinner."

"You came all the way from Naples to ask me to dinner?" She took off her sunglasses.

"I had to," Oliver said and smiled. "A letter would have taken too long, and I didn't have your phone number."

"I had a lovely time," Lily said, biting into a crepe suzette. "How did you know all my favorite things?"

Oliver sipped a black Muscat and thought it had been a spectacular day. They'd started the morning with espressos in North Beach and climbed to the top of Coit Tower. They rode bicycles in Golden Gate Park and saw the collections at the Asian Art Museum. Now they sat at a bistro on Union Street and ate steamed mussels and lamb stew Provençal.

"In your letters you described the Chinese lacquerware at the Asian Art Museum and Pearls on a String exhibit so clearly, I felt like I had already seen them."

"I do ramble in my letters." Lily laughed. "I'm surprised you didn't crumple them up and toss them in the garbage."

"I loved your letters. But there's one thing you didn't tell me." Oliver traced the rim of his glass. "That your parents' house is at the top of Pacific Heights and takes up a city block."

"Would that have stopped you from coming?" she asked.

"Mansions like that usually come with memberships to the country club and marriages arranged at the cotillion," Oliver continued. "Your parents aren't going to be thrilled that you're seeing a struggling waiter."

"For your information, my family has a history of ignoring the restraints of polite society. The house was built during Prohibition and the cellar was crammed with bootleg liquor," she said sharply. "And just because I misplaced my credit cards and live at home, doesn't mean I'm a child. I can see whomever I like."

"I'm sorry." Oliver stumbled. "I just . . ."

"I put my earnings into a savings account and I'm going to open my own store by the time I'm twenty-five." Lily fumed. "Who are you to talk? You won't achieve your ideal life by being a waiter. And what happens when you run out of Giuseppe's cousins?"

"I just wrote my first restaurant review," Oliver retorted. "The *San Francisco Chronicle* is going to print it."

"That's wonderful news!" Lily said and laughed. "We had our first argument before we finished dessert. I'm sure you think this is the worst date ever; you should probably take me home."

Oliver swallowed the wine, and a warmth spread through his chest. Lily wore a silk cocktail dress and diamond earrings and she'd never looked more beautiful.

"You're radiant when you get angry." He touched her hand. "Like a shooting star falling to earth."

"Sometimes I say the first thing that comes into my head." She flushed.

"It's my fault." He put his napkin on the plate. "I was afraid your parents would ask about my prospects."

"Do you want to meet my parents?" Lily asked.

Oliver inhaled her floral perfume and desperately wanted to kiss her.

"Yes," he gulped. "I'd like that very much."

They climbed to the top of Pacific Avenue, and Lily opened the gate. A fog had settled over the bay and the sky was a velvet tapestry.

"I completely forgot. My parents are at a party and won't be home for hours." She fumbled in her purse. "I can't find my key, it must be in my other bag. I'll have to wait until they return."

"You can't sit in the driveway. When the fog rolls in, you'll freeze to death!" Oliver exclaimed. "Surely there's a key hidden under a flowerpot."

"My mother doesn't believe in spare keys." She shook her head.

"I'm staying at Guido's, and his wife is a devout Catholic." He hesitated. "She won't be happy if I bring home a girl."

"Don't worry about me. I can call a friend and ask her to come get me."

"What if you can't reach anyone? I can't leave you." Oliver looked up at the house. "There must be an open window."

"Sometimes my father opens his study window," she remembered. "My mother gets furious. She thinks it's an invitation for thieves to steal the artwork."

"I was a pole-vaulter in high school." He smiled. "This will be a piece of cake."

Oliver nudged open the window and clambered inside. The room was dark, and he walked to the hallway. He found a light switch and gasped.

Crystal chandeliers dangled from the ceiling, and a Chinese cabinet held a Fabergé egg. The floors were black-and-white marble, and the walls were lined with Impressionist paintings.

He descended the circular staircase and discovered salons with Oriental carpets and damask curtains. There was a library with leather-bound books and a Steinway piano.

"I was so worried that you'd fall," Lily said when he opened the front door. "How can I thank you?"

"A shot of brandy would be nice," Oliver said. "Unless there's a Doberman pinscher lurking in the hallway."

"We can't have a dog. My father is allergic." Lily poured two shots of cognac. "My mother does keep a pistol in the safe. But it's been there for decades and doesn't have any bullets."

"Your mother sounds more terrifying than any attack dog." Oliver shuddered. "Maybe I should leave."

"I told you they won't be home for hours." Lily handed him the glass. "Unless you want to go."

Oliver had never wanted anything more than to wrap his arms around her. But he could hardly make love to her on the daybed or carry her upstairs to her bedroom.

"I'd love to stay. But what if they come home early?"

"I suppose you're right," Lily conceded.

"There is one thing I'd like before I go." He hesitated.

"Oh, really." She looked up, and her eyes were the color of amber. "What did you have in mind?"

"I was thinking of this." He kissed her. She kissed him back and tasted of chocolate and raspberries.

"I had a lovely time," Lily said when he released her.

"So did I." He walked to the entryway and smiled. "Perhaps we can do it again tomorrow."

Oliver finished his glass of pineapple juice and glanced at the harbor. It was late afternoon and yachts were teeming with men wearing dark sunglasses and women in bright tunics. The sun glimmered on the water, and it was like a glossy postcard.

Why was he thinking about his first date with Lily when he was sitting on the balcony of his suite on the Emerald Coast? There were still a few hours until dinner. He should go swimming at Liscia Ruja Beach. The water was like a bath, and you could see the green hills and sailboats breezing across the bay.

Or maybe he'd wander down to the marina. He could sit outside at Nikki Beach and have a predinner snack of bruschetta topped with buffalo mozzarella and arugula. After all, he was in Sardinia to write a restaurant review. It would be a good idea to sample the competition.

"Oliver," a female voice called. "What are you doing out there? I thought we were going to take a nap."

Oliver peered through the sliding glass door and saw Angela propped against the pillows. The sheet was drawn around her waist, and she rubbed her lips with ChapStick.

"You were asleep when I got back from the gift shop." He walked inside. "I didn't want to wake you."

"I suppose I did fall asleep. I had a wonderful dream, and you were in it." She sighed. "Do you want me to show you what happened in my dream?"

Oliver put his glass down and stripped off his shirt. The beach would be there tomorrow, and if he had a snack before dinner, he'd ruin his appetite.

"I'd like that very much." He climbed into the bed. Her skin was smooth, and she smelled of shampoo and lavender soap.

"It started with me under the covers." She slid under the sheet.

He felt her mouth against him and stiffened. The sun made patterns on the bedspread, and a yacht's horn sounded in the distance. He let out a moan and felt young and bold and happy.

Chapter Five

LILY WALKED DOWN A COBBLESTONE alley past stands selling olive oil and jars of honey. There were leather shops displaying soft purses and jewelry stores with cases of gold bangles. She inhaled the scent of perfume and cut flowers and thought her first full day on the Emerald Coast was better than she had imagined.

She started the morning at a café, with poached eggs and tea with milk thistle. Then she entered the Lily Bristol store and studied the bright artwork and ceramic pottery and lacquered furniture. Seeing it all come together—the linen chairs where shoppers could sift through piles of fabric, the coffee bar with cappuccino and pastries—made her heart race. The grand opening was in five days, and she hoped it would be a huge success.

Now she had an hour until she met Ricky for lunch. She adjusted her sunglasses, and her heart beat a little faster. It didn't matter that Ricky was a complete stranger; they were just going to share a plate of pasta and a bottle of mineral water. Anyway, she couldn't sit in her hotel room and not talk to anyone except Enzo when he came to refill the ice bucket.

She thought of Oliver and Angela in the adjoining suite, and her stomach clenched. They weren't the reason she'd left the hotel so early. She wasn't in the least bit jet-lagged, and there was so much she wanted to do: pick out a few items for the store; buy Louisa a pretty dress, sample the local fruits and cheeses.

But whenever she entered the hallway she had a prickly feeling, as if a bug had crawled under her skirt. She even brought a paperback book, so if she ran into Angela in the lobby she could pretend she was reading.

Now, for the first time since Oliver had crouched down to help her find her key, she felt relaxed and happy. Sea air was always invigorating; it had nothing to do with being away from Oliver and Angela. And Porto Cervo was charming, with its quaint fishermen's cottages and sleek galleries; she didn't have time to think about anything else.

Lily entered a children's boutique and sifted through the girls' clothing. There were sailor dresses and satin slippers and drawers filled with hair ribbons. She looked up and saw a familiar figure examining a glass bracelet. His hair was freshly washed, and he wore a striped shirt and khakis.

"Oliver!" she exclaimed. "What are you doing here? Did you follow me?"

"Of course I didn't follow you," he answered. "Did you follow me?"

"Don't be silly." Lily took off her sunglasses. "I wanted to buy a present for Louisa. I spoke to her last night and realized how much I miss her."

"I called her yesterday, and she said I must bring her a bracelet like she saw in a magazine." He smiled. "She sent me a picture from the computer."

"You do buy her lovely things," Lily agreed and gasped. "You didn't tell her that we . . ."

"Are practically sharing a hotel suite?" He shook his head. "I can't believe it myself. She's only a child; she wouldn't understand how we ended up in the same place. I just said I was having a good time but miss her very much."

"We aren't sharing anything; I just don't want her to get the wrong idea and think we're together. I miss her too." Lily sighed. "It was easier when I traveled and left her with you. Louisa adores my parents, but if I ask my mother what they had for dinner, she accuses me of not trusting her cooking."

"I'd rather not talk about your mother before lunch," Oliver said stiffly. "It will ruin my appetite."

"Oliver, you know she likes you now. She thinks you're a good father."

"She's impressed that I'm the restaurant critic for the *New York Times*." He bristled. "All those years, she hated telling her friends what I did, and now she drops my name like I'm Anthony Bourdain."

"It was nice to see you, Oliver." She turned away. "I have to go."

"You can't walk away as if I'm a stranger you met in line for gelato," he insisted. "Your Italian is better than mine; we should explore Porto Cervo together. Do you remember when we were in Pisa, and I said the wrong thing to a few thugs and almost got us involved in a drug ring?"

"I knew we shouldn't ask them for directions." She laughed. "How could they afford Gucci loafers unless they were doing something illegal?"

"They could have been knockoffs," he countered. "Join me for a coffee. I already drank two cups at the hotel. If I order regular instead of decaf I'll swing from the trees like Tarzan."

Lily still had time before she met Ricky, and it would be nice to rest her feet. And they weren't doing anything unusual. She and Oliver had drunk coffee and read the newspaper together every morning for years.

"I could use a cold juice," she relented. "But I have an appointment in an hour."

They sat at an outdoor table at La Briciola, and Lily drank sweetened grapefruit juice. Window boxes overflowed with pastel-colored pansies, and the pavement was lined with shiny sports cars. A red Ducati motorcycle gunned its engine, and her face lit up in a smile. She was sitting at a café on one of the most famous coastlines in the world, and the sun warmed her shoulders.

The view from the outdoor café was one of the most beautiful she had seen. When you looked up, you saw emerald hills scattered with juniper trees, and tall pines and beds of wildflowers. In front of her was the ocean, which was almost translucent. It was some exotic jewel from a page in a Sotheby's catalog. You couldn't stop staring at the priceless pink diamond earrings or sapphire necklace owned by a famous movie star.

"In America, a bread basket means a few plain rolls." Oliver handed her a woven basket. "In Sardinia, it comes with goat cheese and sausage and homemade honey. It's a wonder anyone has an appetite for an entrée."

"No thank you," Lily shook her head. "I'm not hungry."

"What do you mean, you're not hungry?" he asked. "Do you

remember when we met in Naples? You accused me of only dating models because I was staring at you eating a croissant."

"That was ten years ago." She sipped her juice. "I've changed."

"You haven't left a thing on your plate our entire marriage. And we've only been divorced for a week." He studied her white dress and gold earrings. "Though you do look different. You look single."

"What does that mean?" she asked.

"You have that air that women have when they know they're beautiful, and men are watching," he explained.

"I don't know what you're talking about." She flushed. "Anyway, you saw me a week ago at the attorney's office."

"I wasn't paying attention," he admitted. "Signing those papers was like entering the Bastille. It's too dark to notice your surroundings, and you're certain you'll never see the sun again."

"Oliver," she said sharply. "We agreed on a divorce because we both wanted to be happy."

"I didn't think it would be this difficult." He sighed. "The dryer shrinks my clothes because I never have a full load, and I eat too much cholesterol because if I don't make a six-egg omelet, the carton will expire."

"Set the dryer to warm instead of hot, and hard boil the eggs and put them in the fridge," Lily replied. "They last for weeks."

"You see, I miss the instructions you always taped to the fridge." Oliver beamed. "Even when you were in San Francisco or Milan, I knew how long to heat up the lasagna or where Louisa kept her guinea pig pellets."

"This isn't helping, and you're hardly alone." Lily looked away. "I'm sure Angela knows how to preheat an oven."

"Angela has never cooked in my apartment." He stirred his coffee. "I haven't even shown her where I keep the coffee beans."

"It's none of my business what she does in your home." She hesitated. "I thought since you brought her to Sardinia that . . ."

"We were on the verge of domesticity?" he finished. "I don't blame you for being upset. I'd be furious if you brought someone on vacation."

"You can bring whomever you like." Lily paused. "It was just a shock. Louisa never told me."

"We met a couple of months ago, and I enjoy her company." Oliver shrugged. "Her boss was angry because she lost a big client, and I felt sorry and invited her."

"But you do like her?" Lily asked.

"Of course I like her, I wouldn't have brought her otherwise." He brushed crumbs from his slacks. "But there's a long way from like to . . ."

"To what, Oliver?"

"To what we had," he said.

"What we had was ruined because we didn't trust each other. You lied to me, Oliver." Her cheeks flushed.

"It was a stupid lie." He fumed. "You knew me better than that. You should have trusted my judgment."

"You can't trust someone who lies," she explained. "How many times have we gone over this? I have to go, I'm meeting someone."

"How many new friends have you made? You've only been here for twenty-four hours."

"This was a bad idea." She stood up. "From now on, let's grunt if we pass each other in the hall. I'm sure Angela wouldn't approve of you having coffee with your ex-wife."

"Don't go," he pleaded. "I don't want to end every conversation with a fight."

"That's why we got divorced. So we wouldn't have conversations." She slipped on her sunglasses. "It was nice seeing you. Don't sit in the sun too long. We're both getting older, and you don't want to get wrinkles."

Lily crossed the *piazzetta* and her heel wedged between the cobblestones. She reached down and tried to dislodge it. The last thing she needed was Oliver assuming she wanted him to run after her.

She should never have agreed to join him for coffee. They might look like any other young couple, with their sunglasses and light tans, but they couldn't stop bickering. They were like children, furiously pushing buttons on a new toy.

She remembered telling Oliver that she had changed. She was different. These days she got her hair cut at expensive salons instead of trimming it herself, and she had replaced the cotton dresses in her closet with Ella Moss suits. And of course, she was a single mother now. She couldn't just think about her own happiness; she had to consider Louisa.

A man with dark hair and olive-colored skin waved, and she gasped. She'd almost forgotten about Ricky! She adjusted her sunglasses and smoothed her skirt. Thinking about her ex-husband was no way to start a relationship with a handsome young businessman.

"Lily, there you are." Ricky approached her. "It's lovely to see you."

"I'm so glad you suggested lunch. I've been exploring Porto

Cervo for hours. I've never seen so many gorgeous shops. I'm tempted to buy all the clothes in the boutique windows."

"You don't have to." Ricky handed her a box wrapped in tissue paper. "This is for you."

"You can't give me another present," Lily protested. "We just met."

"Remember, in Sardinia men give gifts, and women accept them." He pointed to the box. "Open it and see if you like it."

Lily untied the ribbon and took out a straw hat with a red bow. "It's gorgeous, but I can't accept it."

"Of course you can." He took her arm. "It's my mother's birthday next week, and she's addicted to American television. In return, you can update me on *Scandal* or *Modern Family*."

They entered a stucco building with marble floors and a beamed ceiling. There were floor-to-ceiling wine racks, a stone fireplace, and Moroccan chandeliers. Tables were set with white china and high-back chairs were covered with orange upholstery.

"It's gorgeous," Lily breathed. Windows opened onto the harbor, and sleek yachts gleamed in the noon sun. Men and women lingered on the balcony over bowls of fish stew, and the air smelled of floral arrangements and sea salt and butter.

"Renato Pedrinelli is the oldest restaurant in Porto Cervo and is owned by two brothers." Ricky sat opposite her. "They treat all their diners like family. They have been known to sneak George Clooney in the back door and seat him facing the kitchen." He stopped and smiled. "George enjoys the seafood lasagna but isn't fond of tourists begging for autographs."

"I've never been anywhere like the Emerald Coast. You imagine everyone arrived on a yacht or flew in by private jet, but then you meet an old man who eats bread and cheese for every meal and has never owned a television," Lily mused.

"In the 1960s, Prince Aga Khan thought the northern coast of Sardinia was the perfect vacation spot." Ricky tore apart a piece of bread. "He bought all the land and invited his friends to stay at his villa. Princess Grace loved to visit, and King Juan Carlos of Spain was a regular, and his parties were attended by Catherine Deneuve and Cary Grant. He built the marina so his guests could park their yachts and opened boutiques where they could shop, and it became the most exclusive resort in Europe."

Lily studied Ricky's dark hair and tan cheeks and felt the urge to run to the hotel and hide. She didn't have a wardrobe filled with Versace and she'd never been on a yacht in her life. She should call Louisa to remind her to feed Brussels, her guinea pig, or email the office to make sure the caterer was set for the opening.

But then she ate a bite of mussels in wine sauce, and her shoulders relaxed. She was a newly divorced woman; she couldn't only think about Louisa and Lily Bristol; she had to meet new people. And why shouldn't she nibble seafood with a charming Sardinian?

"You look serious," Ricky said. "I hope you're enjoying the restaurant."

The waiter replaced their plates with platters of tuna steak and stuffed artichokes, and Lily smiled. "It's the most delicious lunch I've ever had."

"Tell me why a beautiful American owns her own business," Ricky said when the waiter brought them ricotta cake and bowls of berries. There was a pitcher of coffee and pots of honey on the table. "I thought American women spend their days at the gym and attending book clubs, like on my mother's television programs."

"Your mother must watch too many episodes of *Desperate Housewives*." Lily laughed. "I love being a mother but I couldn't imagine not working. It's wonderful having something of my own."

"Did your husband feel the same?" Ricky asked.

"Oliver was quite supportive of my career." Lily nodded. "He took care of Louisa when I flew to San Francisco or Milan. Though he often forgot to put out her school clothes at night and he was hopeless at school lunches." She smiled. "But no child is going to suffer from wearing the same dress or eating peanut butter and jelly sandwiches."

"Then why did you get a divorce?" Ricky asked.

"We stopped making each other happy," she explained. "If you can't be happy, what's the point?"

"In Sardinia, you only get divorced for two reasons," he answered. "The husband is cheating, and the wife threatens to cut his heart out while he sleeps, or the wife has an affair, and the husband buys a pistol to shoot her lover."

"Marriage in Sardinia sounds dangerous." She laughed. "Is that why you haven't gotten married?"

"I haven't had the opportunity." He stirred honey into his coffee.

"Are you going to become one of those confirmed bachelors who doesn't know what to do with his money?" she continued. "You see them all the time in Manhattan. Their vintage sports cars get older, and the models on their arms get younger, and eventually they're dating women the age of their godchildren."

"I would love to be married," Ricky replied. "My parents have been married for thirty-five years."

"You're good-looking and successful," Lily mused. "I'm sure you've had invitations."

"My store might be filled with designer clothes, but I couldn't marry someone who only cares about the diamonds in her ears and price per ounce of her perfume. I want to meet a woman who can spend the day sitting under a juniper tree and discussing art and politics."

"It's important to have things in common," Lily agreed.

"I'm not talking about knowing the names of the latest books, I'm talking about being in love. You can't wait to be together and, after you part, you replay the evening like a movie you can't get enough of." He looked at Lily and his eyes were serious. "When I find that, I will be the luckiest man on the Emerald Coast."

Lily entered her hotel suite and tossed her purse on the end table. It had been a wonderful afternoon. She and Ricky had browsed in the shops in the marina and Ricky insisted on buying her a bunch of daisies at a flower stall. The air was fragrant and the ocean glittered like a diamond tennis bracelet, and Lily had never seen anything more stunning.

There was a knock at the door, and Lily froze. She almost forgot about Oliver and Angela. But there was no reason for Oliver to be here. They had both decided it was better if they ignored each other for the rest of the vacation.

Lily opened the door, and her shoulders relaxed.

"Oh, Enzo, it's you." She ushered him inside. "What a pleasant surprise."

"You texted me and asked me to come up," Enzo said, taking the phone out of his pocket.

"I did, didn't I?" Lily laughed. "I wasn't sure if you'd check it. You did say I could text if I needed anything. I had the most wonderful time. I wanted to send you pictures of our lunch. The ricotta cake with berries looked like one of the photos you see on Instagram that are so gorgeous they must be photoshopped. And Ricky was handsome and charming. You should take up a second job as a matchmaker. You'd be a great success." She paused. "Not that it's going to become anything serious. Tomorrow we're going to visit the antique stores in San Pantaleo. We'll pack a picnic and drive along the whole coastline."

"Ricky is a lucky man." Enzo nodded. "He gets to show a beautiful young American the Emerald Coast."

"You say the nicest things, you always make me feel good." She paused. "Can I ask you a question? Have you ever lied to your wife? Not about something silly like that you fed Maria and Gia turkey sandwiches and fruit salad for lunch when you really gave them frozen yogurt. Oliver used to do that all the time. He didn't have to; frozen yogurt is delicious on a hot day and it's high in calcium." Her eyes were large. "I mean, lied about something important."

"That's not the kind of question guests usually ask," Enzo responded.

"Please, Enzo," Lily urged. "It's very important. And I know we're friends. You wouldn't have read my texts if we weren't."

"There was the time I told Carmella that my cousin's bachelor party was at my uncle's restaurant, when really the groom and all his men were going to a nightclub," he conceded. "It wasn't up to me. My cousin insisted we keep it secret."

"That's terrible," Lily gasped. "What happened?"

"I decided not to go." He shrugged. "I stayed home, and we ate spaghetti marinara and spumoni."

"What if your wife was working for a dress designer in Paris or Milan and was out of town on the night of the bachelor party?" Lily asked thoughtfully. "She couldn't be sure you stayed home if you lied to her to begin with."

"She would have been angry that I didn't tell her the truth," he plumped the cushions on the sofa. "But she would have trusted me to do the right thing."

Lily stood up and walked to the window. Yachts lined the port like some impossibly beautiful jeweled bracelet, and she heard laughter and music.

"You make marriage sound easy, Enzo." She turned around. "But sometimes it doesn't work out. What if you both mess it up and get divorced? Do you get another chance at love, or will you be alone forever?"

"Everyone finds love on the Emerald Coast." Enzo refilled the bowl of Brazil nuts. "Why would it be different for a young American divorcée?"

"You're right, of course," Lily said and sighed. "Maybe you can come back tomorrow morning and help me pick out an outfit to wear for the picnic. Whenever I'm with you, I think anything is possible."

Enzo left, and Lily stood at the window. It would be lovely to take a swim in the pool or walk along Cala di Volpe beach, with its limestone cliffs and white sand. But she didn't want to bump into Oliver and Angela sipping martinis at the bar or strolling along the shore.

She entered the marble bathroom and unzipped her dress. A

silver dish held scented soaps, and fresh towels were folded next to the pedestal bathtub. She thought about what Enzo had said and turned on the faucet. She remembered when she and Oliver were so young and in love. Every day was perfect, and nothing could tear them apart.

Lily glanced in the mirror of her dressing room and fiddled with her ruby earrings. She usually adored her parents' Christmas party. The house was filled with the scent of nutmeg and decorated with poinsettias and twinkling lights. And the food! Platters of duck pâté and mini eggs Benedict. There was chocolate nougat, and custards in silver bowls.

But she had been looking forward to having Oliver by her side, and now he had to work at the restaurant. She rubbed her lips and wondered if he could have gotten the night off. It was the busiest season, and Giuseppe's cousin had been so kind, letting Oliver stay at his home until he could afford his own apartment.

She snapped a diamond bracelet around her wrist and had a sinking feeling. Was it possible her mother planned the Christmas Open House during the week she knew Oliver couldn't come? That was ridiculous; how could her parents have anything against Oliver? In the three months they had been dating, they hadn't shared more than a few Sunday dinners together, and turkey and stuffing at Thanksgiving.

It was unfortunate that Lily's parents happened to visit the restaurant with Lily just after their first Sunday dinner with Lily and Oliver. It must have been awkward for the waiter to shake her mother's hand and compliment her choice of banana soufflé from the menu. And he might have waited until he and Lily were alone to say she looked stunning in her low-cut evening dress instead of commenting on it in front of the other diners at the restaurant.

Oliver admitted it was his fault. He should have just asked whether everyone at the table preferred the grilled halibut or salmon and not said anything personal. But it wasn't the nineteenth century, and he wasn't an indentured servant. Waiting tables made sense while he built his reputation as a restaurant critic.

Lily descended the circular staircase and gazed at women in glittering evening gowns and men wearing white dinner jackets. She would circulate around the room and say hello to her parents' friends. Then she would slip out the side door and join Oliver at the restaurant.

"Lily. You're more beautiful than I remember!" a male voice said. "Did you let your hair grow? It suits you."

"Roger!" Lily exclaimed. "I didn't know you were in town. Your parents must be thrilled to have you home for Christmas. I've envied you the last year. Ice-skating in Rockefeller Center and watching the ball drop at Times Square. Everyone wants to be in New York during the holidays."

"You could have visited." Roger sipped his martini. "The door was always open."

"I doubt your fiancée would approve of your old girlfriend showing up for eggnog." She laughed. "How is Rachel? It must be exciting to be engaged to a Broadway actress."

"We broke up." He shrugged. "I worked twelve-hour days at the law firm, and she spent all night at the theater. The only thing we had in common was matching pajamas."

"I'm sorry," Lily replied. "I'm sure you'll find someone.

Manhattan is crawling with women looking for a handsome young attorney."

"Didn't your mother tell you? I moved back to San Francisco," he said. "I'm an associate at a firm and I bought a condo on Nob Hill."

"She didn't mention it." Lily moved away. "It was lovely to see you, I'm sure we'll run into each other."

"Lily, wait." He touched her arm. "Can we talk?"

"We are talking," she answered.

"I mean really talk." He led her into the library. He closed the door and perched on an ottoman.

"We probably shouldn't sneak off to the library." She laughed. "People will get the wrong impression."

"But it's the right impression." He fiddled with his tie.

"What are you talking about?"

"Our breakup was rocky, and I felt terrible that I sent you a letter. But the distance was killing me. I had to find another girl."

"That was two years ago." Lily flushed. "I haven't thought about it in months."

"Your mother invited me to lunch. She said you're still in love with me, and now the timing is perfect," he began. "We should take it slowly, I don't want to rush anything. But I miss sailing with you on the bay. No girl looked better in capris and boat shoes."

"You must have heard her wrong." Lily's cheeks turned pink. "I met Oliver in Naples, and we're quite serious."

"Look, maybe I shouldn't have told you what she said. It's awkward to reveal a broken heart," he said, feeling bad. "Why don't we start over? If you're free on Friday, we can have dinner at Boulevard."

"I'm not free any day." She walked to the door. "If you'll excuse me, I have to go."

"Where are you going?" he asked.

Lily turned the handle, and her hands trembled. "To see my mother."

"Darling." Lily's mother stood next to the French doors in the living room. She wore a silver gown and her ash-blond hair touched her shoulders. "That dress suits you. You look lovely in red."

"Can I see you in private?" Lily asked.

"All the guests have arrived." Alice scanned the room. "It isn't a good time."

"It's the perfect time." Lily took her mother's arm. "Everyone is happy drinking eggnog and eating lobster rolls. No one will miss you."

"What is it?" Alice asked when they entered the kitchen. Granite counters were littered with silver trays, and a ceramic vase held red and white roses.

"It's Roger," Lily said. "You didn't mention he was coming."

"Isn't it a lovely surprise? You've been so busy at Gump's, I didn't have time to tell you." She paused. "I forgot how handsome Roger is. He looks marvelous in his white dinner jacket."

"You told him I was in love with him," Lily said furiously.

"You are still in love with him." Alice arranged pralines on a plate. "When I told you he was engaged, you stayed in bed for days."

"I had a fever." Lily fumed. "It had nothing to do with Roger."

"A mother can tell the difference between the flu and a broken heart," she said. "You went to Europe to get over him."

"That's where I met Oliver!" Lily exclaimed. "We're madly in love."

"You can't be in love with Oliver," Alice said. "He is good-looking and fairly charming, but he's a waiter. He doesn't even have his own apartment."

"Oliver's housing situation doesn't affect my feelings," Lily retorted. "And Oliver is very frugal, he saves his money."

"Oliver was a wonderful distraction, but Roger is back, and the timing is perfect," Alice began. "If you start dating now, you'll get engaged next fall and have a summer wedding. In two years, he'll be a junior partner, and you'll open your own store. You'll be San Francisco's *it* couple."

"Roger and I broke up more than a year ago," Lily countered. "He fell in love with someone else."

"It was hurtful the way Roger ended things, but he had a good reason. And it's healthy for young couples to take a break, it makes them appreciate each other," Alice mused. "I could tell by the way he looked at you that he's still in love with you."

"I don't want to marry Roger," Lily insisted. "I want to be with Oliver."

"Oliver is twenty-three, he's not ready to settle down." She shrugged. "And even if he was, what would be your future? At best, he'll write a newspaper column, and you'll live in a flat on Van Ness. This is where you belong." She waved at the beamed ceiling and double ovens. "Giving dinner parties and attending galas."

"I told Roger I wasn't interested in him," Lily said. "If you'll excuse me, I'm going to join Oliver at the restaurant."

"Roger is persistent, and you'll see each other at social functions." Alice patted her hair. "I'm sure you'll come around."

"That's impossible." Lily took a deep breath. "Oliver and I are engaged."

"What did you say?" Alice gasped.

Lily regretted the words as soon as they were out of her mouth. But her mother hated losing an argument, and how else would Roger leave her alone?

"We were going to tell you on Christmas Eve," she continued. "We couldn't be happier."

"You're not wearing a ring." Alice glanced at her finger.

"Oliver's mother is sending his grandmother's ring from Ohio," Lily explained. "We're going to have a spring wedding and go to Portugal on our honeymoon. I heard the Azores are spectacular."

"You can't marry Oliver," Alice insisted. "He doesn't know anything about San Francisco society. And you've always wanted children. How will you afford private school and orthodontists on his salary?"

"We have plenty of time for children, and I'm going to open my own store." She defended her decision.

She really should have made up a different story. She should have said she was going backpacking in Asia or had decided to be celibate for a year. What was going to happen when her parents grilled Oliver about his plans for a college fund?

Oliver! What would Oliver say when she told him she'd pretended they were engaged? They'd never talked about the future; she'd ruined everything. But she couldn't admit to her mother she'd lied. Alice wouldn't stop until Roger led Lily down the aisle of St. Dominic's.

Oliver was right, she should have moved to her own apartment. But she loved the mansion on top of Pacific Heights, and her parents were so busy, they rarely saw each other. And anyway, just because she borrowed her mother's *Vogue*, it didn't mean her mother could tell her whom to marry.

"I know you've been saving money, but opening your own store is expensive." Alice inspected her fingernails. "I can't promise your father and I will help if you marry Oliver."

"We don't need your help. We have each other." Lily gathered her purse. "Merry Christmas, Mother. I'll see you later."

Lily clutched her pashmina and hurried down Columbus Avenue. Ever since she'd left the party, she couldn't stop shivering. She pictured the last few months with Oliver: visiting the redwoods in Muir Woods and taking the ferry to Sausalito. Whole Sundays spent sitting at a café on Russian Hill. Even doing Oliver's laundry at the Laundromat was fun. They took turns doing the *New York Times* crossword puzzle and separating the colors from the whites.

What if Oliver was furious at her for saying they were engaged? Her mother had surprised her, and she'd blurted out the first thing that came to mind. It didn't mean anything.

"I thought you'd be sipping vodka gimlets and nibbling smoked salmon," Oliver said when she entered the restaurant. "I didn't expect to see you for hours."

Oliver looked so handsome in his white shirt and tan slacks. His dark hair touched his collar, and his cheeks were brown and smooth.

"I left the party early." Lily shrugged. "You see the same people year after year. It's quite boring."

"That's not what you told me when you asked me to take the night off." Oliver led her into the kitchen. "You said the oysters are from an oyster farm in Bolinas, and the cognac is from your father's private collection, and the house is lit up like the San Francisco Opera House."

Lily fiddled with her earrings and couldn't keep it from Oliver any longer.

"My mother invited Roger without telling me," she blurted out.

"Roger?" Oliver repeated.

"I'm sure I mentioned Roger. We started dating when I was a junior in high school and he was at Stanford. He went to Columbia Law School, and I attended UCLA, and the relationship didn't last."

"That was ages ago." Oliver smiled. "I didn't think I was your first boyfriend."

"It's a bit more complicated," Lily hesitated. "Roger broke up with me and got engaged to another girl. The engagement ended, and now he's working at a law firm in San Francisco."

"What are you saying?" Oliver stiffened. "Did something happen?"

"Of course not! My mother told Roger I was still in love with him, and he asked me to dinner. I tried to convince her I didn't want anything to do with him, but she wouldn't listen." Lily looked at Oliver and her eyes were huge. "So I told her we were engaged."

"You did what!" Oliver exclaimed.

"It's impossible to win an argument with my mother, and I didn't want Roger calling me. I'm terribly sorry. I'll tell her we called it off. We're still dating, but we decided to take things slowly." She paused and her cheeks burned. "I shouldn't have lied and I haven't even thought about marriage. It was a silly mistake."

Oliver stuffed his hands in his pockets and paced around the room.

"Now that you mention it, it is a good idea," he began. "I don't want to call it off."

"You don't want to call what off?" she asked.

"The engagement," he answered. "Why should we call it off when we're in love? It will be difficult at first, but when we're together I feel like I can accomplish anything. The *Chronicle* loves my reviews, I'm sure they'll hire me full time. Eventually, you'll open your own store, and it'll be a great success. We're going to have a wonderful future."

"You want to get married?" Lily gasped. "That's ridiculous. We're too young, and we've barely started our careers. You don't even have your own apartment."

"You won't marry me because of my living situation?" Oliver protested.

Lily looked at Oliver's blue eyes and suddenly wanted him more than anything. "I won't marry you because you haven't asked me."

Oliver walked over to a pile of linen napkins and loosened a napkin ring. He kneeled on the stone floor and took Lily's hand.

"The last few months have been the best of my life, and I love you more than anything. When we're together, I never know what's going to happen next, and that makes life exciting. I may not be able give you a mansion in Pacific Heights or three weeks on Lake Tahoe every summer, but I'll spend every day making you happy." He paused. "Lily Wallace, will you marry me?"

Lily inhaled Oliver's musk aftershave. They were too young to get married, and with their combined incomes, they could barely afford a studio apartment. But Oliver was handsome and warm, and she couldn't imagine them being apart.

"Yes," she whispered. "Yes, I'll marry you."

He slipped the napkin ring on her finger and kissed her. She kissed him back, and a shiver ran down her spine.

"It doesn't quite fit, it's a little large. I never thought I'd get engaged with a napkin ring." She laughed. "Maybe we'll set a new trend."

"I'm sure Guido knows someone in the diamond business," Oliver suggested. "I have money saved. I'll buy a one-carat diamond on a platinum band."

"You'll do nothing of the sort." She shook her head. "That money has to help pay for furniture and kitchen utensils and a bed."

"Describe the bed." Oliver stroked her cheek.

"King-sized, with a headboard, so we can stay up all night reading," she mused. "And it has to have a firm mattress or we'll end up with bad backs."

"I don't want to stay up all night reading." Oliver pulled her close.

"What would you rather do?" she asked.

Oliver covered her mouth with his. He wrapped his arms around her and held her so tightly she couldn't breathe.

"I love you," he said, pulling away.

"I love you too," she whispered.

The other waiters clapped, and the chef sent a busboy to chill a bottle of champagne.

Her lips were sore, and her heart raced, and she had never been so happy.

Lily slid under the bubbles and closed her eyes. Of course she was nostalgic for the past; they had been young and in love. But she wasn't going to think about all that now. She had to go the hotel gift shop and buy something to wear for her picnic with Ricky. Enzo was right. She was a single young woman staying on one of the most glamorous coastlines lines in the world. Why shouldn't she find romance?

Chapter Six

OLIVER SAT ON A LOVE seat in the hotel lobby and wished he smoked. It was silly to long for a habit that made your clothes reek and gave you cancer. And Louisa would never speak to him. Children were taught that lighting a cigarette was worse than being a criminal.

But the dark-haired man at the bar blowing smoke rings seemed so relaxed. Even the women who were smoking looked sexy, with their gold earrings and cigarettes dangling from their fingertips.

Of course, having his ex-wife staying in an adjoining suite made him nervous. It was like when he'd been a teenager and seen his history teacher at the cinema. He admired Miss Martin, but he didn't want to run into her when he was sneaking into an R-rated movie.

Was he afraid that Lily would interfere with his relationship with Angela, or was it something else? And why did seeing Lily, with her oval sunglasses and Tory Burch sandals, make him want to swallow a packet of TUMS?

He couldn't worry about it now; Angela had gone to the suite to change, and then they were going to swim at Spiaggia del Principe. It was named the Prince's Beach because it was the favorite beach of Prince Aga Khan. An afternoon of splashing in the azure water would be the perfect antidote to his anxiety. He imagined sipping Bellinis with Angela and felt suddenly brighter.

And he was on the Emerald Coast to work. He had received an invitation from the chef at Trattoria Balbacana to sample his *paglia* pasta with sea asparagus. The restaurant was nestled in the town of San Pantaleo at the foot of the Gallura Mountains. It was only minutes from the Emerald Coast, but there weren't any smart boutiques or fancy sports cars—just a village built around a stone church and outdoor market. Maybe he'd go tomorrow and take Angela. A short excursion away from Hotel Cervo was just what he needed.

A woman wearing a straw hat crossed the lobby, and he remembered his first holiday with Lily. They had spent their honeymoon in Portugal and thought life was a string of warm beaches and romantic dinners . . . except for the sudden jealousy that had consumed Oliver and made him behave in a way he instantly regretted.

Oliver sat an outdoor café and squinted into the sun. The fishing village of Salema in Portugal was the perfect destination for their honeymoon. Cobbled streets had whitewashed houses with latticed chimney boxes and blue trim. The wide beach was flanked by sharp cliffs, and restaurants spilled onto the sand. And the people were so friendly! The fishermen taught them how to catch an octopus: you put a jar in the ocean, and the octopus climbed into the glass.

The best part was that it was far from Lily's parents in San Francisco. Her mother had acted as if she were furious that Lily and Oliver had decided to have a small wedding in Carmel, but Oliver suspected she was relieved. Alice didn't have to explain to her friends at the Bohemian Club why Lily was marrying a waiter.

He pictured the wedding reception at the Pebble Beach Lodge and clutched his glass. It wasn't Lily's fault that her father had read out loud an email from Roger saying if Lily changed her mind, she knew where to find him. As soon as her father realized what it said, he'd stuffed the printed email into his pocket. But the memory made Oliver feel like his throat was on fire.

If only Oliver hadn't brought it up on the plane, the moment would have dissolved like the bubbles outside the church. But now Lily kept asking if something was wrong, and he couldn't disguise his anguish. He remembered the photo of Lily and Roger in her parents' den, and his stomach turned over.

He ate muesli with yogurt and berries and wished he had waited for Lily to join him. He usually loved sitting with the sun streaming through the window and watching her do her exercises. But he'd woken with a tenseness in his neck and thought he should leave before they had an argument.

"Excuse me, do you have a lighter?" a female voice asked.

Oliver looked up and saw a blond woman wearing white shorts and a halter top. Turquoise earrings dangled from her ears, and she wore gold sandals.

"I'm sorry, I don't smoke," Oliver said.

"You're American," she replied and pulled out a chair. "Do you mind? The other tables are taken, and I'm desperate for an espresso."

"I do mind, actually." Oliver shifted in his seat. "I'm married."

The woman took off her sunglasses and laughed. "You Americans are so surprising. Your movies are about sex and violence, but you can't share a table or smoke a cigarette."

"I'm not accountable for Hollywood's tastes." Oliver turned back to his omelet. "Anyway, cigarettes will kill you."

"Being alive will kill you eventually." She shrugged. She had some kind of Scandinavian accent, and her fingernails were painted pearl pink. "Americans are so puritanical. In Europe, husbands and wives breakfast with whoever they like without assuming it's an invitation to a noon tryst."

"I didn't think it was." Oliver flushed. "I'm here on my honeymoon, and the only woman I want to talk to is my wife."

"Then why isn't she with you?"

"That's a good question." Oliver thought he couldn't let Lily's mother ruin their holiday. He tossed a wad of euros on the table and grabbed his jacket. "Excuse me, I have to go."

"But you haven't eaten your breakfast," the woman protested.

"You can have it." He turned away. "The fresh orange juice is excellent."

He hurried along the sand and squinted into the sun. Lily had never given Roger any encouragement, and it was all in the past. Anyway, Oliver had plenty of old girlfriends. But they were tucked away in Michigan, and he didn't have to worry about their sports cars roaring down Lombard Street.

They were on their honeymoon in Portugal and they should be eating grilled squid and drinking Madeira, and making love on crisp sheets. And the scenery was spectacular. A wooden boat swayed at the shore and a young fisherman taught a woman how to fish. His hands were wrapped around her waist, and she tugged at the pole. She turned and laughed, and he realized it was Lily.

"Bloody hell!" Oliver said out loud. He ran down to the shore and grabbed the fishing pole. "Get your hands off my wife."

"Oliver!" Lily exclaimed. "What are you doing?"

"I thought you were in the room doing your deep knee bends, and instead you're letting this fisherman behave like an octopus." He fumed.

"He was teaching me how to fish." Lily's eyes flashed.

"You don't need to know how to fish, they serve it to you at restaurants with a slice of lemon." He waved the rod at the man. "I suggest you take this, or I'm going to shove it where it doesn't belong."

Lily said something to the man in Portuguese. She adjusted her straw hat and ran down the beach.

"Where do you think you're going?" Oliver chased after her.

"I was going to join you for breakfast, but you were busy with some model or flight attendant." Lily turned around. "I decided to take a walk, and Carlos asked if I wanted to learn how to fish."

"She asked if I had a cigarette lighter," Oliver protested. "And just because I was talking to a woman doesn't mean you should strike up a friendship with a stranger."

"If you weren't so moody, this wouldn't have happened," she snapped. "Every time you look at me, you're wondering if I think I should have chosen Roger. I told you a million times, I'm in love with you and that's why I married you."

"When you told me about Roger, I didn't think anything about it," he began. "But your mother mentions his name more often than she discusses the weather. Then your father read Roger's email, and it was the last straw. Every face in that room looked like they thought you'd made a mistake."

"Isn't my opinion the only one that matters?" Lily demanded. "If you're jealous about every little thing, how will we survive?"

"Can't a woman ask me for a light for her cigarette?" He was suddenly angry. "And you're lucky I discovered you before Carlos decided you'd learn to fish better from the back of his boat."

"You don't smoke, and she still sat down with you," Lily retorted. "And I would never get into a boat with a strange man."

"I've been out of sorts and I'm sorry." He took her hand. "I love you and I can't get over the fact that we're married. Every morning I wake up and imagine I'm back at the train station in Naples, and it was all some incredible dream."

"Most of the time I'm so happy." Her eyes filled with tears. "But we have to trust each other, or we don't have anything."

Oliver noticed a fisherman dragging his boat onto the shore. He hurried across the sand and reached into his pocket. He ran back to Lily and took her hand.

"Where are we going?" she asked, clutching her hat against her head.

"We're going fishing." He lifted her into the boat and climbed in beside her.

"You can't just take someone's boat." Lily sat on the wood bench. "What if we get stuck and can't paddle back in?"

"I paid him more than he'll make selling fish," Oliver said. "And I spent a dozen summers on Lake Michigan. I know how to handle a boat."

He rowed until they were surrounded by turquoise water and the harbor was a hazy blur. He tossed the anchor over the side and sat next to Lily.

"How do you know this is the right place to fish?" She shielded her eyes from the sun. "And I hardly took one lesson, I don't know how to fish at all."

Oliver pulled her into his arms and kissed her. God, she was beautiful! Her breasts were high and her legs were smooth and she wore a floral perfume.

"That's not the kind of fishing I'm talking about," he said softly.

He found a blanket and spread it over the planks. He took off his shirt and tossed it on the bench. Her skin was warm, and her breath was sweet, and he'd never wanted anything more.

"What if someone sees us?" she whispered into his ear.

Oliver glanced at the blue sky and orange sun and high white clouds. He lay on the blanket and pulled her down beside him.

"We're perfectly safe." He grinned. "I doubt the seagulls are interested."

He kissed her neck and breasts and the curve of her thigh. Her body twisted, and he wondered how he could have let anything get between them.

"I love you," she said. "I'm very glad I married you."

"You better be," he whispered. "Because you're never getting rid of me."

She opened her legs, and Oliver slid inside her. Lily wrapped her arms around him and urged him to go faster. The boat rocked, and their bodies moved together, and he came with an incredible force.

"We were both being stupid," Lily said when they lay with their heads propped against the bench. Oliver's heart raced, and he felt like he could do anything.

"That didn't feel stupid," he answered. "That was fantastic."

"I mean before; worrying about other people." Lily turned to him. "I'm in love with you, and we're perfect together."

"There's only one thing we have to worry about." He pulled her onto the blanket and covered her body with his.

"What's that?" she asked.

"Not getting a sunburn," he murmured. "I want to stay here and make love to you all day."

"A little sunburn might be worth it." Lily kissed him. "There's nowhere else I'd rather be."

"Everything smells divine." Lily put down the menu. "I don't know how to choose."

Oliver sipped a glass of sangria and thought it had been a wonderful day. After they'd returned the boat, they explored the narrow alleys and vibrant piazzas. There were galleries and quaint shops and cottages with painted front doors.

Now they were having dinner at the finest restaurant in Salema. Agua Na Boca was perched above the village and had views of the whole coastline. Fishing nets hung from the ceiling, and waiters carried platters of clams with cilantro and melted butter.

"You could let me choose," Oliver suggested. "I am the new restaurant critic at the *San Francisco Chronicle*."

"What do you mean?" Lily asked.

"I received an email while you were in the shower," he explained. "I start full time when we return. I'll have a weekly column and my own office and an expense account."

"That's the best news I've heard! We'll get invited to all kinds of openings and have so much fun." She dipped a focaccia into olive oil. "If I'm not careful, I'll get fat."

"I doubt that could happen." Oliver studied her brown eyes and small pink mouth and wondered how he got so lucky.

He reached into his pocket and brought out a package wrapped in tissue paper.

"I bought you a present." He handed it to her.

Lily untied the bow and discovered a bolt of colored fabric.

"I found it at the market this morning," Oliver said. "It will be the first item in your store."

"It's gorgeous, but it will be ages before I open a store." Lily hesitated. "We have to save up the money."

"I also have this." He took a piece of paper out of his pocket. "It's my bank statement. I saved almost everything Guido paid me, and he added a little extra. His children are grown, and he doesn't know what to do with his money."

Lily glanced at the deposits on the bank statement and gasped. "Guido gave you ten thousand dollars! We can't accept that."

"Apparently a real-estate developer offered to buy the restaurant," Oliver explained. "Guido is going to sell it and move back to Italy."

Lily leaned over the checkered tablecloth and kissed him. "I'll start looking for spaces when we get home. The store will be stocked with linens from Spain and earthenware from Tuscany and antique furniture bought at estate sales in Provence."

"What will you call it?" Oliver asked, eating potato and kale soup.

"Lily Bristol, of course." She traced the rim of her wineglass. "It will have black awnings and Lily Bristol written in gold letters in the window."

The waiter served octopus baked in garlic and onions. There was rice cooked with white wine and tomatoes. They talked about visiting castles in Lisbon, and Oliver felt light and happy.

"Here's the check." He handed her the bill. "I'm going to use the restroom."

"Why are you giving me the bill?" Lily finished the last spoonful of rice pudding.

"I didn't want to carry my wallet, so I put a fifty euro in your purse." Oliver stood up. "Don't tip too much. They already charge a fortune because we're tourists."

Oliver returned from the restroom, and they stood up to leave. They walked outside and strolled along the cobblestones. Lily stopped and frowned. "I'm sorry, I forgot my purse. I must have left it on the table when I paid the bill."

"I'll get it." He kissed her. "Wait here, and I'll be right back."

Lily's purse lay on the table, and he picked it up. It fell on the floor, and he gathered the contents. There was a piece of paper, and he noticed it was the bill. On the bottom was the note: "To the beautiful American. Please come tomorrow night, and we will finish our conversation. You must sit in my station, and I promise you a delightful evening."

He crumpled the note and strode onto the street. As he reached Lily, his hands shook.

"Are you all right?" she asked. "Did you find my purse?"

"Your purse is right here." He handed it to her. "And there was a note inside. Apparently you made an impression on the waiter when I was in the restroom."

Lily scanned the paper and looked up. "He happened to speak English, and we talked for a minute. He asked where I was from, and I complimented the cooking."

"It sounds like he wanted to make a date," Oliver stormed. "Maybe you should take him up on it."

"I can't help what he wrote, but I didn't give him any encouragement." She handed him the paper. "Let's forget about it."

"Waiters don't hit on diners for no reason," he persisted. "If he did that all the time, he'd get fired."

"I told you it was nothing, but if you don't believe me, you can ask him yourself," she said, and her eyes blazed. "Good-bye, Oliver. I'm going home."

Oliver waited until he had cooled off and then walked along the alley. As soon as Lily left, he realized he had overreacted. Lily was hardly going to make a date with a Portuguese waiter, even if he did have a physique like a bullfighter. He had been upset and said the first thing that came out of his mouth. But what did she mean, she was going home?

He turned the corner and saw a young woman huddled on the hotel steps. She wore a linen dress and carried a beige purse. He recognized Lily's brown hair and realized she was crying.

"I'm sorry, I shouldn't have gotten so upset," he began. "The waiter had those chiseled cheeks and white teeth that belong in a toothpaste commercial."

"How could you accuse me of making a date?" Lily looked up. "I have no interest in other men."

"I apologized," Oliver pleaded. "You're so beautiful, I think every man wants you."

"We promised we'd trust each other, and you went back on your word."

"I'm very sorry." Oliver touched her hand. "It will never happen again."

Lily's eyes were huge, and she took a deep breath. "Maybe this isn't working, and we should stop now."

"What are you talking about? We're on our honeymoon."

"Maybe we're not good at being married, not everyone is, you know. My parents have made each other miserable for years." She looked at Oliver. "We should end it before someone gets hurt."

"We don't give up on the whole thing because of a few hiccups." Oliver waved his hand. "Of course, being married takes adjusting; it's like buying a new car. You have to learn how to work the windshield wipers and use the air-conditioner. But once you take it out on the freeway, it's the best feeling in the world."

"Do you really think I'm a car?" she said and suddenly laughed.

"You're the most wonderful girl I've ever met, and I'm lucky to be your husband."

"And we won't doubt each other anymore?" she asked.

He crossed his heart, and his face broke into a smile. "Scout's honor. Now let's go upstairs." He pulled her up. "Checkout is nine AM. We may as well get a lot of use out of that bed."

He picked her up and carried her into the hotel. He entered their room and fumbled with her zipper.

"You shouldn't have carried me up the stairs." She laughed. "You'll hurt your back."

Oliver tore off his shirt and drew her onto the quilted bedspread. He kissed her and whispered, "Let me show you what I can do."

Oliver glanced around the Hotel Cervo's lobby and sighed. Of course he had been jealous. What twentysomething male didn't act like a bull in heat? And in the end, he had reason to be jealous; what Lily had done in San Francisco was unbearable. But of course it didn't excuse what he did next. He had been like a wounded animal; he needed female reassurance. If only he hadn't lied to her about that night in Manhattan in the first place, he never would have set off the chain of events that ended their marriage. He was as sure of that now as he was that the tasting menu at Eleven Madison Park was worth it, even when he had to pay for it himself.

The double doors opened, and Angela appeared. She wore a crepe blouse and pleated skirt. Her hair was tied in a knot, and she wore leather sandals.

"I thought you were going to the suite to change." Oliver rushed across the lobby.

"I did change," Angela answered. "I bought the skirt at a boutique on Via La Passeggiata. It's Roberto Cavalli; it cost me one hundred euros."

"But we're going to the beach." Oliver pointed to his board shorts and thongs. "You're dressed for an afternoon performance at Carnegie Hall."

"Not Carnegie Hall, Stella Maris Church. It was built in the 1960s by a famous Italian architect and contains a seventeenth-century pipe organ." She paused. "The beach sounds lovely, but we spent all day yesterday at the pool. I thought it would be interesting to visit local monuments."

"The only times I go to church are on Easter Sunday and Christmas," he protested. "We're here to lie on the sand and eat overpriced seafood linguini."

"That may be why you're here, but you never asked why I came." Angela pursed her lips. "I like being with you, and the Jacuzzi tub in the suite is appealing. But I've been crazy about Sardinia since I did a project about it in the eighth grade. I eat Sardinian *malloreddus* at Arco Cafe on the Upper West Side and buy Sardinian wine at Eli's List on Third Avenue, and I attended the gallery opening for a Sardinian artist in Chelsea."

"When do you have time to do those things?" Oliver asked.

"We only see each other a few times a week." She shrugged. "What do you think I do the other nights? Put on pajamas and reheat Chinese takeout?"

"You could have said something." Oliver wondered why he felt cheated. Wasn't it good that Angela wanted to explore the culture of Sardinia? But he thought of the bikini on Angela's bedside table and grimaced.

"Said what, Oliver?" she demanded. "That I'm not a live Barbie doll who's only interested in floral bouquets and drinking Blue Jasmines at the Flatiron Lounge? We've never attended the ballet or seen an Off-Broadway play."

Off-Broadway plays were often boring, and the theater never had comfortable seats. And he couldn't afford an evening at the ballet; the champagne at intermission was so expensive.

But Angela was gorgeous and sexy, and he enjoyed her company.

"Every New Yorker dreams of drinking limoncello and sailing on the Emerald Coast." He sighed. "But we'll go to Stella Maris Church. We can even drive to Arzachena to see the ancient Nuragic sites if you like."

"That might be too much history for one day." She took his arm. "Let's start with the church and see how we do."

"You see, Oliver," Angela said, sitting on a wood bench, "churches can be interesting."

Oliver sat beside her and thought it had been a fabulous afternoon. The church was perched on a cliff, with views of the green hills and the jagged coastline. Myrtle bushes were scattered over the grounds, and there were oleander trees and beds of lavender.

The best part was when Angela had kneeled down at the altar to blow out a candle. There was something about seeing her making the sign of the cross that was incredibly sexy.

"It says here that the church was designed by Michele Busiri Vici," Oliver said, leafing through the brochure.

"Didn't you hear the guide?" Angela asked. "Prince Aga Khan hired noted architects to build villas and hotels and churches. The church's pews are made of juniper wood, and the bronze doors were created by the Bolognese sculptor Luciano Minguzzi."

Oliver had been too busy admiring Angela's legs to listen to the tour guide. Now he wondered how she remembered everything the guide had said.

"You're looking at me like I'm speaking a foreign language." Angela inspected her fingernails. "Ohio isn't all barns and cornfields. Toledo has many fine churches and museums."

"But you don't like museums. And how do you know so much history? You told me you didn't go to college."

"You asked me once if I wanted to spend the afternoon at the Guggenheim. I said no because I had a summer cold," she explained. "And not everyone has the money to go to college. That doesn't mean I don't like to learn."

He hadn't assumed Angela was uneducated; he hadn't thought about it all. Angela was like a delicious meal presented at a Michelin-starred restaurant. You didn't ask where the bamboo shoots were grown; you were just grateful they arrive stuffed with curry and smothered in butter.

But now he felt shame mixed with a sudden joy. Maybe he and Angela could have a future together. He pictured weekends with Angela and Louisa at the Natural History Museum. They could drive to Poughkeepsie to see the leaves change without running out of things to say.

"I forgot to get Louisa a present at the souvenir stand." He stood up. "Would you like to come?"

"No, thank you." Angela stretched out her legs in front of her. "I'll stay here and soak up the sun."

Oliver clutched his parcel and ran down the stone steps. He searched the garden, but Angela had disappeared.

"Oliver, I need you." She waved at a man standing across from her. "That man whistled and tried to look up my skirt. Then he asked my name, and I told him to leave me alone."

Oliver glanced at the man's thick chest and gulped. He was at least six foot two, and looked like he spent his free time splitting tree trunks. If Oliver threatened him, the man could knock him out.

"He's not bothering you now, we should probably leave," Oliver suggested.

"We can't leave, or he'll do it to someone else," Angela insisted. "A woman should be able to wear a miniskirt without being harassed."

"You're right, and if this was Manhattan, I'd go and tell him that's no way to treat a woman." He looked up nervously to see if the man was walking in their direction. "But what if he doesn't speak English and takes it the wrong way? I could end up with his fist in my mouth."

"It's still not right." Angela fumed. "Somebody needs to tell him how to behave."

"Perhaps he was only trying to compliment you. In Sardinia, men are taught to admire women," he tried again. "And you're so unusual, with your copper hair and alabaster skin. Maybe he's an artist and needed inspiration."

"Do you think so?" Angela patted her hair.

"I'm positive. I saw paint splotches on his shirt." Oliver took her hand. "I've had enough of churches, let's go to the beach. We'll take an evening dip in the ocean."

Angela adjusted her sunglasses and smiled. "That's an excellent idea. I'll wear the maillot I bought at Missoni."

Oliver filled two glasses with champagne and waited for Angela to step out of the shower. The beach at sunset had been magnificent. They lay on striped towels and drank vodka gimlets. The sand was tinged with gold, and sailboats skimmed along the waves.

Now Angela entered the bedroom and shook out her hair. She wore a peach robe, and her toenails were painted pink.

"Back at the church"—she tied the robe around her waist—"why weren't you jealous of the man who tried to pick me up?"

"What do you mean?" Oliver handed her a champagne flute.

"I don't know, Oliver. Sometimes I feel like you're an actor reciting his lines. You're in the scene, but you're not really here," she continued. "My last boyfriend would have punched him in the jaw."

"I'm a restaurant critic for the *New York Times*. I don't solve problems with my fist," Oliver answered. "And I don't know what you're talking about. There's nowhere I'd rather be than with you."

"I'm not a mannequin you can practice kissing on." She walked to the bed. "I like you, Oliver. But I need you to try harder."

"We're in an oceanfront suite, and I ordered oysters and champagne." He waved at the ice bucket. "What more can I do?"

She slipped off her robe and peeled back the sheets. "You could start by calling me your girlfriend."

Had he ever called her his girlfriend? He couldn't remember. And he hadn't used that term since college. But her hair was fanned out on the pillow, her lips were coated with lipstick, and his heart pounded.

"Of course, you're my girlfriend." He lay down beside her.

"Do you really mean it?" she asked. "You're not just saying it to appease me?"

"Of course I mean it." He nodded. "You are bright and beautiful, and when I'm around you, I feel like I matter. I'm the luckiest guy to be able to call you my girlfriend."

"I can't tell you how happy that makes me, Oliver." She played with her necklace. "Now I'll show you what a girlfriend can do."

She climbed on top of him. He lay on his back and couldn't remember the last time he'd done this with a woman. She ground into him, and he gasped and thought he had gone to heaven.

"I'm going to make you come," she whispered in his ear. "Like you've never come before."

Oliver groaned and flipped her onto her back. He slid inside her, and her nails dug into his flesh. Her stomach was rounded, and her breasts were heavy, and suddenly he couldn't slow down. He grabbed her shoulders and came with one endless thrust.

"You see, Oliver. I thought you'd like that," she murmured.

"We're not quite done." He lay beside her and stroked her

thighs. His palm moved in circles, and she let out a small moan. She clutched the pillow, and her whole body shuddered.

"Maybe I was wrong," Angela said, when they both lay on their backs. The ceiling fan turned overhead, and Oliver tried to catch his breath.

"Wrong?" he wiped his forehead. How could anything be wrong when he felt like Joe DiMaggio after he'd won the World Series?

"You don't need to try harder." She closed her eyes. "That was perfect."

Oliver stepped onto the balcony and closed the sliding glass doors. It was almost midnight, and the *piazzetta* teemed with men and women in glittering evening clothes. Sports cars idled on the cobblestones, and a driver in a red uniform stood next to a gleaming silver Rolls-Royce.

He turned and studied the yachts in the harbor. Their wooden decks were lit up like a fireworks display on the Fourth of July. Sleek figures dove into swimming pools, and Jacuzzis resembled fizzy glasses of champagne.

Angela had fallen asleep, but Oliver was suddenly restless. A stunning redhead had just been straddling him. Why did he feel empty? He was incredibly attracted to Angela. And look how well he'd performed. After he'd finished, she was like a kitten with a warm bowl of milk.

It wasn't just her looks and her actions in bed. She was easy to talk to. She valued his opinion, and when he was with her, he felt needed.

How was he supposed to know she wanted him to punch the

guy at the church? Didn't women these days carry cans of mace so they could protect themselves? It didn't mean he wasn't jealous; he'd just stopped behaving like a boy with a BB gun.

He gazed at the round portholes and knew he was kidding himself. Earth-shattering sex didn't mean anything if, the minute you rolled off, you wondered if it was too late to order a pizza. And he hadn't really matured. He didn't see the point in poking out another man's eyes because he'd looked up Angela's skirt.

He opened the sliding glass door and approached the bed. He took off his robe and slipped in beside her. Angela was right. If she was going to be his girlfriend, he needed to try harder.

Chapter Seven

LILY BRUSHED HER HAIR WITH a wooden hairbrush and rubbed her lips with lipstick. She had spent the morning choosing floral arrangements for Lily Bristol's grand opening in four days. There were going to be jugs of purple daisies and wreaths of wild-flowers.

She debated what to wear for her picnic with Ricky. She tried on the straw hat, and a shiver ran down her spine. It was lovely to dress up for someone. And he really was handsome, with his dark eyes and white smile.

She studied her reflection in the mirror and knew she was being silly. What was the point of seeing Ricky if she was going home in a few days? But when she'd met Oliver in Naples, she'd thought he was just a ride to Florence.

Oliver! She hadn't said his name so often since he'd moved out. And why shouldn't she explore Sardinia with Ricky? She didn't want to drive the winding roads by herself, and there was more to the Emerald Coast than boutiques and gourmet food stores.

What if he wanted to kiss her? She made a face in the mirror and laughed. If she got this nervous before a picnic, how would she survive a romantic dinner? She had to go with him or she'd spend her life doing sales projections for Lily Bristol and buying Louisa new ballet slippers.

Her phone rang, and she picked up.

"Lily?" a male voice said. "I'm glad I caught you."

"Ricky!" Lily walked to the window. "I was debating whether to pack a swimsuit. It's a gorgeous day, and I've been working all morning."

"I'm afraid I can't make our picnic," he began. "The Greek shipping magnate, Christoff, arrived and is having a lunch party on his yacht. He has a wife in Athens and mistresses in Portofino and Monte Carlo. He buys three of every outfit in my boutique. He doesn't want to send the wrong gift."

"He sounds horrible." Lily grimaced.

"I abhor his morals, but I can't afford to turn him away," Ricky explained. "And I have to go to his party. Every boutique owner on the Emerald Coast wants his business."

"I understand." Lily nodded and wondered why she felt deflated.

"I wonder if you could meet me there," he continued. "His yacht is called the *Hercules*. It's royal blue and has a shuffleboard court."

"You want me to join you?" she asked.

"Of course," he answered. "What did you expect?"

"I just thought . . ." She hesitated.

"We made plans, and Sardinians keep our word." He stopped, and she wondered if she had lost the connection. "And besides, there's nothing I'd rather do than be with you."

"I'll bring my bathing suit after all," Lily said and laughed.

"You'll probably think it's boring. It's not cut up to my stomach or threaded with gold."

"As long as you're wearing it, it will be the prettiest swimsuit on the yacht." He paused. "I'm glad you're coming. I can't wait to see you."

Lily shielded her eyes from the sun and frowned. She was positive she'd written down the name of the yacht, but now she couldn't find the paper. And it wasn't as if she could walk along the dock until she spotted Ricky. There were dozens of yachts, and some of them were larger than buildings.

"Lily, what are you doing here?" a male voice asked.

"Oliver!" Lily turned around. "Don't you think it's odd that we keep running into each other? And where is Angela? I would have thought you wanted to spend all your time together."

"Porto Cervo is a small place, it would be hard not to run into each other." He shrugged. "And I'm working. I'm researching a background piece for the *New York Times*. You know: the Emerald Coast is the playground of Russian oligarchs and European royalty who arrive on yachts outfitted with more precious jewels than the Taj Mahal."

"They can't be worth that much," Lily said and laughed.

"That yacht over there," he pointed to a four-story yacht with a helicopter pad. "It's owned by an Arabian prince and has a bowling alley and aquarium."

"Who wants to bowl when you're sailing on the Mediterranean, and why do you need an aquarium when you're surrounded by fish?"

"When you're fabulously wealthy, you can buy whatever you

like," Oliver said. "It's like being a child without parents to spoil your fun."

"Being that rich doesn't appeal to me," she mused. "I like driving a Volvo, and I'd get tired of wearing designer clothes. I'm happy in a cotton dress and sandals."

"Unfortunately, Angela doesn't share your view." Oliver sighed. "She's at Trussardi, trying on their fall collection."

"Why aren't you with her?" she asked. "I thought you'd like to help her shop."

"I was afraid that if I commented on the dress, I'd end up handing over my credit card," he explained. "You know how much I earn. If it wasn't for my expense account, I couldn't afford a bag of figs."

"Being the restaurant critic for the *New York Times* is a huge achievement."

"It looks good on a Twitter handle, but it will never pay for one of these." He waved at a catamaran. "You were the one who brought in real money. That's why you kept the farmhouse, and I'm living in an apartment I can't afford. But Louisa can't stay with me in a walk-up in Harlem."

"Oliver, this isn't the time." Lily turned away. "I have to go, I'm already late."

"Where are you going?" He followed her. "There's nothing here but yachts."

She bit her lip and hesitated. It wouldn't hurt to tell Oliver; maybe he could help her.

"If you must know, I was invited onboard a yacht." She turned around. "I wrote down its name, but I can't find the piece of paper."

"Invited by who?" Oliver asked.

"That's none of your business," she said and started walking. "I shouldn't have told you. I'll figure it out myself."

"I'm happy to help, I've always loved word games." He raced after her. "Do you remember anything about it?"

"I think it was the name of a god." Lily stopped.

"Roman or Greek?" he asked. "Did you know Zeus is the same as Apollo? I learned that from watching Louisa's Disney movies."

"Greek, I think." She sighed. "It's no use, I'll go back to my suite and look for the paper."

"You can't do that, the yacht will leave without you," he protested. "You must remember something. What was the first letter?"

"It started with an H."

"Was it Helios, the god of the sun, or Heracles, the son of Zeus? That's the Greek name for the Roman god Hercules."

"That's it, Hercules!" Lily said, and a smile spread across her face. "How did you know?"

"Louisa and I watched the DVD until it wore out. The musical score is superb." Oliver pointed to a blue yacht with gold trim. "That's it, over there."

Lily looked up and gasped. The decks were gleaming walnut, and there was a marble bar. And the people! The women had bronze skin, and the men wore chrome watches, and they all looked like ornaments on some fabulous Christmas tree.

"I should take a picture and send it to your mother." Oliver whistled. "She'd be happy you're hobnobbing with the rich and famous. Maybe if I owned a yacht like this, we'd still be together."

"That's a horrible thing to say." Lily's cheeks flamed. "My mother never had anything to do with our split, it was all in your head. And the man who invited me works very hard. He just happens to have wealthy friends."

Why had she told Oliver anything about Ricky? They were divorced, and Oliver had a girlfriend. Lily could date whomever she liked.

"Believe that if you want to," he answered. "Everything revolves around money, even sex."

"When we got together, you didn't have a penny, and the sex was wonderful."

"It was, wasn't it?" Oliver perked up. "We were like puppies that couldn't get enough of a ball." He paused. "If only you had trusted me. I never would have done anything to hurt you."

"You lied about where you were that night, Oliver." She bristled. "You can't trust someone who lies."

"Once I asked Louisa if she ate a piece of fruit for breakfast, and she said she had a banana. I couldn't find a banana peel in the whole apartment."

"She's six and doesn't like bananas," she said. "Maybe that's the only kind of fruit you had."

"I'm just saying there can be different reasons to lie, and not all of them are bad."

"I don't want to argue, that's why we got divorced." Lily fixed her hat. "We said if we kept making each other miserable, we would stop trying."

"I never stopped trying, it just didn't work," he mumbled.

"Good-bye, Oliver," she said. "Thank you for helping me remember the name of the yacht."

"Watch your step." He pointed to the wooden planks. "You don't want to get your sandal caught."

She walked along the dock, and her shoulders tightened. The next time she saw Oliver she would run in the other direction. He still made her feel like she did when she shared Louisa's cotton candy. It tasted delicious until your head buzzed from the sugar and you felt slightly ill.

What did Oliver mean, saying that money was the cause of their problems? She'd never cared how much Oliver earned. Even owning Lily Bristol wasn't a means to get wealthy. She adored her stores as if they were her children.

She remembered when she and Oliver had flown to Milan for the opening of the new Lily Bristol. It was their first time away from Louisa together, and they were as giddy as newlyweds. Milan was glamorous and intoxicating, and Lily had everything she'd ever wanted.

Lily stood at the window of their room at the Hotel Baglioni and thought she had never been anywhere so fashionable. Even Rue St.-Honoré in Paris wasn't like Milan's Golden Quadrangle. Via della Spiga was lined with Versace and Prada, and the female shoppers reminded her of greyhounds. Their hair was slicked back, and they wore narrow slacks and ankle boots.

The lights of Milan Cathedral twinkled in the distance, and Lily let out her breath. Oliver was in the bathroom shaving, and then they were going to the grand opening of Lily Bristol Milan.

It had all happened so quickly. A year before, she'd been on a buying trip and entered a design store in an eighteenth-century palazzo on the Corso Venezia. The exterior was all creamy granite and iron latticework, but inside there were teak floors and chrome walls and bright leather furniture.

She had a lively discussion with the owner about Milan's fashion houses and how people actually wore what they saw on the runway. It was the only city in the world where women could wear a dress made of feathers, and no one batted an eye. And the food! Milan served the darkest espresso and sweetest cannoli and better veal cutlets than in Rome.

A few months later, the owner had called and asked if Lily wanted to buy the store. Lily had only opened Lily Bristol San Francisco two years before, and was having so much fun. Every morning, she left Louisa with the babysitter and chatted with Presidio Heights matrons looking for the perfect serving bowl and young professionals furnishing their apartments in the Marina.

If she opened a store in Milan, she would have to hire a manager and staff. She would be away from Louisa for longer periods, and what if something went wrong? She couldn't hop on a plane if the roof leaked or there was a problem with the credit card machine.

But Oliver convinced her she couldn't pass it up. Milan was the most important design center in Europe. She could attend estate sales on Lake Como and pick out glass vases in Murano.

Oliver appeared in the doorway and fiddled with his cuff links. His dark hair was freshly washed, and he had a shaving nick on his chin.

"I sent my shirt to get pressed, and it cost more than my whole wardrobe." He grimaced. "And I haven't eaten a thing since we got off the plane. But the macadamia nuts in the minibar are the price of a pair of loafers."

"Why are you complaining?" Lily turned around. She wore a black cocktail dress and silver pumps. "You're the one who wanted me to open a store in Milan."

"I'm just uncomfortable that we left Louisa with your parents. Your mother will point out all the things the other girls have and she's missing: private singing lessons and Gymboree classes. She doesn't miss an opportunity to show I'm a terrible provider."

"Louisa is two and a half. The only thing they discuss is whether to watch *Dora the Explorer* or *The Wiggles*. And you're being too harsh on her. My parents did book us a room at the Hotel Baglioni as an anniversary present." Lily waved at the black-and-white marble floor and sideboard set with Italian chocolates. "If you relaxed, we might enjoy ourselves."

"How can I relax when she keeps telling me I'll never be able to save for a college fund?" He smoothed his collar. "She's right, of course. If Lily Bristol wasn't doing well, we'd still be living in a studio apartment."

"What does it matter who earns more, as long as the money ends up in our bank account? And you're a wonderful father. Louisa has a better vocabulary than any of her friends." She stopped and laughed. "Though I did hear her mutter a swear word."

"It was probably after we came back from a Sunday dinner with your parents." He grimaced. "I don't see why we have to subject ourselves to your mother's inquisition. Last week, she asked if I'd thought of being a firefighter. They have good benefits, and the protective clothing makes it perfectly safe."

"You're the restaurant critic for the *San Francisco Chronicle*. You're famous all over the city," Lily said.

"The homeless man who waves at cars on Van Ness is famous, but he doesn't have a 401(k) either." Oliver unwrapped a chocolate truffle.

"I don't enjoy our dinners any more than you do, but it's important that Louisa knows her grandparents. And my parents are behaving better." Lily fixed her hair. "Last week they took us to the Bohemian Club. It was the best prime rib I ever tasted."

"Your mother wanted you to run into your old friends: Buffy, who's married to a hedge fund manager, and Chloe, whose husband started an Internet search engine." He paused. "The members of the Bohemian Club might wear threadbare blazers, but they own real estate worth more than small countries."

"We've been married for five years and have a beautiful two-year-old daughter. When will you realize it doesn't matter if Chloe Burke sports a five-carat wedding ring? I'm in love with you," she said stiffly. "And I've never had a friend named Buffy."

"All the names sound the same." He sank onto the sofa. "I just feel like I'm not enough."

"You're more than enough." She sat beside him. "You're everything I wanted."

"I love what I do, and I love you and Louisa," he said. "I just wish I could pay for a fancy preschool and our own vacations."

"You're perfect." She kissed him. "Now let's go to the grand opening before the guests eat all the canapés, and we have to come back and order overpriced room service linguini."

The chrome walls were illuminated by pinpoint lighting, wood floors were covered with patterned rugs, and it all looked so inviting. There was an antique table Lily found at a farmhouse in Tuscany and earthenware from a ceramic factory in Spain.

"The owner has excellent taste," a man commented. He wore a dark suit and tasseled shoes.

"I'm Lily Bristol." She held out her hand. "To be honest, I was petrified it wouldn't come together. But I'm in love with the Moroso leather ottoman, and I adore the jacquard slipcovers. It's all perfect."

"If my wife was here, she'd buy up the store." He paused. "I just got transferred to Milan and came ahead to furnish the apartment." He looked at Lily. "Perhaps you could come and take a look? I'm hopeless when it comes to design, and it would be a relief to turn it over to someone."

"I'd be happy to." Lily handed him her card.

"I hate to interrupt." Oliver appeared beside Lily. "The bartender wants to know if the Negronis should be served with a lemon peel or a slice of orange."

"Oliver, this gentleman wants me to look at his apartment." She turned and smiled. "He's interested in having me furnish it."

Olive gulped his martini. "I'm sorry, my wife doesn't make house calls."

"What did you say?" she gasped.

"Lily Bristol is a home furnishings store, not an interior design firm." He waved his drink. His words were a little slurred, and he took Lily's hand. "You'd better come with me. The caterer is using too much garlic and ruining the ricotta crostini."

"I'm terribly sorry." Lily turned to the man. "I'll get in touch with you tomorrow."

"What the hell was that about, Oliver? And you're tipsy. This is a store opening, not a cocktail party," Lily raged. They faced each other in the back room, and she couldn't stop shaking.

"I may have been thirsty and downed a couple of martinis, but that doesn't change what you just offered. You can't go to a strange man's apartment," Oliver said hotly. "You may as well put up a sign that you're an escort service."

"I own a furnishings store. Why shouldn't I go to people's

homes?" she demanded. "Anyway, he's married. His wife is coming from London."

"If you believe that, you might believe in Santa Claus." Oliver laughed. "He's not wearing a wedding ring, and he drives a red sports car."

"How dare you question my integrity," she challenged. "Lily Bristol is a business, and I need to make a profit."

"Because one of us has to pay for the imported vodka and fancy finger food?" he fumed. "I'd rather eat peanut butter sandwiches and drink Louisa's apple juice than have you pick out a strange man's bed linens."

"You don't know a thing about sales projections or cost per square foot," Lily snapped. "If we lose money on this, we'll never own a home or be able to go away on weekends."

"You see." Oliver's face twisted. "It's starting."

"What's starting?"

"You're blaming me for things we can't afford. Remember when I proposed and said I'd never be able to give you three weeks in Lake Tahoe every summer?"

"I didn't ask for three weeks in Lake Tahoe," she said. "I just want a car that doesn't break down on the Golden Gate Bridge."

"It doesn't make sense to own a decent car when you live in the city," he insisted. "It's too easy to get broken into."

"My parents own two Audis and never have any trouble."

"Then stay with them. Or better yet, go to Roger." He walked to the door. "Your mother said he just bought a Mercedes."

"I'll tell you what I did ask for," she called after him. "All I wanted was a marriage where we loved and respected each other."

Lily gulped Oliver's martini and set it on the table. How dare Oliver bring up Roger every time they had a fight? The room swam before her eyes, and she needed fresh air. She stepped into the alley and leaned against the wall. A cat sprang across the pavement, and she wrapped her arms around her chest.

Of course there were things she craved: a full-sized washer and dryer and a proper dining room table. But she never blamed Oliver for not having them. He had been so supportive of Lily Bristol: giving her the money from Guido, watching Louisa so she could work on weekends. And it had been her idea for Oliver to be a restaurant critic.

Lily Bristol was doing well; soon they'd be able to afford family holidays. Why should they argue about money now? And what was the point of any of it if they didn't make each other happy? But she couldn't act as if nothing had happened. It was her grand opening, and Oliver had behaved like a child. She would go inside and mingle with the guests. Then she'd go back to the hotel and take a bath. They could talk about it in the morning.

There was a rustling sound, and Lily turned. A figure was slumped against the wall. She squinted under the street lamp and recognized Oliver's gold cuff links.

"What are you doing out here?" she demanded. "I thought you were a cat rummaging through the garbage can."

"I couldn't stomach eating canapés and making small talk. But I didn't want to desert you by going back to the hotel." Oliver fiddled with his cuffs. "I thought I would wait here until the party was over."

"Oliver . . ." Lily began.

"You don't have to tell me I acted like I child, I already know," he cut in. "Of course I'm proud of you. I tell everyone my wife is the owner of Lily Bristol." He paused. "I had too much to drink and thought that man was hitting on you. I apologize."

"You were horrible and you spoiled one of the most important nights of my career." She walked over to him. "But I forgive you."

"You do?" He looked up.

"I couldn't have built Lily Bristol without you. And I know you're going to be a success as a restaurant critic." She paused. "The important thing is to make each other happy."

"Sometimes I don't deserve you, but I always love you," he said.

"I love you too, Oliver." She leaned down and kissed him.

"You know what would make me happy?" He stood up. "A cup of black coffee and two aspirins."

"We're in Italy, they have the best espresso." She took his hand. "Let's go back inside and find some."

Lily sat in a striped armchair in their room at the Hotel Baglioni and slipped off her pumps. It had been a whirlwind three days since the store opening. They climbed to the roof of the Duomo and admired the pink Candoglia marble statues and ornate spires. They visited La Scala opera house and marveled at Leonardo da Vinci's *Last Supper.*

Now she wanted to relax with a book and a cup of hot chocolate. She thought of Louisa and brightened. Being in Milan with Oliver was heavenly, but she couldn't wait to see Louisa. There was a new doll and a pair of pink slippers in her suitcase.

"There's my beautiful wife." Oliver entered the room. "Please get dressed, I have a surprise for you."

"We've eaten Milanese saffron risotto and Tuscan lamb. We've sampled pistachio ricotta and eaten too much gelato." Lily looked up and smiled. "I'm too tired to go out. I want to lie here and think of all the things I'm grateful for: a wonderful husband and a healthy daughter and a bright future."

"Your wonderful husband has planned an evening you won't forget." He leaned down and kissed her. "Wear the cocktail dress you wore to the opening. A car is picking us up in half an hour."

"Where are we going?" Lily asked.

"It's a secret." Oliver's blue eyes sparkled. "I promise it will be worth it."

"We can't afford this," Lily gasped, admiring the restaurant's sleek marble floors and alabaster walls. There was an aquarium filled with neon-colored fish and racks stacked with hundred-year-old wine bottles.

A town car had picked them up and delivered them to Ristorante Cracco; Carlo Cracco was the most famous chef in Milan. The restaurant had two Michelin stars, and Carlo was known to stop by the table to make sure the egg yolk spaghetti with chili was served al dente.

"Tonight we can afford anything," Oliver said, and Lily thought he looked like a schoolboy on awards day. His dark hair was tousled, and he wore a white shirt and striped tie.

"We already drank Campari at the Foyer bar to commemorate our anniversary, what are we celebrating now?" Lily said and felt almost giddy. It was lovely to see Oliver not worrying about her mother or Louisa's college fund.

"You're looking at the new restaurant critic for the *New York Times*."

"What did you say?" she asked.

"I applied a few months ago, but I never thought I had a chance," Oliver began. "Their critic usually has a degree from Cornell and a certificate from a Cordon Bleu cooking school."

"But we'd have to move to New York." Lily's throat was dry, and she couldn't swallow.

"I start in four weeks, we have plenty of time to find an apartment." He picked up a breadstick. "I've always wanted to live in New York! We can take Louisa to the Bronx Zoo and the Museum of Natural History. We'll pick apples in the Hudson Valley and buy maple syrup in Vermont."

"What about Lily Bristol?" she reminded him. "I can't leave San Francisco."

"I thought you'd be pleased, you love Manhattan." He was surprised. "I'd earn a decent salary, and you could be bicoastal. You can open a Lily Bristol in New York. And think about Louisa. She'll grow up visiting the Guggenheim and the Met. New York is the center of the world."

"It's too soon to expand with another store." Lily wished she had ordered a cocktail. "I'm still involved in the day-to-day operations of Lily Bristol San Francisco."

"You can hire a manager for the San Francisco store. Can you imagine your own furnishings store in the West Village or Chelsea?"

Lily wanted to open more stores eventually, but Lily Bristol Milan was barely off the ground. And they couldn't move Louisa across the country; she adored her grandparents, and they would have to find a new nanny.

"It's a wonderful opportunity, but it's not the right time." She refolded her napkin. "Louisa is already enrolled in preschool, and it's too soon to open a new store. I don't have the capital, and if I overleverage, the whole thing might fail."

"We'll take out a loan to open a new store and sign up Louisa at the best preschool in Manhattan. I'll ask the editor in chief for a recommendation." Oliver waved his hand.

"I'm sorry, Oliver. Maybe in a few years." She shook her head. "But not now."

"You were willing to move to New York before." Oliver clutched his wineglass.

"What are you talking about?" She looked up.

"Your mother said you planned on moving to New York when Roger graduated from law school," he said slowly.

"That was different. I was young and didn't have any commitments." She fiddled with her earrings.

"You're right, this is different." Oliver's voice shook. "I'm asking you to support your husband. If I don't do this now, I'll always be a second-rate columnist at a provincial newspaper. But maybe that isn't as important to you as being the wife of a partner at a law firm." He threw his credit card on the table and stood up. "If you'll excuse me, I lost my appetite."

Lily handed the driver five euros and stepped out of the taxi. How dare Oliver apply for the position without asking her? And they couldn't just move to New York like college kids whose belongings fit into a duffel bag.

She hurried up the steps of the Hotel Baglioni and entered the glass foyer. Bellboys carried soft leather luggage, and an uneasy feeling formed in the pit of her stomach. She and Oliver were married; weren't they supposed to support each other?

Maybe Oliver was right. Being the *New York Times* restaurant critic was like starring in a Broadway show. She imagined his by-line in the *New York Times* and felt a thrill of pride.

Her mother adored Central Park in the spring and New York Fashion Week in the fall. She would have a dozen reasons to visit Louisa. And it would be exciting to open a Lily Bristol store in Manhattan.

Couples mingled in the hotel lounge, and she wondered when it had all gotten so difficult. They wanted the same things, but they seemed to come from opposite directions. It was like one of Louisa's Lego structures. Every time you added a piece, you were in danger of toppling everything you had built.

She walked past the restaurant and saw a man sitting at the bar. He wound spaghetti around his fork and cradled a shot glass.

"I thought I'd find you here." She sat down beside him.

"I'm sick of pretentious dishes: tortelli with mint and aspara-gus cream, and apricot-stuffed quail with roasted goose liver. You know what's the best Italian food? Spaghetti with butter and grated Parmesan cheese. It doesn't even have to be the real stuff. I'm perfectly happy with the Kraft cheese they sell at the super-market."

"That doesn't sound like something the *New York Times* res-taurant critic would say," she replied.

"You'll have to write and ask how he likes his pasta," he snapped. "I'm sure his contact information will be on the website."

"Do you remember when we drove to Florence, and I asked what made you happy? You said the usual stuff: a pretty girl and a good book and delicious food. I said you can't answer 'the usual stuff' to every question, and you said that I made you happy because I'm so unusual." She paused. "When did we stop making each other happy?"

"You do make me happy." Oliver put down his fork. "I know I get irritable, but I'm so lucky to have you."

"How can I make you happy when we argue about everything?" she sighed. "We're about as happy as turkeys on Thanksgiving morning."

"But that's what marriage is about," he explained. "You can't imagine we would agree on everything."

"You stormed out of the restaurant." She frowned. "I thought you were furious."

"I am furious. The job means everything to me." He nodded. "But I'm still in love with you."

"So you wouldn't be disappointed if we didn't move to New York?" she asked.

"I would do everything I could to convince you." He paused. "But if the answer was still no, I'd get over it eventually."

Lily inhaled deeply and shivered. Oliver was smart and handsome and he was her husband.

"Owning three stores might be difficult at first, and we'll have to buy Louisa a proper winter wardrobe. But we'll have so much fun. We'll take her ice-skating in Rockefeller Center and buy gumdrops at Dylan's Candy Bar." She took a deep breath. "It's a fabulous opportunity, and you can't pass it up."

Oliver threw a wad of euros on the bar and jumped up. He took her hand and ran to the elevator.

"Where are we going?" she asked.

"That spaghetti tastes like something for a five-year-old." He pressed the button. "We're going to order room-service Iberian pork with turnips and mustard, and Italian cheeses with dried fruit and honey for dessert."

"You said you were tired of fancy food, and room service is terribly expensive."

The elevator doors opened, and he pulled her inside.

"That was before I was the *New York Times* food critic." He kissed her. "Now I want the most exotic item on the menu, and we can afford it."

"I knew when we got married I'd worry about getting fat." She kissed him back. "We're going to have to do some strenuous lovemaking to work it off."

"The best move I ever made was asking you to marry me," he whispered. "You're everything I ever wanted."

Lily walked along the dock and approached Christoff's yacht. Maybe it had been a bad idea to stay at the Hotel Cervo once she knew Oliver was there. He was like a deep conditioner she couldn't get out of her hair.

They had been so young and in love; they'd thought talking could solve anything. But all the talking in the world couldn't fix things that were broken. She'd destroyed Oliver's trust and then he'd done something she couldn't forgive.

The advice articles said you had to move on from people in your life who weren't working. Look how much happier they were now. Oliver had a girlfriend, and she was having lunch with a sexy Sardinian. How could she complain when she was about to board a fabulous yacht?

"Lily," a male voice called. "Up here. I was afraid you got lost."

Lily looked up, and her shoulders relaxed. Ricky's dark eyes smoldered, and he looked like an ad for men's cologne.

"I'm terribly sorry. I forgot the name of the yacht." She ran up the steps.

The deck had polished wood floors and chaise longues and a pink marble bar. Creamy leather sofas were littered with silk cushions, and there was a tennis court and a Jacuzzi.

"Oh, it's gorgeous," Lily breathed. "I want all these fabrics for my store."

"Christoff's girlfriend is an interior designer," Ricky explained. "The yacht has been featured in *Architectural Digest*."

"The mistress in Portofino or the one in Monte Carlo?" Lily said and laughed. She had to learn to enjoy herself. Isn't that what people did on the Emerald Coast?

"I didn't ask him." Ricky took her hand. "Come, I'll show you the whole yacht."

There was a salon with white carpets and white sofas and a white grand piano. Abstract art lined the walls, and vases were filled with white roses. There was an entertainment room with a billiard table and a movie theater with plush velvet chairs. And the guest rooms! Cabin after cabin filled with crisp linens and sea foam towels. They drank champagne and slurped oysters and talked about swimming and sailing.

"It's like a luxury resort with a view of the ocean from every window." Lily leaned over the railing.

Men and women wore bright swimwear and carried frosty glasses. Music played over the loudspeakers, and the air smelled of suntan lotion and cologne.

"In Greece, everyone owns a yacht." Ricky stood beside her. "I know a Greek jeweler whose yacht has a parking garage. He buys

Bugattis and Aston Martins, but then he parks them on the yacht and never drives them. They're like performance art."

"I love buying Louisa pretty dresses but I could never spend money like that." Lily fiddled with her earrings.

"What would you do with a lot of money?" he asked.

"Open more Lily Bristol stores and give some to charity," she mused. "There are so many people who don't have opportunities."

"Visitors think all of Sardinia is like the Emerald Coast, with its white sand beaches. But in 2012, the coal mining industry collapsed, and many miners are still out of work," Ricky began. "Every month, I take books and food to villages in Carbonia. Someday I hope to build a library. It's nice to meet someone who wants to help people who are less fortunate."

Lily remembered Ricky saying he had to be with a woman who shared similar interests and a felt a thrill of anticipation.

"I'm terribly thirsty." She smoothed her skirt.

"I'm failing as a host." He touched her arm. "I will ask the bartender to make blood orange mojitos."

Lily waited for Ricky to return and shielded her eyes from the sun. Sailboats skimmed over the waves, and she felt warm and happy.

"It's spectacular, isn't it?" A woman approached her. She wore a pastel-colored sarong and gold earrings. "Christoff spends more money feeding his guests for one week than some hedge fund managers earn in a month."

"It's the most stunning yacht I've ever seen," Lily said. "And everyone is so glamorous. I've never been around so many fabulous-looking people. I feel completely underdressed."

"I haven't seen you before, are you new? I'm Marjorie." The

woman held out her hand. "I join Christoff every summer. We start in Crete and stop in Portofino and Capri. I like the Emerald Coast the best. The water is clear, and you don't bump into tourists with bulky cameras and terrible sunburns."

"I haven't met Christoff yet," Lily replied. "My name is Lily, and I'm here with Ricky. He went to get some drinks."

"You're here with Ricky?" Marjorie raised her eyebrow.

"Is there something wrong with that?" Lily suddenly wondered if Ricky had a girlfriend.

"I've known Ricky for years, and he usually likes women who are blond and well-endowed." She laughed, and Lily noticed her teeth were white as pearls.

"We've only known each other a few days," Lily answered. "I'm American and I'm opening a home furnishings store in Porto Cervo. It's called Lily Bristol, you should come to the opening."

"That explains it. Ricky loves everything American." Marjorie nodded. "He always asks Christoff to show American movies, and Ralph Lauren is his favorite designer. And he adores New York. He visited last summer, and all he talked about was Bloomingdale's and Barneys."

"What's wrong with that?" Lily asked. "The department stores in New York are famous."

"Perhaps if you're American. But in Europe, the great fashion centers are Paris and Milan." She shrugged. "I should go, I'm late for a game of shuffleboard."

Lily rubbed her lips and wondered why Ricky hadn't told her he had been to New York. But they'd just met, and there were plenty of things she hadn't mentioned: she was afraid of snakes and adored Jane Austen and was always losing things.

What did it matter anyway? She was only seeing Ricky because she didn't want to explore the Emerald Coast alone. They hadn't been on a proper date or even kissed.

"Is something wrong?" Ricky approached her. He handed her a glass and rested his elbows on the railing.

"I must have had too much sun." Lily sipped the drink and tasted oranges and berries. "I'll drink this and I'll be fine."

"I can't have you fainting." He took her hand. "Come with me, there's something I wanted to show you anyway."

Ricky led her down a staircase with inlaid mosaic tile steps and a gold railing. The hallway had portholes made of tinted glass and rich paneled walls. He opened double brass doors, and they entered a room with a pink-and-white marble floor and gold-flecked walls.

Lily looked around and gasped. It was like standing in the middle of some fabulous museum. There were glass cabinets filled with ancient pottery and priceless jewelry. She saw a statue of a girl wearing a gold dress and holding a snake made of sapphires.

"Christoff is a serious collector of ancient artifacts." Ricky opened a case and took out a terra-cotta bottle. "This was a terra-cotta baby bottle discovered in a Messapian tomb; it's twenty-four hundred years old." He put it back and waved his hands over the glass. "There are oil lamps used in Ancient Greece and dolphin-shaped brooches worn by fashionable women in Crete. Last year, he bid on the oldest musical instrument ever discovered. It was found in a cave in Slovenia and is sixty thousand years old. He keeps it in a safe and only brings it out on special occasions."

"I can understand why," Lily said. There were cabinets of black and red painted bowls, and marble busts and bright silver coins. It was like visiting a fantastic exhibit at the Met, but she could touch whatever she liked. "How exciting to be able to surround yourself with such treasures."

"This is my favorite room on the yacht." He stood beside her. "But today it holds an even greater treasure."

"Where?" Lily scanned the space. There was a limestone bust of a bull from 3000 BC and a painting in a gold frame from the Byzantine Empire.

"Right here." He leaned forward and kissed her. His lips tasted of berries and some kind of delicious liqueur.

"I don't know if I can compete with a two-thousand-year-old Minoan flute," she said and kissed him back. "But I'm very happy to be here."

Lily and Ricky strolled along the dock, and Lily thought it had been a spectacular afternoon. The yacht cruised to La Maddalena Archipelago, and they explored the green inlets. The water was like a photo in a magazine where the colors had been enhanced so you couldn't believe it was real. And the flowers! Cliffs were covered with bougainvillea, and fields were dotted with poppies, and it was like Central Park during a flower show.

Then they clambered back on the yacht and ate scampi with watermelon marinade and platters of suckling pig in sweet-and-sour sauce. There were berries and cream for dessert.

By late afternoon, the hills were a muted purple. Her shoulders were bronze from the sun, and she was filled with an incredible lightness. For the first time since Oliver had left, she felt happy.

"You're a strong swimmer. Some of the men were upset." Ricky grinned. "Europeans don't like to be beaten by a woman."

"When I was a child, we spent three weeks every summer in Lake Tahoe," Lily explained. "All we did was swim and sail."

"So we have something else in common," Ricky mused.

"Something else?" Lily wondered whether he was going to tell her he had visited New York.

"We both own businesses and are not afraid to work hard," he said. "The women you meet on Christoff's yacht only think about whether they should eat another bite of cheesecake or if a sapphire necklace looks good with their tan."

"The yacht!" Lily gasped. "I left my straw hat on board, and now it's gone."

"We can go back and find it," Ricky offered.

"I don't remember where I put it. It could be anywhere," she said worriedly. "You must think I'm hopeless. You gave me a gift, and I lost it."

"You're not hopeless at all." He touched her cheek. "You're very unusual."

"You think I'm unusual?" She looked up.

"In a good way," he answered. "You're successful, but there's something fresh and original about you. And you like to enjoy yourself but you're not sure how."

"When you're married, you put the other person first," Lily began. "The advice books say that's wrong, but that's how marriage works. Then you get divorced and you can't remember what flavor of coffee you like or whether you prefer to eat at a restaurant or stay home. It's easier when Louisa is around, of course. Then I don't have time to do anything except fix peanut butter sandwiches and make her brush her teeth. But when I'm by myself, it's more difficult."

"I can help you," Ricky suggested. He stood so close she could smell his aftershave.

"Help me?"

"Help you enjoy yourself. We'll start by going to dinner tonight at the Yacht Club. It's the most famous restaurant in Porto Cervo, and it's packed with film stars and Arab sheiks."

"But it's almost evening, and we just ate lunch." She laughed.

"No one on the Emerald Coast eats dinner before nine PM." He shrugged. "You have plenty of time to get an appetite."

Lily felt a warmth spread through her chest. "Yes, I'd like that very much."

He kissed her and tasted of almonds and honey. She kissed him back and her lips throbbed with pleasure.

"I have to go." She glanced at her watch. "It's nine AM in New York, and I promised to call Louisa before she goes to camp."

"Lily," he called after her.

"Yes?" She turned around.

"I had a wonderful time," he said and smiled. "I can't wait to see you tonight."

Lily entered her hotel suite and set her purse on the side table. The drapes were open, and the harbor was tinted glass.

She stepped onto the balcony and pictured the yacht with its gleaming staterooms, and the kiss on the dock.

Music drifted up from the *piazzetta*, and she remembered Ricky saying she was unusual. She took out her phone to call Louisa and gasped. She knew why she suddenly felt unsettled. The last person who'd said she was unusual had been Oliver, and she had married him.

Chapter Eight

OLIVER STROLLED ALONG THE *piazzetta* and admired the okra-colored buildings and lacquered window boxes. Men and women kissed each other on the cheek, and a Bentley idled on the pavement, and it resembled a secret club that would never accept him as a member.

Ever since yesterday, when he'd decided he was going to try harder with Angela, the sun had seemed brighter and even his poached eggs had tasted better. He felt like when he made a New Year's resolution to go to the gym. Even while he was taking the subway to 24-Hour Fitness, the anticipation of working out made him feel healthy.

The concierge suggested he take Angela to dinner at the Yacht Club, and Oliver balked at the prices. Could you really charge one hundred euros for a plate of crustaceans that had clung to the bottom of a boat? But every night, the Yacht Club overflowed with models and actors. Angela would be impressed by the Baccarat crystal and front-row view of the yachts.

Now he entered a boutique and thought he would buy her a pair of sandals or a quilted evening bag. He glanced at the price tag on a crocheted top and gulped. It was hot pink and looked like something Louisa could have made in art class.

He hadn't even known Angela liked designer clothes until she'd entered the hotel suite with shopping bags from Gucci and Prada. Angela insisted they were "investment pieces." When would she be so close to the center of high fashion again?

And he was pleased that wedding florists in New York earned more than he imagined. He wouldn't feel guilty if Angela Uber-ed home from his apartment or paid for Sunday brunch at Tartine's in the West Village.

"Can I help you find something?" a female voice asked.

Oliver looked up and frowned. Once a saleswoman engaged you, you were trapped. They had a way of making you feel like you were avoiding the IRS if you said you were only looking and tried to slip out the door.

"I was looking for a present," he said uncertainly.

"Is it for your wife?" the woman asked. She wore a gold tunic, and her blond hair was pulled into a chignon.

"No," Oliver said and felt suddenly proud. "It's for my girl-friend."

"What would suit her?" she asked.

Oliver pictured Angela's coppery hair and curvy hips and felt a thrill of excitement. "She looks good in anything."

"Certain colors flatter different complexions," she prodded. "Do you have a photo?"

Oliver took out his iPhone and marveled at technology. When he was dating Lily, he often bought a blouse or skirt she never ended up wearing. Now all he had to do was hand the salesgirl his phone, and she would make the decisions for him.

"Is that your girlfriend?" She raised her eyebrow.

"Well, yes." Oliver wondered if by accident she had clicked to the photo of the middle-aged female chef he'd interviewed for his latest review.

She gave Oliver back the phone. "She's stunning. She would look breathtaking in a vintage Romeo Gigli dress."

Oliver never heard of Romeo Gigli, but he was confident he was out of his price range. In his experience as a food critic, the more obscure items—the Le Pin bordeaux from Saint-Émilion in France, the lobster the chef discovered on holiday in Scotland—cost more than anything else on the menu.

"It depends on the price," he hesitated. The dress had an orange bodice and wide tulle skirt, and looked like an overgrown tulip. "I was hoping to spend under one hundred euros."

The saleswoman put the dress back on the rack. "Perhaps you should try somewhere else."

"All the tourists in Porto Cervo wear Versace and Fendi," he sighed. "I can't buy her something from a local seamstress who works at a sewing machine in her living room."

"What do you want the gift to say?" she asked.

"To say?" Oliver repeated.

"A silk scarf says 'It's nice to spend the weekend together,' while a cocktail dress says 'I'm serious about you.'" She paused. "We do have a selection of La Perla underwear. The nude camisole is popular."

Oliver flushed and looked away. Then he glanced at the photo of Angela on his phone, and his heart surged.

"I want it to say 'I can't live without you,'" he said and puffed out his chest. "I don't care about the cost. Give me the best you've got."

———

Oliver clutched his parcel and strolled though the *piazzetta*. Once he acknowledged that Angela was his girlfriend, even his step was lighter.

He passed an outdoor café and decided to have an aperitif. The tables were filled with men and women with European accents. They flicked cigarette lighters and drank golden liqueurs, and it was so decadent, Oliver was almost dizzy.

He ordered peach sorbet and iced coffee with amaretto. The sun sparkled on the silverware, and the air was as sweet as honey. It felt so good to buy Angela something special; why hadn't he thought of it sooner?

He sipped his drink and remembered when he and Lily had first gone to New York. They had both wanted to please each other so much; they were like children adding syrup to scoops of ice cream.

Oliver stirred sugar into hot coffee and thought there was no point in ordering iced coffee in Manhattan in August. By the time it appeared, the ice cubes melted and you were left with murky water. He pushed the cup away and decided if he had any more caffeine he'd have a stroke. Then he'd end up in the hospital, and the whole trip would be wasted.

He and Lily had left Louisa with Lily's parents and come to New York to find an apartment. But the places they saw had cramped rooms and fire escapes advertised as balconies. The last one had had ants in the kitchen and a hole in the bedroom ceiling.

"What did you think of the apartment on West Eighteenth Street?" he asked Lily. "The second bedroom had a window, and the building's supervisor said he would install air-conditioning."

"The window looked over the garbage cans, and if we pay an additional one hundred dollars a month, he'll put a wall unit in the living room." Lily leaned against the diner's booth. "But Louisa's room will still be a furnace, and we can't afford the rent now."

Oliver's salary at the *New York Times* was respectable, but apartments in New York were obscenely expensive. If they took out a loan to open a Lily Bristol, they would hardly have anything left for necessities.

"The real estate agent said young couples are moving to Brooklyn," he suggested. "The sidewalks have trees that aren't protected by barbwire, and there's a thriving arts scene."

"If I open a store in Manhattan, I'll spend all my time on the subway." Lily put down her spoon. "It was so simple in San Francisco. I could walk to the store, and the babysitter brought Louisa to visit in the afternoons. I don't know what to do, it all seems hopeless."

Oliver looked up from his cheese omelet and gulped. If he didn't take the position, he would always wonder what he had missed. But Lily's shoulders sagged, and she looked so unhappy.

"Why don't we go back to our hotel and look through Craigslist," he offered.

"Our room is so hot I can barely breathe," she answered. "And we've read every newspaper in New York. It's no use, we'll never find a decent apartment we can afford."

"I've already given the *Chronicle* my notice." He fiddled with his fork. "If we go back to San Francisco, I'll end up as the food critic at the *Palo Alto Gazette*."

"Maybe this isn't the right time to open a Lily Bristol," she said slowly. "We'll take the money we were going to borrow to open the store and get a weekend cottage outside the city."

"You have to open a Lily Bristol," Oliver insisted.

"I'll still fly to San Francisco to check on the store and make trips to Milan," she answered. "We agreed you had to take this job, and now we have to make it work."

Oliver's heart melted. Lily adored Lily Bristol but she would give it up for him. He thought of everything they'd done together. Strolling along the River Arno in Florence. Eating lobster on their honeymoon in Portugal. Seeing Lily push through the pain of childbirth and being handed the most exquisite bundle. Everything that made him happy was because of Lily.

"I have an idea," he said suddenly. He put some money on the table and took Lily's hand. He ran into the street and flagged down a cab.

"Where are we going?" she asked.

"First we're going to check out of that fleabag motel and get a room at the St. Regis." He climbed into the taxi. "My expense account is the best thing about this job and it's time to use it. We're going to drink Bloody Marys at the King Cole Bar and watch cable television. Then tomorrow, I have a surprise for you."

"You forgot the best part." She rested her head on his shoulder.

"What's that?" he asked.

"We're going to turn on the air-conditioning and fall asleep under cotton sheets. In the morning, we'll order muesli with fruit salad and fresh-squeezed orange juice."

"Will we be naked when we climb into bed?" Oliver wondered aloud.

Lily reached up and kissed him. "We'll definitely be naked."

———

"Oh, Oliver, there are apple trees and a pond." Lily waved her arms. "Louisa could have a dozen goldfish and that tiger fish she saw at the pet store."

Lily clutched a red apple, and Oliver was reminded of the girl eating a peach at the Naples train station. Lily's brown eyes sparkled, and a smile lit up her face.

They had taken the train to Wilton, Connecticut, and met with a real estate agent. She'd shown them a cottage in the woods and a colonial house in the center of town. Now they stood in front of a clapboard farmhouse with a sloped roof and a barn.

"So you like it?" Oliver asked.

"I love everything about it." Lily turned to him. "The dormer windows and secret space under the stairs. And the garden! It's like something out of a Virginia Woolf novel. But we can't afford it."

"Why don't we discuss it over ice cream?" he suggested.

"There's no point talking about it," she sighed. "We're just looking for two bedrooms and a shed for buckets and shovels."

"We'll ask the agent to drop us at off on Main Street." He took her arm. "Then we'll figure it out."

"You know what Wilton doesn't have," Oliver said, eating a bite of chocolate ice cream.

They sat at a window table at Carvel and shared a banana split. Lily's hair was pushed back, and she looked like the cover of his sister's old *Seventeen* magazine.

"It has everything." Lily licked her spoon. "A bookshop and a children's clothing store and an old-fashioned pharmacist. There's even a tack shop with a saddle in the window."

"It doesn't have a home furnishings store."

"I suppose it doesn't." She wiped her mouth with a napkin. "It would be a wonderful place to open a store. The locals all wear Italian loafers and drive Audis and Range Rovers. And the weekenders would spend a fortune."

"There's a vacant space across the street." Oliver pointed to a brick building with black awnings. "You should open a Lily Bristol."

"How would I do that if we lived in Manhattan?" she asked.

"We wouldn't live in New York." Oliver said. "We'd live in a white clapboard farmhouse with a barn. Louisa would ride a bicycle to school when she's older, and in the summer, she'd build sandcastles at the beach."

"I thought we were looking for a weekend cottage. How could we afford to live here full-time?" she asked. "A farmhouse in Connecticut must be expensive."

"The agent said the owner would lend us the money himself. He wants the house to go to a young family who will fill it with love," he explained. "And the store across the street has been empty for ages, we could get a great deal."

"But you'd have to be in the city almost every night," Lily said doubtfully. "Louisa and I would barely see you."

"You could take the train in on some evenings and meet me," he suggested. "It would be like when we were dating, except we would eat at Michelin-starred restaurants." He took her hand. "Do you recall when we met in Naples, and I asked what you wanted to do when you weren't getting stranded in train stations? You said you wanted to collect furnishings from all over the world and open your own store." He paused. "You can't stop now. You could open Lily Bristols in Paris and London and Amsterdam."

"You've always wanted to live in a city, what if you hate it here?

And the farmhouse needs a lot of work." She hesitated. "You'll spend weekends patching walls and replacing shingles."

"I worked on my parents' lake house every summer in Michigan." He paused. "Remember when we stopped in the village of Spello on the way to Florence, and you asked what my ideal life would be? I said I wanted a rewarding career and a loving family and plenty of money." He looked at Lily. "I have all that now, but it doesn't mean anything if you're not happy."

"Oh, Oliver, if you really think so!" She clapped her hands. "We'll be stretched financially at first. We'll eat ham sandwiches and sleep on foam mattresses." She laughed. "But I'll fill Lily Bristol with wooden chests from Cape Cod and maple furniture from Vermont. Louisa will climb trees, and we'll lie on the porch at night and gaze at the stars."

Oliver leaned forward and kissed her. Her mouth was soft, and she tasted of bananas and nuts.

"I forgot the most important thing." She kissed him back. "We'll be so happy."

Oliver ate the last bite of sorbet and glanced around the *piazzetta*. For the first time since he and Lily had separated, he felt optimistic. Look at how Angela had surprised him. She was not only gorgeous, she enjoyed art and culture too.

He paid the check and scooped up his package. If he hurried, he might convince Angela to take a nap before dinner. What would she say when she unwrapped the tissue paper, and how would she thank him?

———

"It's the most spectacular restaurant I've ever seen," Angela breathed. "And did you look at the crowd? I swear I saw Kate Moss and Calvin Harris."

Oliver thought the Yacht Club was like one of those E! specials about the rich and famous you couldn't help watching. The tile floor was covered with red carpet, pewter urns held flowering orchids, and glass chandeliers dangled from the ceiling. And the view! The yachts were parked so close, Oliver could see staterooms with leopard-skin rugs and silk bedspreads through the portholes.

"Remind me never to let Louisa go to a place like this when she's older," he muttered, noticing a woman in a spandex dress and stilettos. "I've seen more clothing on Louisa's dolls when they take a bath. That woman may as well be wearing a Band-Aid."

"Relax, we're on the Emerald Coast!" Angela laughed. "Part of the fun is wearing outrageous designs and doing crazy things. I read about a movie star who got thrown out of the Yacht Club for drinking champagne out of a slipper."

"Well, you look sensational. The dress suits you." Oliver studied the vintage Romeo Gigli and thought the saleswoman had been right. The color enhanced Angela's coppery hair, and the style showcased her figure. Gold earrings shimmered in her ears, and he was proud to accompany her. He remembered their predinner frolic and sighed.

"Thank you, it really was a thoughtful present," Angela said and gasped. "Is that Johnny Depp? I heard he's about to get engaged. I should give him my card."

"You can't waltz over to a celebrity you've never met," Oliver protested. "And how do you know he's getting engaged? It's probably Internet gossip."

"Part of my job is knowing who's getting engaged. Or how would we get the big clients?" she asked. "I do work for one of the best florists in New York. Johnny Depp would be lucky to have Dalton Faye design his wedding. I'll be right back."

"You're not really going to give him your card?" Oliver fumed. "What if he asks the maître d' to kick you out?"

"Do you really think he would have me kicked out?" She tossed her hair over her shoulders. "I don't want to work for someone else forever. If I don't try, I'll never get ahead."

Angela crossed the room, and Oliver searched for a waiter. He really needed some bruschetta while they waited for a table. The concierge insisted the reservation be for nine PM or they wouldn't see the fashionable people. But now his head felt light, and he had a hollow feeling in his stomach.

A couple entered through the glass doors, and Oliver noticed the woman's silver taffeta gown. It had a tight bodice and full skirt, and she wore diamond earrings.

He looked more closely and had a clammy feeling that started at his toes and worked its way to the base of his neck. What was Lily doing at the Yacht Club, and who was the dark-haired man beside her?

He and Angela could sneak out the side door and try another restaurant. But it would be impossible to get a reservation at this hour. And if they went back to their suite, room service would take ages.

But would Angela be comfortable dining in the same room as his ex-wife? And what was Lily doing with a guy who looked like one of those Tom Ford ads plastered on the side of a bus? You hated everything about the male model: his chiseled cheekbones and smoldering eyes and Rolex watch . . . until you remembered it was just an ad and he probably worked nights as a waiter, like every struggling actor/model in New York.

"Oliver!" Lily approached him. "What are you doing here?"

Oliver turned and gulped. It was too late now; he had to make the best of it. And anyway, he was having dinner with his girl-friend. Lily was all dressed up for someone she barely knew.

"Lily, what a surprise," Oliver answered. He turned to the man and held out his hand. "I'm Oliver Bristol, Lily's ex-husband."

"This is Ricky Perilli," she introduced them. "Ricky and I met a couple of days ago. He owns a boutique in the marina."

"The Emerald Coast seems like an excellent place to own a store." Oliver nodded. "I visited a boutique this afternoon and practically turned over my life savings. I haven't seen such high prices since I reviewed Masa. It's the most expensive restaurant in New York, and a prawn cocktail costs two hundred dollars."

Oliver thought he should keep quiet. He was babbling, and nothing he said made sense.

"Here's Angela, let me introduce her to Ricky." He sighed with relief. "She was just talking to Johnny Depp."

"Are you sure it's Johnny Depp?" Lily peered across the room. "That man looks too young, and he doesn't have a pierced ear."

"Oliver." Angela joined them. "You didn't tell me you invited another couple."

"We ran into each other," Oliver stammered. "You remember Lily, and this is Ricky. He owns a boutique in the marina."

"We could all have a drink while we wait," Lily said, and her eyes sparkled. "Ricky knows the bartender. He'll make us Tan-queray and tonic with guava juice."

Oliver had to stop this before it got worse. He signaled the maî-tre d' and took Angela's arm.

"Another time. Our table is ready." He nodded at Ricky. "It was a pleasure meeting you."

Oliver sipped ice water and leaned back in his chair. Why would Lily invite them for a drink? Perhaps she wanted to show off her date. But that wasn't like Lily; she never cared about Oliver's looks or wardrobe.

But how well did he know Lily now? He had never seen that taffeta gown, and how did she know Johnny Depp pierced his ear?

"You're not listening to me, Oliver." Angela looked up from the menu. "I just said that wasn't Johnny Depp, it was a French actor based in Cannes. His sister is getting married next year, and he's going to recommend me for the job."

"I didn't know Johnny Depp had a sister," Oliver said, and realized his mistake. He signaled the waiter and thought he must get Angela drunk. It was the only way she wouldn't notice his hands were shaking.

"Are you all right?" Angela asked. "You're acting strangely, and you look a little peaked."

How could he explain to Angela that eating at the same restaurant as Lily made him anxious? Even if he didn't have feelings for her, there was a connection like an invisible thread.

"Is it because you're not comfortable around ambitious women?" Angela asked, buttering a breadstick.

"What did you say?" Oliver asked.

"Ever since I said I was going to give Johnny Depp my card, you've been a little off," she continued. "Some men have trouble with women who have careers. I thought you'd be different."

"Different?" he repeated. If he had something in his stomach, he thought, he could think clearly and follow the conversation.

"Since your wife was successful, I thought you wouldn't mind that I want the same thing," she explained. "I've read a few articles about Lily Bristol, and Lily is quite impressive. She owns stores on three continents, and all her employees are women."

"You never said you knew anything about Lily." He fiddled with his glass.

"I didn't really put it together until we met at the hotel." She shrugged. "I'm not a fangirl or anything, I just admire what she's achieved. I want the same things: my own floral business and a family."

"A family?" Oliver looked up.

"I could never be one of those career women who comes home to a briefcase full of papers and grilled salmon from Zabar's. I am an Ohio girl, after all. Family is important to me." She looked at Oliver. "You do want more children, don't you?"

"I hadn't thought about it." Oliver loosened his collar.

"You're only thirty-three, and I'm sure Louisa would like a brother or sister." She leaned forward. "All children want a sibling."

Oliver opened his mouth and stopped. He was having dinner with a beautiful woman at the most exclusive restaurant on the Emerald Coast. Why make a fuss about the future?

"Of course." He swallowed his gin and tonic. "Why wouldn't I want more children?"

They ate gnocchi with garlic foam and paprika. There was goat with cheese sauce and some kind of flavorful risotto. Oliver told stories about sampling seven-course tasting menus at Per Se and eating hundred-dollar plates of sashimi at Kurumazushi.

"Tell me what I should have for dessert." Angela handed him the dessert menu. "Something light without too much sugar."

Oliver looked up and noticed Lily and Ricky at a table near the window. Lily was talking animatedly, and her cheeks glowed in the candlelight.

"Oliver," Angela repeated. "The waiter would like to know what we want for dessert."

"The tiramisu with lemon zest is excellent," the waiter said. "I just recommended it to another couple." He pointed in Lily and Ricky's direction.

"Did you say they were having the tiramisu?" Oliver asked.

"Yes, but there's more in the kitchen," the waiter answered. "It's our most popular dessert."

"Is it made with cinnamon?" Oliver asked.

Lily was allergic to cinnamon; it made her eyes water and gave her a rash. Surely she wouldn't have ordered the tiramisu. But knowing Lily, she'd forget she was allergic. She was used to Oliver ordering for her.

"I believe it is." The waiter nodded.

Oliver looked up and saw another waiter place a silver dish in front of Lily. He pushed back his chair and raced across the room. He grabbed the dish and held it in the air.

"Oliver, what on earth are you doing?" Lily jumped up.

"The tiramisu is baked with cinnamon," he explained. "You'll have an allergic reaction!"

Lily's eyes flickered, and she held out her hand. "I requested it without cinnamon. Please give me back my dessert."

Oliver stepped forward and tripped over the rug. The bowl

flew out of his hands and clattered on the floor. He slipped on custard and landed on his back.

"Are you all right?" Ricky got up from his chair and crouched beside Oliver.

Oliver wiped off his slacks and stood up. Lily's mouth trembled, and he had never seen her so angry.

"I'm fine." He nodded and turned to Lily. "I'm very sorry. I'll order you another dessert."

Oliver took off his blazer and folded it on the love seat. It was almost midnight, and the sound of laughter and music drifted up from the *piazzetta*.

After he had wiped off the custard, he returned to their table and tried to eat dessert. But all he could see was the horrified look on Lily's face when he grabbed the bowl. He'd only been trying to help; how could he know Lily ordered it without cinnamon?

Now Angela was changing in the bedroom, and he wondered if she would make him sleep on the sofa. He couldn't blame her. He'd embarrassed her in front of the entire dining room.

"Oliver." Angela opened the bedroom door. She wore a peach robe, and her hair cascaded over her shoulders. "Why aren't you getting undressed?"

"I thought . . ." He walked to the bar and poured a glass of scotch.

"Thought what, Oliver?" she interrupted. "That I would be upset that you tried to save your ex-wife from having an allergic reaction?"

"It can be terrible. Lily's eyes water as if she's been chopping onions, and her skin itches for days."

"I don't mind at all. You make a charming knight in shining armor." She paused. "Unless you still have feelings for her. But you don't, do you?"

"Of course not." Oliver downed the scotch. "We're divorced."

"I didn't think so, or you wouldn't call me your girlfriend. I'm glad you're friends with Lily." She stood close to Oliver. "It's important to have a good relationship with your ex, especially when children are involved." She rubbed his chin. "You have a bit of custard on your chin. Why don't you shower before we go to bed?"

"That's an excellent idea." He put his shot glass on the bar. "I could use a shower."

Oliver stood under the water and massaged his neck. He pictured Lily demanding her dessert, and Ricky crouching beside him, and was glad the evening was over. It could have been worse; at least Angela was understanding.

The shower door opened, and Angela stepped inside. She was naked, and water pearled up on her breasts.

"Have you ever done it sitting down in the shower?" she asked.

"I beg your pardon?" Oliver gulped.

"Sit down." She motioned to the tile bench. "And lean against the wall."

Oliver sat on the bench, and Angela climbed into his lap. The water sprayed her hair, and he buried his mouth in her neck.

He wrapped his arms around her, and she moved on top of him. Steam filled the shower, and he was so hard he was afraid he would come too fast.

"Say my name," she whispered.

"Angela," he breathed, kissing her breasts.

God! He had never experienced anything like it. Her nipples were erect, and her skin glistened, and she was like some incredible mermaid.

"I want you, Oliver." She tossed her hair over her shoulders. He was about to answer, but the water droned in his ears. Tension built inside him, and he came with an unbearable force.

"Come into the bedroom when you're ready." She climbed off him and grabbed a towel. "I'll keep the bed warm."

Oliver knotted a towel around his waist and wondered how he'd gotten so lucky. Even thinking about what he and Angela had just done made him groan.

He remembered her saying she wanted children, and was suddenly apprehensive. Most women in their twenties said that; it didn't mean anything. And he and Angela had never said they loved each other. They were just having a good time.

He rubbed his wrists with cologne and entered the bedroom. Angela's hair spilled over the pillow, and she looked like an angel. He dropped his towel and slid into bed beside her.

Chapter Nine

LILY STROLLED ALONG THE *piazzetta* and inhaled the scent of coffee and hyacinths. It was mid-morning, and the sun glinted on the harbor. Lily had never seen that shade of blue. The water was like one of Louisa's watercolor activity books, but the only colors were turquoise and magenta, mixed with gold.

She and Ricky had had a wonderful time the night before, drinking champagne and dancing. She'd forgotten what it was like to hold hands in the moonlight. The harbor had been lit up like a thousand fireflies, and pearl-colored yachts swayed against the shore. When they kissed in front of the hotel, her heart expanded and she felt light and happy.

Ricky was handsome and charismatic and they had so much in common. He had a niece Louisa's age, and he knew all about Hello Kitty. And Ricky wanted to learn everything about Lily: her favorite foods and books and movies.

Lily entered a market and picked up a basket. They were going to drive to Porto Rotondo and have a picnic. It was the prettiest stretch of beach on the Emerald Coast, and the sea was almost transparent. Afterward, they would have a romantic dinner at S'Astore Ristorante tucked high in the hills.

She selected *pane carasau* and dried beef and a packet of ricotta cheese. She added a bag of figs and walked to the cash register. The clerk rang up her purchases, but she couldn't find her wallet.

"Are you looking for this?" a male voice asked.

She turned around and saw Oliver holding her leather wallet. His hair was freshly washed, and he wore khakis and loafers.

"What are you doing here, Oliver?" she demanded. "And where did you find my wallet?"

"You left it next to the almonds." He pointed to a barrel of nuts. "I was going to say something, but you were engrossed in your shopping."

"I must have taken it out when I looked for my list." She grabbed the wallet. "This can't be a coincidence. I haven't seen anyone in Porto Cervo this often except Enzo, my butler."

"I saw you leave the hotel." He shuffled his feet. "I came to apologize."

"To apologize?" Lily looked up.

"For the scene last night at the Yacht Club," he began. "I was only trying to help."

"You didn't have to do anything. I'm perfectly capable of taking care of myself."

"Last Thanksgiving, you ate a slice of pumpkin pie with cinnamon at Louisa's class party," he reminded her. "You couldn't stop itching for days."

"You embarrassed me." Lily shuddered. "The Yacht Club is the most exclusive restaurant in Porto Cervo."

"Angela thought I did the right thing," he said and stopped. "Apparently, she's quite a fan of yours."

"What are you talking about?" she asked.

"I'd rather not discuss it here." He pointed at shoppers standing at the cash register. "Why don't you pay, and I'll wait outside?"

Ricky was meeting her in an hour, and she needed to pick up a sponge cake at the *pasticceria*. But it had been kind of Oliver to stop her from eating the tiramisu. And they were both going in the same direction. There was nothing wrong with talking while they walked.

"What is it, Oliver?" She stepped onto the *piazzetta*. "I'm in a hurry."

"How can you be in a hurry on a morning like this?" Oliver waved at boats gliding across the bay. "It's a perfect day to sit at an outdoor café with a paperback book and an iced chocolate."

"I'm going on a picnic," Lily said.

"With Ricky?" he inquired. "Isn't this a bit sudden? You've seen him every day since you arrived."

"That's none of your business," she answered. "You said you wanted to talk about something."

"Angela read some articles about Lily Bristol, and she's impressed with your success." He bit into an apple. "She's quite serious about her career."

"That's very flattering," Lily answered. "And why shouldn't she be serious about her work? I'm sure she's intelligent, or you wouldn't be seeing her." She paused. "Unless there's another reason you're together."

"If you're implying I like her for her physical attributes, you're wrong," Oliver retorted. "I admire her ambition. But she also said she wanted to have a family. She asked if I wanted more children."

"Why are you telling me? If you want relationship advice, you should write to *GQ*." She paused. "But that's not unusual. Most women want a husband and children."

"We've only known each other for two months," Oliver explained. "Isn't it too early to talk about the future?"

"Honestly, Oliver, I don't want to have this conversation." She walked faster. "But it's never too early to think ahead, if you have feelings for someone. The whole point of a relationship is to move forward."

"The last time I mentioned Angela, you said our relationship seemed rushed," he protested. "Now you think it's all right if she wants to know if Louisa wants a half sibling?"

"All I'm saying is I don't blame her for talking about her plans." Lily turned to Oliver. "Excuse me, I have to go."

"Wait." Oliver touched her arm. "The only reason you would change your mind is because of Ricky. You can't be serious about a Sardinian you met in the *piazzetta*?"

"I didn't meet Ricky in the *piazzetta*. He's a friend of Enzo's sister," she corrected him. "And he's intelligent and charming."

"You've known him for three days, he could be a serial killer!" he spat. "You can't think this is long term."

"I doubt the Emerald Coast has any serial killers." She smiled. "And I'm not thinking about anything. I'm just enjoying myself."

"I don't believe you," Oliver said stubbornly. "You'd be up in arms about what Angela said if you weren't thinking the same things about Ricky yourself. Ricky lives halfway across the world, it's ridiculous."

"I didn't ask you for dating advice," Lily snapped. "Good-bye, Oliver. Thank Angela for the kind words."

"Do you remember when we were in Naples, and I took you to Mergellina to see the sunset? You were so excited by the ancient buildings and lights twinkling on the bay. I thought if I could always see the world through your eyes, I'd be the luckiest guy alive."

He tossed the apple core onto the pavement. "We're both smart people, and we can be so stupid."

"What do you mean?" She turned around.

"If we had trusted each other, none of this would have happened."

"We had reasons not to trust each other. You lied to me about Mirabelle, why would I believe you again? And you never accepted the fact that I was over Roger." She adjusted her sunglasses. "We can't change what happened, that's why we got divorced. You enjoy Angela, and I'll go on a picnic with Ricky. I'll see you later."

Lily hurried along the alley and then realized she'd forgotten the sponge cake. She didn't want to go to the *pasticceria* and risk running into Oliver. She and Ricky would have to buy dessert in Porto Rotondo.

Could Oliver be right, was she falling in love with Ricky? That was impossible; she had to think about Louisa and Lily Bristol. She couldn't stay on the Emerald Coast forever.

She wasn't even thinking about love. It was Oliver who'd brought it up. She suddenly remembered Oliver saying they should have trusted each other. Oliver had lied to her; how could she have trusted him?

She clutched her shopping bag of picnic items and remembered the first tremor in their marriage. It was like the earthquakes in San Francisco when she was a child. She was never sure they really happened, until she saw a broken vase in the living room and wondered if she would ever feel safe again.

———

Lily strolled through the West Village and admired the lacquered window boxes and striped restaurant awnings. It was early evening, and couples hurried into the Waverly Inn to eat lamb shanks and Fedora to sample the braised duck with rhubarb jam.

Fall really was the best season in New York. The trees were orange and yellow, the women wore wool scarves, and the air smelled of damp leaves. She turned onto Christopher Street and was thrilled to be joining Oliver at Mirabelle, Manhattan's most exciting new restaurant.

The last three years of living in the farmhouse had been exhilarating. Everyone in New York read Oliver's reviews, and he was a local celebrity. Whenever Lily's friends heard she was married to Oliver Bristol, they demanded to know where they should eat in the city.

He wore Brooks Brothers shirts and was invited to sporting events and art openings. Lily watched him sipping vodka gimlets at summer parties in the Hamptons and knew they had made the right decision.

And the new Lily Bristol was a success! The store had white linen sofas and woven baskets filled with seashells. Clients drank fresh lemonade and admired pastel-colored fabrics and wooden hutches. On the weekends the showroom was so busy, she hired an assistant.

The farmhouse needed more work than they had anticipated and sometimes they were terrified they'd gotten in over their heads. But Lily could spend hours puttering around the kitchen, and she adored the sloped floors and beamed ceilings.

And the endless projects were worth it when Lily watched Louisa performing cartwheels on the lawn. In the summer, Louisa chased butterflies and slept in a tent on the porch. Her legs and arms grew tan, and she learned to ride a bicycle.

There were parts of their life Lily wished were different: She often prepared Oliver's favorite dinners and fell asleep before he arrived home. Oliver was too busy to accompany her on buying trips, and she had to travel to Europe alone. But they were both thriving and in love.

Now Lily climbed the steps of a brownstone and opened the door. Mirabelle had glass tables and high-backed velvet chairs. Recessed lighting illuminated abstract paintings, and there was a marble fireplace.

"Excuse me." Lily approached the desk. "I'm meeting Oliver Bristol for dinner."

"I believe your husband is waiting at the bar," the hostess greeted her. "It's such an honor to have you with us."

Lily followed her and smiled. Dining out with a *New York Times* restaurant critic was like being with a pitcher for the Yankees. She and Oliver were treated to bottles of vintage wines and chanterelles grown in Provence. And the desserts! The chef always insisted they sample the fruit tarts and macaroons. Sometimes Lily was so full she was tempted to fold them in her napkin and pretend she'd finished them.

"There you are." Oliver waved. He was sitting next to a blonde wearing a white blouse and tan slacks. "I was afraid you weren't coming."

"I'm terribly sorry. The train was late, and Midtown traffic was a nightmare." Lily approached the bar. "I was tempted to get out and walk."

Oliver introduced them. "This is Mirabelle. She trained under the chef at the Palace Hotel in Montreux."

"It's a pleasure." Mirabelle extended her hand. She was in her late twenties and wore diamond stud earrings. "I was trying to bribe your husband into giving us a good review, but he refused."

"I doubt you have to bribe me. Every chef in New York wants to replicate your celery root–saffron soup." Oliver smiled broadly. "I read in the *New York Post* that the chocolate ganache was worth skipping the entrée for."

"Everyone knows Oliver Bristol's review is the only one that matters," Mirabelle said. Lily noticed her eyes were green, and she wore shimmering lipstick.

"I only write about what's put in front of me." Oliver shrugged. "You have nothing to worry about."

"I'll have plenty to worry about if I don't get back to the kitchen." She stood up and turned to Lily. "It was a pleasure meeting you."

The hostess escorted them to a table, and Lily sat stiffly in the chair. She buttered a slice of pumpernickel and looked at Oliver.

"Mirabelle is very pretty," Lily commented, and for some reason her heart beat faster.

"Is she?" Oliver looked up. "I didn't notice."

"She could be on the cover of a magazine," Lily continued. "She had one of those moles on her cheek that always makes you wonder whether or not they added it in Photoshop so the model wasn't completely perfect."

"I stopped looking at women when you stepped out of the shower at the hostel in Naples," Oliver mused. "You wore that blue bathing suit, and your hair clung to your head like a bathing cap. You looked like a water sprite."

"Everyone looks at women in New York, Oliver. The sidewalks are a moving catwalk," she pointed out. "And you were having a drink with her. Your knees were practically touching."

"It was a cramped bar, and I don't drink alcohol before a meal. It dulls the palate." He paused. "You're not jealous?"

"She just acted so familiar." Lily bit her lip.

"All chefs butter me up. I received a gold pen from the chef at the Four Seasons for my birthday. It's part of the job."

"I suppose you're right." She sighed. "Sometimes I miss being together every night. Connecticut is wonderful, but it's another planet. While Louisa and I are watching fireflies, you're sampling wines and eating off bone-white china."

"And counting the hours until I walk through our door." Oliver smiled. "Let's ask the babysitter to spend the night and get a room at the W. We'll stay up eating M&M's and watching movies."

"Audrey charges us a fortune to sleep over, and I have to get home," Lily said. "I'm leaving for San Francisco tomorrow."

"Then we'll make out on the train like teenagers who ride the subway all night because nothing else is open."

Lily looked at Oliver, and the knot in her chest loosened. He was the same Oliver he had been from the day they met, and she was being silly.

"I'm acting like a typical suburban wife." She picked up the menu. "Let's have dinner and forget I said anything."

They ate salad of asparagus with bacon, and chicken with fingerling potatoes. Lily nibbled baby fennel and thought Oliver was right; Mirabelle really was a talented chef. But she was still uncomfortable when Mirabelle insisted on making their soufflé at the table. The custard was too sweet, and the nougat got stuck in her throat.

"Do you think you could ever fall in love with someone else?" Lily asked when they walked onto the sidewalk. The street lamps glowed, and a light mist touched her shoulders.

"What are you talking about?" Oliver asked.

"I mean, if something happened to me. Say I was killed in a plane crash or an earthquake in San Francisco. Would you get married again?"

"That's a silly question," Oliver said. "Planes are safer than cars, and San Francisco hasn't had a catastrophic earthquake in almost thirty years.

"I'm just asking if you could be attracted to another woman," Lily prodded. "Louisa would need a mother. And you're hopeless at doing laundry. If I'm gone for more than a few days, Louisa runs out of underwear."

"I suppose I could if I had to." He debated. "But it would be like having to learn Chinese when you spent your whole life speaking English."

"Women would line up to be with Oliver Bristol, restaurant critic for the *New York Times*."

"Is this about Mirabelle again?" He took her arm.

"I walk into a trendy restaurant, and you're being cozy with a blonde at a bar." She paused. "You are an attractive man, and you meet dozens of women every day."

"You're the only woman I ever wanted, and I'm lucky to have you," he said and kissed her.

Lily could smell Oliver's cologne. She kissed him back, and he tasted of vanilla and almonds.

"I know you're lucky, Oliver," she said playfully. "Just don't forget it."

Lily stood at the window of her room at the Westin St. Francis and thought the sunset in San Francisco was spectacular. The sky was purple, the cable cars were bright red, and the Bay Bridge was a silvery outline.

She had been in San Francisco for four days and now she couldn't wait to get home. But her meetings ran long and she had to postpone her flight.

Her phone rang, and she picked it up.

"I was supposed to pick you up at JFK in five hours. But you sent a text that you're not on the plane." Oliver's voice came over the line.

"I'm sorry. My bookkeeper told me she's five months pregnant, and I have to hire a new one," Lily explained. "I have to stay for two more days."

"But tonight is the eighty-fifth anniversary party of the Rainbow Room," Oliver reminded her. "We were going to drive straight from the airport. It's the event of the season."

"Then you'll have to go without me," she said.

"You don't mind?" he asked.

"You can't have a foodie event in Manhattan without the critic for the *New York Times*." Lily smiled.

"I'll take pictures of the food spread," Oliver replied. "There's going to be a caviar bar and lamb flown in from Singapore."

Lily hung up the phone and decided to get clam chowder at Fisherman's Wharf. Her phone rang again, and she wondered if she'd forgotten to give Oliver the flight number.

"Lily, you're still here," her mother said. "I was afraid you were on the plane to New York."

"I spoke to you this morning, Mother." Lily clutched the phone. "I told you I had to stay until Friday."

"I'm glad you haven't left," Alice continued. "I'm having a dinner party tonight, and you must come."

"Sorry, I can't. I have to study résumés," Lily answered.

"Gavin Newsom and his wife, Jennifer, are invited, and they're redesigning their cabin in Tahoe," Alice said. "They're the ideal clients for Lily Bristol."

"I don't have time," Lily replied. "I have four interviews tomorrow."

"The Newsoms are San Francisco's premier couple, you can't pass up the opportunity," Alice insisted. "Plus, they have a daughter Louisa's age. You have a lot in common."

Lily fiddled with her earrings and thought she didn't really want to eat dinner alone. And Jennifer Newsom seemed lovely in her photos.

"All right, Mother," Lily agreed. "I'll come."

"Excellent," Alice replied. "Cocktails are at seven."

Lily rushed up the stone steps of her parents' house and rang the doorbell. She heard the clatter of heels, and her mother opened the door. Her ash blond hair fell to her shoulders, and she wore a cream dress and diamond earrings.

"I'm sorry I'm late." Lily entered the marble foyer. Crystal vases were filled with orchids, and the air smelled of expensive perfume. "It was impossible to get a taxi."

"I don't know why you don't stay here when you're in San Francisco," Alice remarked. "Your room is the same."

"I'm a thirty-one-year-old career woman, I can afford a hotel," Lily said and stopped. She was determined not to let her mother upset her. "I love staying on Union Square. I bought Louisa a dress at Neiman Marcus and picked up a shirt for Oliver at Wilkes Bashford."

"The Newsoms aren't here yet anyway." Alice led her into the living room. "But there is someone you haven't seen for ages."

Lily followed her mother and gasped. Roger sat on the sofa, nursing a gin and tonic. She hadn't seen him since before her wedding, but he looked the same. His blond hair was perfectly cut, and he wore a navy suit and tasseled shoes.

"Roger!" Lily exclaimed. "What are you doing here?"

"Your mother invited me to dinner." He stood up. "Gavin and I are friends, we serve on the same committees."

"Roger is doing so well," Alice cut in. "He's a partner at his firm, and thinking about going into politics."

"It's wonderful to see you." Roger beamed. "You haven't changed a bit, you look lovely. Alice showed me a photo of Louisa. She has your eyes and smile."

"I've always thought Louisa looks like Oliver," Lily said and turned to her mother. "Could I see you in the kitchen?"

"How dare you invite Roger without telling me?" Lily fumed. "Oliver would be furious if he knew."

"Why shouldn't you attend a dinner party with an old friend?"

Alice arranged a bouquet of peonies. "And Roger knows a lot of people in San Francisco. He can send you clients."

"Lily Bristol is doing very well, I don't need Roger's help," Lily snapped. "I know what you're doing. You're trying to interfere with my marriage."

"Oliver could have come on your trip. I would have loved to see Louisa." Alice sighed. "I don't know what you're doing in Connecticut anyway. Your friends and family are here, you belong in San Francisco."

"Oliver loves his job and Louisa is happy in school." Lily bristled. "I don't believe the Newsoms are even coming; you lured me here to see Roger. How could you? I'm in love with my husband, and I'm not the slightest bit interested in Roger's accomplishments."

"It's always nice to be surrounded by successful young people." Alice's tone softened. "Let's go back and join Roger. Your father will be home soon, and we're having sirloin tips and roasted potatoes."

Lily grabbed her purse and walked back to the living room.

"I'm terribly sorry, I remembered I have an appointment," she said to Roger. "Have a wonderful dinner. I'll see you another time."

"Lily! You can't just leave." Alice followed her to the foyer. "What will I say to the Newsoms when they arrive?"

"You'll think of something." Lily turned to her mother. "You're very good at twisting words."

Lily sat on the sofa of her hotel room and sipped a cup of tea. She had ordered a Caesar salad. Now she leaned against the cushions and wished she were home in bed with Oliver.

It was almost midnight in Connecticut. She wondered if it was too late to call him again. She had tried his cell phone a few times, but each time it went straight to voice mail. Oliver never charged his phone at night; it was probably sitting on the bedside table.

She dialed the home number and pressed send.

"Hello, the Bristol residence," a female voice answered.

"Audrey?" Lily asked. "I didn't think you'd still be there. Is Louisa all right?"

"She's fine," the babysitter replied. "She's been asleep for hours."

"Oh, good." Lily let out her breath. "I was looking for Oliver."

"He called earlier and asked if I could sleep over," Audrey said. "He had to stay in the city."

"Oliver is staying in the city?" Lily repeated and felt something hard press against her chest.

"He has his cell phone with him. I'm sure you can reach him."

"Of course," Lily answered. "Thank you for being so flexible. Please tell Louisa I can't wait to be home, and I bought her a present."

Lily hung up and stared at her phone. She wondered if something had happened, and Oliver had gotten in an accident. But he would have told Audrey.

She flipped through her phone and clicked on Oliver's Instagram account. She recognized the floor-to-ceiling windows and crystal chandeliers of the Rainbow Room. There was a photo of Oliver talking to a blonde in a black cocktail dress. She zoomed in and realized it was Mirabelle.

Her hands shook, and she walked to the window. She tried Oliver's number one more time, but it went through to voice mail. There was nothing to worry about. Oliver probably had a perfectly good reason to stay in the city. He had to file an early morning story or he lost his wallet and couldn't afford the train fare.

But Oliver always took the last train home, even when he was on deadline. And she was the one who lost things; he never misplaced his phone or car keys.

It was late, and she was upset by her mother and Roger. She would call Oliver in the morning, and he would explain everything. A chill ran down her spine, and she wondered how she would ever fall asleep.

Lily slipped off her pumps and poured a cup of coffee. She had held interviews all day, and now it was almost evening. A soft fog drifted over San Francisco Bay, and Coit Tower was bathed in a golden light.

She had tried calling Oliver in the morning, but his phone had gone straight to voice mail. Now she curled up on the upholstered love seat and dialed his number.

"I haven't spoken to you all day," Lily said when Oliver answered. "How was the Rainbow Room?"

"The scallops were soggy, and the upside-down martinis gave me a headache. I came home and took two aspirin and went straight to bed."

"Was Audrey still there when you arrived?" she asked.

"Of course she was here," he replied. "She wouldn't leave Louisa home alone."

Lily had never run out of things to say to Oliver. But suddenly her throat was parched, and she couldn't form any words.

"There's a new Basque restaurant in the East Village I've been wanting to try. Why don't we have a romantic dinner tomorrow on our way home from the airport?" Oliver suggested. "I'll rub your thigh under the table and tell you how much I've missed you."

"That sounds wonderful." Lily gripped the phone. "I can't think of anything I'd like better."

Lily hung up and wondered why she hadn't asked Oliver if he'd stayed in the city. But Oliver had lied to her before she got a chance.

Her teeth chattered, and she felt like she was coming down with the flu. She searched the bathroom for some aspirin but all she could find was a pink bottle of Pepto-Bismol. She grabbed her purse and took the elevator to the lobby.

"Lily," a male voice called. "I was about to ask the front desk to call your room."

"Roger?" Lily turned around. "What on earth are you doing here? Don't tell me my mother sent you."

"She told me where you were staying, but I came by myself. I want to apologize." He stuffed his hands into his pockets. "I'm sure you didn't have to rush off to an appointment last night. You were the victim of an ambush."

"It's nothing against you," Lily assured him. "But my mother shouldn't have invited you without telling me."

"I completely agree." He nodded. "If I had known you were coming, I would have declined the invitation."

"You would have?" she repeated.

"You're married, with a beautiful daughter," he continued. "I understand if you're not comfortable around me."

"Of course I'm comfortable around you." She suddenly felt flustered. "I really should go. I have to buy some aspirin, I'm coming down with a fever."

"Aspirin won't do anything to help that." He looked at Lily. "And you do look a little pale. Why don't we order a brandy at the hotel bar?"

Lily's head ached, her eyes burned, and she longed to sit down. "All right." She nodded. "A brandy sounds lovely."

The Clock Bar had paneled walls and oriental rugs and red velvet booths. Lily leaned against the cushions and sipped a Toasted Almond. The Kahlúa was sweet, and the amaretto was rich, and a warmth spread through her chest.

"I haven't drunk one of these in years." She stirred her drink. "We drank Toasted Almonds at the Dakota Bar when I visited you at Columbia. I'd never even heard of it. It sounded like a jelly bean flavor," she giggled. "I didn't believe something that tasted like a milkshake could affect me."

"You started singing 'Silent Night' in front of the whole bar, and I had to carry you out." Roger laughed. "I didn't mind. You were light as a sparrow."

"I've never been a good drinker," she mused. "Oliver had to finish my glass of champagne, or I wouldn't have been able to dance the first dance at our wedding."

"I still remember everything about that Christmas you visited me in New York," Roger said slowly. "It snowed all night, and when we woke up, the streets were covered in a white blanket."

"I'd only seen snow a few times in Tahoe," she recalled. "Manhattan looked so pretty. The lights twinkled in Rockefeller Center, and Central Park was hushed, and everything was magical."

"Do you ever wonder what would have happened if I never

posted that letter?" Roger finished his martini. "We'd be living in an apartment on Fifth Avenue, and I'd be a partner in a Manhattan law firm. You could have done anything you liked: decorated houses and traveled and served on charity boards."

"I'm happily married," Lily said stiffly. She remembered the Instagram photo of Oliver and Mirabelle and felt a searing pain. "I should go. I have an early morning flight."

"I'm sorry, I didn't mean to offend you." He rubbed his brow. "It was the martini talking. Can we still be friends?"

"It would be impossible not to be friends with my mother around," Lily said and smiled.

She opened her purse and rifled through her lipsticks. "I must have left my key in the room. I'll get another from the front desk."

"I'll tell the concierge you aren't feeling well and ask for a key." Roger led her to the elevator. "I'll only be a minute."

Lily's cheeks were flushed, and she felt slightly dizzy. "Are you sure you don't mind?"

"I'll only be a minute." Roger led her to the elevator.

Lily sat on an ottoman and noticed a couple standing near the gift shop. The woman had blond hair and reminded her of Mirabelle. She remembered Oliver and Mirabelle's knees touching at the restaurant, and a prickle ran down her spine.

Could Oliver have spent the night with Mirabelle? Lily had been traveling a lot; perhaps Oliver felt neglected. Or he couldn't resist the attention of a beautiful young chef. Why else would he have lied? Oliver told the truth about everything.

Roger returned from the front desk, and Lily tried to stand up. He had only been gone for a few minutes, but she felt ill. She shouldn't have drunk the Toasted Almond, but it had looked so innocent, like one of Louisa's smoothies. Her knees buckled, and she sank onto the ottoman.

"I can't have you fainting in the elevator. Your mother will never forgive me." Roger took her arm. "Let me help you to your room."

"It's just a chill," Lily protested. "I'll be fine."

"I was a Boy Scout for years." He pressed the button. "I can't abandon a woman in distress."

Lily inserted the key in the door and entered her hotel room. She placed her purse on the coffee table and poured a glass of mineral water.

"Once I caught a bug in Singapore and was stuck in bed for a week." Roger followed her inside. "Maybe you should stay an extra day. You don't want to get on a plane with a fever."

"I'm sure it's a twenty-four-hour thing," she said. "All I need is a good night's sleep."

Suddenly Roger pulled her close and kissed her. A warmth flooded her chest and, for a moment, she kissed him back. Then she started and pushed him away.

"What do you think you're doing?" she demanded.

"There was something different about you tonight," he urged. "I could sense it."

"I wasn't feeling well and needed a drink." She recoiled. "You imagined anything else."

"You kissed me back," he insisted. "Whatever we had is still there."

"I think you should leave," she said and smoothed her skirt.

"Lily, I never should have let you go." Roger walked to the door and turned around. "You're the loveliest woman I ever met. You deserve to be happy."

Lily stood at the window and tried to stop her heart from racing. Roger just left and she was alone. Had she led him on? She had been feeling ill and needed to sit down, nothing more.

The lights twinkled over the bay, and she touched her mouth. What would Oliver say if she told him? And had he already done something she couldn't forgive? She closed her eyes, and tears streamed down her cheeks.

Lily hurried along the cobblestones from the *piazzetta* and shielded her eyes from the sun. She shouldn't have stopped to talk to Oliver while she was shopping. Now it was almost noon. Ricky was meeting her at the Hotel Cervo to go on the picnic, and she needed to pack a swimsuit.

Oliver was wrong; it wasn't just that they hadn't trusted each other. They'd both done something impossible to forgive. That was why they'd divorced, so they had a chance to be happy.

A car honked, and Lily looked up. Ricky jumped out of a red convertible. He wore wraparound sunglasses and held a bouquet of daisies.

"You're early! And where did you get that gorgeous car?" Lily laughed.

"My brother-in-law lent it to me." Ricky opened her door. "It's a crime to drive along the Emerald Coast in anything but a convertible."

"I'm not ready, I haven't packed a bathing suit." Lily climbed into the passenger seat.

"We'll buy one in Porto Rotondo." He slid in beside her. "If we don't leave now, we'll get stuck in traffic."

Lily inhaled the scent of eucalyptus and men's cologne. The

tension ebbed away, and all she could think about were the turquoise ocean and clear horizon.

"Happy?" Ricky asked, squeezing her hand.

Lily studied his chiseled cheekbones, and her heart lifted. A smile crossed her face and she nodded. "Very happy."

They pulled up to the sand at Spiaggia Capriccioli, and Lily jumped out of the car. The beach was surrounded by lush foliage and tall pine trees. Limestone boulders fell down to the sea, and the sand looked like vanilla icing on top of a cake. And the water! Lily had never seen anything like it. It changed from turquoise to sapphire as if she were turning a kaleidoscope. There were brightly colored starfish and clusters of underwater plants.

"This can't be real." Lily ran back to the car. "It looks like the pictures in a magazine. Models in white bathing suits relax at a beach that's so remote it can only be reached by a tiny plane. There are shots of them diving into azure water and swimming with the fish." She sighed. "When you close the magazine, you feel like you've been on vacation, even though you're standing at the supermarket checkout."

"Spiaggia Capriccioli is one of the most intimate beaches on the Emerald Coast." Ricky pointed to the horizon. "That's the island of Soffi, and you can see Mortorio and La Camere." He carried the basket to the shore. "The best part is there are hardly any tourists. We don't have to worry about sharing our olives and ricotta cheese with anyone but the seagulls."

"I'm too excited to eat." Lily pulled off her caftan to reveal the blue swimsuit she found in the glove compartment of the car. "All I want to do is swim. The water is so clear, you don't need a snorkel to see the fish."

Lily raced into the sea and dove under the water. Ricky joined her, and they rolled and splashed like sea lions. There were schools of neon-colored fish and groupers.

"This is the best afternoon I've had in ages." She collapsed on the sand. Then she lay on her back and spread her arms and legs.

"What are you doing?" Ricky stood over her.

"I'm making a Christmas angel," she said and laughed. "I used to make them in the snow when we went to Lake Tahoe. Try it, it's the best feeling in the world."

Ricky lay down on the sand and waved his arms and legs. Lily sat up and burst into laughter.

"What's so funny?" he asked, sitting up and dusting sand from his chest.

"I've never seen a grown man make a Christmas angel before," she said. "I haven't done that since I was ten years old."

He leaned forward and kissed her. She kissed him back and tasted sea salt.

"I've been coming to this beach since I was a boy," he said when they pulled apart. "But I've never had so much fun."

After they dried off and ate their picnic lunch, they got back into the car. They drove along the coast, past Spiaggia dei Sassi Neri and Spiaggia Rudargia. Lily leaned out the window and inhaled the scent of pine trees and juniper.

Finally, they pulled into the town of Porto Rotondo, and Ricky parked the car. Porto Rotondo had brightly painted cottages and sleek galleries, and a horseshoe-shaped harbor. They explored the stone amphitheater and visited San Lorenzo Church and drank iced coffee in the Piazzetta San Marco.

Now it was early evening, and they sat at an outdoor table at S'Astore. The restaurant had a white tile floor and white curtains billowing in the breeze.

"I should have brought a cocktail dress." Lily glanced at women in miniskirts and metallic sandals. "I didn't realize everyone would be so dressed-up."

"S'Astore is the most popular restaurant in Porto Rotondo." Ricky sipped his wine. "It has a view of Cugnana Bay and the best grilled shrimp on the Emerald Coast."

"I've never seen a sunset with such gorgeous colors." She buttered a piece of bread. "Do you ever get tired of so much beauty?"

"What do you mean?" he asked.

"Everywhere you look, there are elegant villas and sparkling yachts." She sighed. "It's wonderful, but it must get exhausting."

"I disagree," Ricky said slowly. "Life is more exhilarating when you are surrounded by beauty. And when you meet someone with lovely brown eyes, you want to look at her forever."

Lily looked up and noticed Ricky's dark eyes sparkling. He gulped his wine and set the glass on the table.

"You order for me," Lily murmured. "I'm sure you know the best things on the menu."

After dinner, they drank digestivi and danced on the terrace. The drive back to Porto Cervo along the winding road was intoxicating. Lily's hair blew in the breeze, and Ricky kept his hand on her knee, and the sky was studded with stars.

Now Ricky pulled up at the Hotel Cervo and turned off the ignition.

"I had a wonderful time." He took her hand.

"So did I, everything was perfect. The red convertible and the white sand beach and the delicious meal." She smiled.

"Do you know what the best part of the last few days has been?" he asked. "It wasn't cruising on Christoff's yacht or eating oysters at the Yacht Club. It was spending this afternoon at Spiaggia Capriccioli. We splashed in the waves and swam with the fish and you were like a young girl."

"I've always loved the ocean," she agreed. "All I need is the sand and sea and I'm happy."

"When we met, I said I was very serious about love. I just hadn't met the right woman." He touched Lily's cheek. "I think I found that woman."

He leaned forward and kissed her. Lily kissed him back, and his mouth was warm and tender. Then she pulled away and was suddenly nervous.

"We just met," she said hesitantly. "You don't know anything about me."

"You're effervescent and lovely, and I can't stop thinking about you." He took a black velvet box from the glove compartment and handed it to Lily.

She snapped it open and gasped. There was a ruby pendant with an antique clasp.

"I can't accept this," she protested. "I'm leaving in a few days. What if we never see each other again?"

"It's only a necklace." He took out the pendant and snapped it around her neck. "It would make me happy if you wore it."

Lily fingered the rubies and suddenly felt glamorous and sexy. She was divorced and sitting in a red convertible on the Emerald Coast. Why shouldn't she accept a gift from a handsome man?

"Are you sure?" she asked.

"I've never been more sure about anything," he said and kissed her.

"I can't stop thinking about you either," she answered and kissed him back. "It's a beautiful necklace and I'd love to wear it."

Lily entered her suite and took a deep breath. Soft lighting illuminated the living room, and she was reminded of how pretty it was. The rug was pale pink, and the window seat was scattered with ivory cushions; it was like the inside of a seashell.

There was a knock at the door, and she answered it.

"Enzo, I'm glad you're here! I have so much to tell you," she exclaimed. "I just got back from Porto Rotondo. We had a wonderful time."

"I am glad Ricky is treating you well." Enzo carried a silver tray of assorted chocolate truffles. "He is lucky to have the company of a beautiful young woman."

"I can't thank you enough, Enzo. If it weren't for you, I would be sitting by the hotel pool like every other tourist. Instead, I'm seeing all the beaches and towns of the Emerald Coast." She took a truffle from the tray and popped it into her mouth. "Can I ask you something serious? How soon did you know you were in love with your wife?"

"I can't remember." He shrugged. "We've been married for thirteen years."

"You must remember; it's one of the most important days of your life. Besides your wedding day and the births of your daughters." She paused. "Was it soon after you met, or did it take months to realize?"

"We were seventeen when we met," Enzo recalled. "I was

working as a valet. One of the guests tore her zipper, and the hotel's seamstress had gone home. The concierge told me to take the dress to a seamstress near the *piazzetta*. I knocked on the door, and a young woman answered. She was about my age, with dark hair and green eyes. She took the dress and went into the back. When she reappeared and handed it to me with a new zipper, I knew I was in love."

"You can't fall in love that quickly." Lily laughed. "You didn't even know her name."

"Love is about how the other person makes you feel," Enzo said. "When I look at Carmella, I'm the luckiest man in Sardinia."

"So you really think love could be possible after a few days?" she asked

"There are no rules to love," he answered. "That's what makes it different from anything else in the world."

"You always say the perfect thing, Enzo." Lily beamed and took out her phone. "I took some pictures to show you. You must take Carmella for a special dinner at S'Astore in Porto Rotondo. The views are spectacular, and the sunset is so romantic."

Lily sat at her dressing table and brushed her hair. Ricky was warm and vibrant, and she'd had a wonderful time. But Lily Bristol's grand opening was in in three days, and then she was flying back to Connecticut.

She studied her reflection in the mirror and wondered if Enzo was right. Could she fall in love so quickly, and what would happen if she did? She'd worry about the future tomorrow. Tonight, she was a young woman on holiday, wearing a ruby pendant.

Chapter Ten

OLIVER STEPPED ONTO THE TERRACE of Cala di Volpe and thought it resembled the paperback books his mother read when he was a child. The covers displayed women in shimmering evening gowns and stilettos. A mysterious man hovered in the shadows, and you knew the book was full of sex and scandal.

Oliver was surprised that Angela had suggested meeting at Bar Pontile; it had the highest prices in Porto Cervo. Cala di Volpe was the most exclusive hotel on the Emerald Coast and frequented by super models and Russian billionaires. There was a kidney-shaped swimming pool and chaise longues littered with striped cushions.

Maybe Angela was hoping to hand out her card to potential clients. He thought about what he was about to tell her and felt a surge of joy. Angela was going to be so pleased; he wondered how she would reward him.

Angela sat at a table by the pool, and he thought she'd never looked more striking. She wore a flower-print dress and red sandals. Her hair was protected by a wide-brimmed hat, and she wore oversized sunglasses.

"Is that a new dress?" Oliver approached her. "It's stunning."

"I discovered it at a boutique in the marina," Angela replied. "The dress is vintage Cavalli and the sandals are next year's Gianvito Rossi. They won't arrive in New York until the spring."

"I didn't know you had such an interest in clothes." Oliver pulled out a chair.

"You have to fit into your surroundings, Oliver," she explained. "How can I convince clients I understand their floral needs unless they feel comfortable around me?"

"I can't imagine fitting into these surroundings," Oliver mused. "The guests look like they belong to an international drug ring. It could be the setting of a Bond movie."

"It *was* the setting of a Bond movie," Angela said. "They filmed *The Spy Who Loved Me* at this hotel. I thought you knew that. You said you were doing background research on the Emerald Coast for your review."

"I am doing research. But I did something more exciting this afternoon," he began. "I can't wait to tell you."

"I have some news too," she answered.

"Do you mind if I go first? I've been bursting with anticipation." He picked up the menu. "But first let's order. We'll want to celebrate."

The bartender brought out a silver cart with a cocktail shaker and ice bucket. He mixed almond syrup and lemon juice and added shots of vodka. The glasses were frosty, and each one contained two raspberries.

"It's delicious. One more of these and I won't flinch when he brings the bill." Oliver sipped his drink. "I was in the Hotel Cervo lobby and noticed a skinny man wearing jeans and a T-shirt. You'll never guess who it was, Dominique Ansel, the creator of the Cronut!

"I offered to buy him a drink and he accepted. I wrote a glowing review when he was the pastry chef at Daniel, and he's never forgotten. Did you know that he arrives at Ansel Bakery every morning at four AM to make sure the people waiting in line for Cronuts have water? And he is a pastry genius. The strawberry rhubarb Cronuts are exceptional, and Martha Stewart raves about his frozen s'mores."

"I'm pleased you met one of your idols, but what's your news?" Angela asked.

"I'm getting to that." Oliver leaned back in his chair. "First we talked about his upbringing. Dominique was born in a working-class suburb of Paris and spent three years as a military chef in French Guiana. Then we discussed his philanthropy. He started the Cronut Mission a few years ago and raised millions to provide nutritious meals for the homeless during the holidays."

"This is fascinating, Oliver," Angela said impatiently. "But I'm sure I can read his biography at Barnes & Noble."

"Then he let drop that he's holding a huge charity event next spring. It's going to be the event of the season. All the celebrities love his Cronuts," he finished triumphantly. "I said I knew the perfect florist, and she's staying in Porto Cervo. He's going to join us for cocktails this evening."

"I am impressed, Oliver! That was very thoughtful," Angela exclaimed. "I'm a fan of his Cronuts . . . though I'd never wait in line for a croissant wrapped in a donut. It will be fabulous, it could launch my company."

Oliver sat back and was quite pleased with himself. It felt so good to do something nice for Angela.

"What did you want to tell me?" he asked. "It can't be as good as my news."

"It's quite different," she said. "I visited a doctor this afternoon."

Oliver gulped. He wanted to be a good boyfriend. But what if Angela had a rare disease like on the Lifetime movies Louisa's babysitter watched on television?

"A doctor?" he repeated.

"It's always a good idea to get a professional diagnosis, even though the tests these days are so conclusive," she continued. "Did you know you can test before you miss a period? It says so on the packet."

"What kind of test?" Oliver clutched his drink.

"A pregnancy test, Oliver." She looked at Oliver and took a deep breath. "I'm pregnant."

"You can't be pregnant!" he spluttered. "We just met."

"We've been together for two and a half months," she reminded him. "That's plenty of time."

"You're a modern woman. Surely you're on the Pill," he floundered. "I saw the plastic container in your cosmetics case."

"You were looking through my cosmetics case?" She raised her eyebrow.

"It was on the bathroom counter," he explained. "I knocked it over when I reached for my shaving cream."

"When we met, I was tired of men and had sworn myself to celibacy." She fiddled with her drink. "Apparently it happened before I resumed taking the Pill."

"You weren't on the Pill and didn't tell me?" Oliver was so angry he couldn't contain himself.

"It was only a couple of times," she replied. "It doesn't matter how it happened. I'm pregnant, and I'm not having an abortion."

"Pregnant," Oliver gasped. Jet Skis skimmed the waves, and he wondered if this was what it felt like to get a terminal cancer diagnosis. One minute you were savoring the hint of raspberry in your martini, the next you were thinking of how to enjoy the time you had left.

"Here's the thing, Oliver," Angela said. "I like you a lot. You're a little sexually repressed, but that's understandable for a guy who's newly divorced. You're bright and personable." She wet her lips. "I could even imagine falling in love with you.

"But we're not going to become one of those couples who hash things out for weeks." She paused. "Whatever you say next about this pregnancy is going to stand between us forever." She stood up. "So I'm going back to the suite, and you're going to think about what I told you. When you're ready to say the one thing you really mean, you know where to find me."

"You can't leave." Oliver jumped up. "That's like dropping the atomic bomb on Hiroshima and not waiting to see the destruction. I don't know anything about your plans or your medical history. Do twins run in your family, and are there any cases of diabetes? Being pregnant is the most climactic news in the world; you don't just mention it over cocktails."

"You know the only two things that matter." Angela gathered her purse. "I'm pregnant, and you're the father."

Oliver sat down and sipped his drink, but the almond syrup was too sweet and the raspberry got stuck in his throat. How could Angela be pregnant? He remembered all the times they had sex: sitting on the bench in the shower, Angela straddling him on the bed. That wasn't the kind of lovemaking that produced a baby; those were a teenage boy's fantasies come to life.

He signaled the waiter and felt like he'd been punched in the stomach. It was all very well for Angela to say she wanted a family, but she couldn't be pregnant now. He didn't even know her shoe size or how she celebrated Christmas.

For a moment, he wondered whether she'd gotten pregnant on purpose, but that was ludicrous. Oliver was a newspaper columnist with an ex-wife and child support payments. Angela was stunning; she could marry a hedge fund manager or a sports agent.

The waiter refreshed his glass, and he pictured Louisa's freckled cheeks. Louisa was the best thing that ever happened to him, but he and Lily had been married and madly in love.

Lily! What would she say when he told her Louisa was going to have a half sister? Neither of them had expected this to happen so quickly. They were still getting used to transporting Louisa's guinea pig from the farmhouse to Oliver's apartment.

Oliver moaned and buried his face in his hands. He remembered when Lily came home from San Francisco with her news. He'd reacted by doing the one thing she couldn't forgive and he would always regret.

Oliver entered the farmhouse and placed his briefcase on the side table. It was early evening, and the living room looked so inviting: the cushions on the floral sofa were plumped, books were arranged on the coffee table, and there was a brandy decanter with two glasses.

He checked his blazer pocket for the tickets and smiled. The tickets had taken more effort to secure than a fake ID in high school. But it was worth it if they made Lily happy.

Ever since Lily had returned from San Francisco a week ago,

something was different. She said it was just the flu, and all she needed was a good night's sleep.

But she'd spent three days in bed and sent back Oliver's trays of chicken soup. She refused to see the doctor, and when Oliver touched her cheek, it was perfectly cool.

He asked if anything was wrong, but she just shrugged and bit her lip. Then she busied herself preparing Louisa's lunches, and Oliver was left to puzzle it out alone.

Now he entered the kitchen and found Lily standing at the stove. Her dark hair was tucked behind her ears, and she wore a yellow dress.

"I didn't know you'd be home for dinner." She looked up. "I made Louisa macaroni and cheese, but I could put a lasagna in the oven."

"Aren't you going to eat?" Oliver asked, peeling a banana.

"I had a sandwich earlier," Lily replied. "I'm not hungry."

"Maybe we can grab a burger at Bar Americain when we get into the city," he said. "I have a surprise for you."

"Why would we go into the city? You just got home." She frowned. "And what kind of surprise?"

"This kind of surprise." He handed her an envelope. "Two tickets to see *Hamilton* on Broadway."

"Hamilton!" She examined the tickets. "Where did you get these?"

"Someone gave them to the editor in chief, and he couldn't use them." Oliver's eyes sparkled. "Four of us fought over them. I had to trade box seats to a Yankees game and a weekend at a bed-and-breakfast in Maine. But it's the best show on Broadway, and we're going to have a fantastic time."

"I can't get dressed and go into Manhattan with an hour's notice," she protested. "I'm sorry, Oliver. I'm just not up to it."

"What do you mean you're not up to it?" He fumed. "You can't get a ticket unless you're the president. I could sell these on StubHub for the price of plane tickets to Australia."

"Maybe you should." She turned back to the stove. "I'm sure it's not too late."

"What could you be doing that's more important than seeing the hottest musical in the country?"

"Louisa has a birthday party tomorrow." She buttered a slice of bread. "We have to write the card and wrap the present."

"I asked Audrey to babysit. She knows how to write a birthday card." Oliver's voice softened. "We'll ask her to spend the night and stay in town. We'll have brunch at Murray's Bagels and spend the afternoon at the Guggenheim. When was the last time we ate bagels and lox and visited museums, like regular New Yorkers?"

"You called Audrey without asking me?" Lily turned around.

"What's wrong with that?" He shrugged.

"Do you always ask her to do things behind my back?" she asked.

Lily's mouth trembled, and he had never seen her so upset.

"I was trying to do something nice. I thought you'd be thrilled," he pleaded. "Something has been bothering you since you got home. And you won't tell me what it is."

Lily turned off the stove and wiped her hands on her skirt.

"When I was in San Francisco, I called to say good night. It was late, and I thought you might be asleep," she began. "Audrey answered the phone and said you were staying in the city. I went on Instagram and noticed a photo of you and Mirabelle at the

Rainbow Room." She stopped, and her eyes were giant pools. "The next day, I asked you about the party. You said you came home early and went straight to bed."

"What are you implying?" he asked.

"You lied to me, Oliver, and there's only one reason. It's so typical; celebrity columnist fawned over by a pretty young chef. His wife is three thousand miles away, so he tumbles into her bed. I thought you were different, but I was wrong."

"What do you mean, you thought I was different?" he exploded. "You know me better than I know myself. Nothing is going on between us. It's perfectly innocent."

"Then explain it to me," she said. "I'm listening."

Oliver sank onto a stool and put his head in his hands.

"I ate a bad oyster at the Rainbow Room and got food poisoning. I knew I couldn't get to Grand Central station and make it home." He looked up. "Mirabelle offered to let me stay at her place. At first I said no, but the room kept spinning. She called a cab, and we went to her apartment. I didn't even take off my socks, I slept fully clothed on the sofa."

"Why would you lie if that's what happened?" Lily asked warily.

"I saw the way you reacted when we had dinner at Mirabelle." He twisted his hands. "The minute you saw Mirabelle, you were like a cat showing its claws."

"She was all over you, Oliver." Lily turned away. "I still don't believe you. Why didn't you tell me the truth?"

"I wanted to. I regretted the lie the minute it left my mouth," he pleaded. "I swear nothing happened. It was wrong to go to her place, but I had no choice. I couldn't sleep it off in the cloakroom."

"Why should I believe you?" she demanded. "If you're capable of lying, you're capable of anything."

"Telling a small lie is different from sleeping with another woman," he said angrily. "You can ask anyone who was at the party. I hardly looked like I was sneaking off to a clandestine affair. My skin was the color of putty, and my shirt was drenched in sweat."

Lily walked to the door. She turned around, and her mouth trembled. "Well, you shouldn't have lied. Now you've ruined everything."

Oliver followed her upstairs and knocked on the bedroom door. Lily lay facedown on the bed. He sat beside her and stroked her hair.

"I wish you had talked to me when you arrived home," he began. "I would have told you the truth right away. I'm terribly sorry, it will never happen again."

"It's too late, you don't know what you did," Lily said into the pillow.

"I didn't do anything, and now it's over," he assured her. "Let's shower and go into the city. Wear that navy dress you bought in Milan."

"You don't understand." Lily sat up. "I was so upset after I talked to Audrey, I thought I was coming down with the flu. I went to the hotel lobby to buy aspirin and ran into Roger."

"Roger!" Oliver bristled.

"My mother invited him to dinner the night before, but I walked out," she explained. "He came to apologize and offered to buy me a brandy. Then he was afraid I'd faint in the elevator and escorted me to my room." She paused and her voice was a whisper. "He kissed me, and for a moment I kissed him back."

"Roger kissed you?" Oliver jumped up.

"It was completely unexpected. One minute I was pouring a glass of water and the next moment he was kissing me," she said. "I know I shouldn't have let him up to my room. But I was so angry with you, Oliver. I was sure you were with Mirabelle."

"How could you?" Oliver asked.

"I pulled away and asked Roger to leave," she said. "It was nothing, a couple of seconds."

"I don't care how long it was!" He seethed. "His mouth was on my wife's lips."

"I never would have accepted a brandy if you hadn't lied," Lily insisted. "And you don't know how tortured I've been. I didn't want him to kiss me."

"Are you sure?" he wondered. "You kissed him back, and you could have stopped him at the door. Maybe your mother was right. You've loved Roger all along."

"That's a terrible thing to say." Lily's eyes flashed. "I love you, and thought you were with another woman. It was a momentary slip."

Oliver wanted to take her in his arms. But he pictured Roger in his designer suit and clenched his jaw.

"I'll see you later." He walked to the door.

"Where are you going?" Lily demanded.

"I'm going to see *Hamilton*," he answered. "We can't let both tickets go to waste."

Oliver sat at the bar at Alfie's and sipped his second bourbon on the rocks. He thought it was his second; it could have been his third. He would know when the bartender handed him the check.

The performance of *Hamilton* had exceeded his expectations. He kept wishing Lily was sitting beside him, so they could gush over the costumes and musical numbers.

It had seemed perfectly natural to walk to Alfie's for a post-theater supper. He and Lily often shared a plate of cauliflower cheese after a Broadway show.

Now he ate a Brazil nut and thought it had been a bad idea. He should have taken the train straight back to Connecticut. But he had been afraid of saying something to Lily he would regret. It seemed better to let off steam alone.

He peered out the window and told himself he hadn't picked Alfie's because it was on the corner of West 53rd Street, a block from Mirabelle's apartment. It wasn't likely she'd walk by. She was probably already at home.

But if he did run into Mirabelle, she would understand that he had been wronged. Of course, he shouldn't have lied to Lily. But Lily shouldn't have kissed Roger at the first opportunity.

He would go home and sleep in the guest room to show Lily how angry he was. Then, tomorrow morning, he would cook French toast. They'd make up and spend the day in bed.

The door opened, and a woman entered the bar. She wore a wool jacket and carried a leather purse.

"Oliver?" Mirabelle asked. "I saw you through the window. What are you doing at Alfie's?"

Oliver looked up and flushed. He couldn't tell her that he'd picked the bar because he knew there was an industry event nearby and hoped she might be walking home. Mirabelle wore a black dress, and her blond hair was knotted in a bun.

"I was having a post-theater cocktail," he explained. "I saw *Hamilton*, the musical."

"Where's Lily?" she asked.

"She's at home." He fiddled with a napkin. "I'm alone."

"You saw a *Broadway* show, and now you're sitting in a bar while your wife is in Connecticut?" She raised her eyebrow.

"I guess so," he agreed.

"Why don't I buy you a cup of coffee." She signaled the bartender. "And you can tell me what's wrong."

Oliver sipped black coffee and told Mirabelle how he'd lied about spending the night at her apartment. He started to mention Roger and stopped. He couldn't say anything bad about Lily.

"I don't blame Lily for being upset," Mirabelle said when he'd finished. "You're an attractive man. Of course she thought something was going on."

"We've been married for nine years. She never had a reason to doubt me."

"Your wife is lovely, but no one feels completely secure in a relationship," she mused. "I had a boyfriend who brought me azaleas every day and cheated on me with the hostess."

"But I didn't do anything," he protested. "I ate a bad oyster and couldn't get home."

"It's not going to get better if you're sulking in a Midtown bar," she said. "Go home and apologize."

"You're right," Oliver sighed. Then he thought of Roger, and his chest constricted. "I'll finish this bourbon first."

"Getting drunk isn't a good idea." Mirabelle frowned. "It's my fault that Lily is angry with you. The least I can do is make sure you get home. Why don't you pay, and I'll flag a cab?"

Oliver left some money on the counter and walked outside.

"Here's a taxi." Mirabelle stood at the curb. "Next time you're in the city at night, stop by the restaurant. My wild mushroom crostini is delicious."

Oliver leaned forward to peck Mirabelle on the cheek. Suddenly, he changed his aim and kissed her on the lips. Her breath was sweet, and he pressed his mouth against hers.

"I'm sorry," he said, when he pulled away. "That wasn't a good idea."

Mirabelle touched her mouth, and her green eyes sparkled. "It probably wasn't. But I enjoyed it."

Oliver entered the farmhouse and hung his jacket in the entryway. The lights were off, and he hoped he could creep upstairs.

How could he have kissed Mirabelle? Once his lips brushed her cheek, he couldn't resist. All it took was a shift in his position, and his mouth was on her lips. Her mouth was round and soft like a raspberry on top of a crepe suzette.

A light turned on, and Lily appeared from the kitchen. A robe was wrapped around her waist, and she clutched a ceramic cup.

"I was having tea with a shot of brandy," she said. "Would you like some?"

"No, thank you," he said stiffly. "I've had enough alcohol for one night."

"How was the show?" She entered the living room.

"It was terrific." He nodded. "I'm tired. I'm going to bed."

"Oliver, wait." Lily touched his arm. "No matter how angry I was, I shouldn't have let Roger into my hotel room. It was wrong, and I'm sorry."

Oliver took a deep breath. He could accept Lily's apology and go upstairs. But he had to tell her about Mirabelle. There couldn't be any more secrets in their marriage.

"After the show, I went to Alfie's and had a couple of bourbons." Oliver perched on the sofa. "Mirabelle walked in, she lives on the next block. She asked why I was alone. I told her you were furious because I lied about staying at her apartment." He paused. "I know I shouldn't have. I guess I wanted someone to say I wasn't a bad guy.

"She went outside to call me a cab, and I pecked her on the cheek good-bye." He looked at Lily. "But the peck turned into a kiss on the mouth. And it wasn't a small kiss; it lasted a few seconds."

"You kissed Mirabelle?" Lily gasped.

"I didn't mean to." Oliver realized the magnitude of what he'd done. "It was a stupid error."

"How could you, Oliver?" she demanded. "Were you trying to get even with me? You acted like Louisa when one of her friends scribbles in her favorite book."

"I suppose I wanted to know how you felt when you kissed another man," he said slowly.

"I told you how I felt. It was wrong, and I regretted it the minute it happened," Lily snapped. "But obviously you weren't listening. Or you wouldn't have done it in the first place."

"We're both exhausted and need a good night's sleep," he pleaded. "Let's go to bed, and talk about it in the morning."

"I have nothing to say." She walked to the staircase. "You can sleep in the guest room. The sheets are in the closet."

———

Oliver peeled off his socks and climbed into the double bed. He remembered thinking he would sleep in the guest room to show Lily how angry he was. Now he would do anything to be lying beside her under their duvet.

It was like a game of telephone he'd played as a child. Of course Lily shouldn't have kissed Roger. But that didn't mean he should kiss Mirabelle. Lily was right; if Louisa behaved like that, they would admonish her.

He looked up and noticed a crack in the plaster. With his luck, there would be one of those rare Connecticut earthquakes, and the ceiling would collapse. That wouldn't be the worst thing to happen. The worst thing would be if Lily never spoke to him again.

Oliver sat at a table at Mirabelle and ate a spoonful of almond parfait. It had been three weeks since the kiss, and the October weather had turned chilly. Leaves were scattered on the ground and the wind tossed a stray flyer in the air.

He told himself he was only there to show Mirabelle his review in the *New York Times*. And she had suggested he stop by the restaurant when he was in the city at night.

He nibbled a praline and knew the real reason he was there. He was tired of arriving home to an empty kitchen. Lily always left a chicken with instructions on how to reheat it. He couldn't even complain that she made him do the dishes. He left them in the sink, and the next morning they magically disappeared.

But she refused to talk to him, except to remind him about back-to-school night. He slept in the guest room, and she locked the door when she showered. He pictured the way she'd looked when she stepped out of the shower in Naples all those years before; he would give anything now to see her wet hair and bare shoulders.

A few times, he asked how long this would last, and she said she didn't know. Once, after a couple of brandies, she admitted she wanted to solve things. But she didn't know how. He said he'd do whatever she wanted, and she ran upstairs and shut the bedroom door.

Now the restaurant's kitchen door opened, and Mirabelle entered the dining room. She wore a yellow blouse, and an apron was tied around her waist.

"Oliver, what a surprise." She approached his table. "You should have told me you were here. I would have insisted you try the duck breast with baby fennel."

"I didn't want to disturb you," Oliver answered. "The meal was superb. The lamb medallions were tender, and the dessert selection is exquisite."

"I'm proud of my almond parfait. I use imported cocoa." She pulled out a chair. "But what are you doing here? I would have thought you always tried new restaurants."

Oliver wanted to remind her that she'd said to stop by. But instead, he handed her a newspaper. "I brought you a copy of the review in the *New York Times*."

"I already bought out the newsstand." She grinned. "I have enough copies to paper my apartment."

"You deserve it." He was suddenly nervous. "It was an exceptional dining experience."

"Why isn't Lily with you?" Mirabelle asked, smoothing a napkin.

"We're in a bit of a freeze," Oliver admitted. "She hasn't talked to me since I told her I kissed you."

"You told her!" Mirabelle gasped. "I can imagine that didn't go over well."

"If I hadn't lied to her in the first place, none of this would have happened," he insisted. "I couldn't keep any more secrets. I had to tell her the truth."

"Relationships can be as tricky as taking a soufflé out of the oven." Mirabelle stood up. "Why don't you have a cognac on the house? I'll come say good-bye before you leave."

Oliver swirled Grand Marnier in his glass and leaned back in his chair. The restaurant was closed, and he knew he should leave. But a fire flickered in the fireplace, and it had started to rain.

He checked his watch and wondered if Lily would be in the living room when he arrived home. It hardly mattered. As soon as she heard his key, she would go upstairs to the bedroom.

"I wasn't sure you'd still be here." Mirabelle appeared from the kitchen. "I always clean the stemware myself. It's the only way I can be sure there aren't any spots."

"You certainly are hands-on." Oliver laughed. "Most chefs would leave the cleaning up to the staff and go home."

"Would you like to see the kitchen?" she asked. "I have a La Cornue stove imported from France."

"I'd love to." Oliver followed her into a room with steel counters and a tile floor. There was a silver fridge and a coffee station with blue-and-white ceramic cups.

"We cover the counters with tablecloths so we know how the

food will look on the table. And we use iridescent lighting so the color palette is the same as in the dining room." She stopped and laughed. "I stole those ideas from Per Se. Thomas Keller runs the best kitchen in Manhattan."

"It's stunning," Oliver agreed. "The best summer of my life was working at a restaurant in Naples. I could never get rid of the smell of garlic from my shirts. But there's something so satisfying about serving customers the perfect spaghetti marinara."

"You're the food critic for the *New York Times*," she commented. "You're too young and successful to be nostalgic about the past."

"I don't feel successful," he muttered. "I ruined my marriage."

"You didn't come for the cheesecake tartlets," Mirabelle began. "You came because you thought if your wife isn't talking to you, you might as well take advantage of the situation."

"What do you mean?" he asked.

"You want to kiss me and see if it was worth it."

Oliver gulped and thought he could just leave. But the cognac warmed his throat, and the rain splattered the window, and he leaned forward and kissed her.

Mirabelle kissed him back, and he wrapped his arms around her. Suddenly, he wanted nothing more than to stroke her breasts. He caressed her blouse, and an electric shock surged through his body.

"Oh, God." He sighed. "You're so lovely."

"Slow down," she whispered. "If you're going to kiss me, you should enjoy it."

She took his hand and slipped it beneath her bra. His fingers touched her nipples, and he let out a moan. Then his mouth was on hers, and all he could think about was the exquisite taste of her lips.

"I should get to the train," he said finally. He straightened his collar and ran his hands through his hair.

"We can share a cab," she suggested. "Have a nightcap at my place."

"It's late." He put on his jacket. "Perhaps next time."

"Oliver, you're quite handsome, and any woman would want to kiss you." She smoothed her skirt. "But you're not happy. Go home and figure things out."

Oliver pulled into the driveway and turned off the ignition. Mirabelle was wrong. He hadn't kissed her because he wanted to see if it was worth it; he'd done it to extinguish any hope. It was like shooting a lame horse. He couldn't fight with Lily; he had to put himself out of his misery.

It was one thing to turn a peck on the cheek into a kiss. It was completely different to hold another woman in his arms. There had been a moment when he'd yearned to slip his hand under Mirabelle's skirt. He was as guilty as if they'd made love on the kitchen counter.

He entered the farmhouse and took off his shoes. The light was on in the living room, and Lily sat on the floral sofa.

"You're home." She looked up. "I called your phone. Louisa has a fever, and I wanted you to pick up some Children's Tylenol."

"I can buy some now," Oliver suggested, draping his jacket over an armchair.

"She already fell asleep." Lily shrugged. "You look terrible. Maybe you're coming down with the same flu."

"I got soaked getting off the train." Oliver sat opposite her.

He studied Lily's pale cheeks and watery eyes, and his stomach turned over. He couldn't tell her what had happened; their marriage would be over. She was all he ever wanted, and he would do anything to keep her.

"Do you remember when we were in Portugal on our honeymoon?" he began. "I was out of sorts because your father read Roger's email at the wedding. I went to breakfast alone, and you thought I was flirting with some blonde. Then I saw you on the beach with that fisherman and almost punched him in the jaw.

"You said if I was jealous of every little thing, we would never survive," Oliver finished. "That's all this is. I was jealous that Roger kissed you, so I kissed Mirabelle. I love you; we can't let anyone come between us."

"I said most of the time I was so happy," Lily remembered. "But we have to trust each other or we don't have anything."

"You can trust me. I never meant to lie, but I didn't do anything wrong. You have to give me another chance," he implored.

She picked up his jacket and hung it in the foyer. A piece of paper fell out, and she reached down and picked it up.

"I think this is for you." She handed it to him and ran up the staircase.

"Where are you going?" He followed her. "We were talking about our marriage."

Lily stood at the top of the stairs ten minutes later, holding an overnight bag. She walked downstairs and stood in the foyer.

"You can't leave," he insisted. "We have to make this work."

"I'm not leaving. You are." She handed him the bag. "The Comfort Inn has free Wi-Fi. Good night, Oliver."

Oliver put the bag on the floor and remembered the piece of paper. He turned it over and read:

Oliver, that was fun. If you want to do it again, you know my address. Xox Mirabelle.

Oliver crumpled the paper and gasped. He picked up the bag and ran through the rain. He opened the car door and rested his head on the windshield. Horses were lucky. One bullet, and it was all over.

Oliver glanced around the terrace of the Hotel Cala di Volpe and groaned. It had only been an hour since Angela had delivered her news about the baby, but it felt like an eternity. Waiters flitted between tables, and he could hear the tinkling of ice cubes. He would give anything to be worrying about something else: the exorbitant price of cocktails or whether he had enough background information for his review.

When you were married, the only time you thought you would have to deal with an unwanted pregnancy was when your daughter became a teenager and dated a musician. He suddenly pictured Louisa in her floral smocks and smiled. Once you had a child, you realized there was no such thing as an unwanted pregnancy. Louisa was the most important thing in the world.

But what part would he play in the new baby's life? Have his name on the birth certificate and receive birthday party invitations? And what would happen when Angela got married? He would become the extra man who appeared at athletic events and graduations.

One of his greatest regrets in the divorce was missing out on half of Louisa's life. And children needed a father. He'd taught Louisa to tie her shoelaces and not to be afraid of spiders.

And he hated living alone. He felt like a failure every time he went to Trader Joe's and couples were filling carts with salmon steaks and bottles of sauvignon blanc. He needed someone to tell him to clear his desk and remember to shave.

Angela was gorgeous and ambitious, and they had more in common than he'd thought. Why shouldn't they stay together? She even said she could imagine falling in love with him.

They'd get one of those fancy strollers and walk in Central Park. Maybe he'd even join a playgroup that met on Saturdays in Washington Square Park. On the weekends when they had Louisa, she could help run a bath. They'd all go out for dim sum, and people would comment that they were a beautiful family.

Suddenly he pictured Lily strolling through the *piazzetta* and was gripped by a terrible pain. But he couldn't think about Lily now. He had to concentrate on the tiny cells growing beneath the curve of Angela's stomach.

He took care of the bill and hurried down the stone steps. He raced to the Hotel Cervo and entered their suite.

Angela was perched on a love seat, scrolling down her computer screen. Her coppery hair cascaded over her shoulders, and she sipped a glass of sparkling water.

"I'm reading about the things to do during pregnancy." She looked up. "One needs to drink six glasses of water a day and avoid salty foods. And never sleep in constricting clothing, it's best to sleep naked."

"I thought over what you said." Oliver sat opposite her. "Of course I want to raise our child together. We'll turn my office into a nursery. The apartment will be a little cramped when Louisa is there, but babies don't take up much space. The West Village has great playgrounds, and when he or she starts school, we can move to the suburbs."

Angela closed the computer and walked to the balcony. The sea was a sheet of glass and the dock was lined with long white yachts.

"Do you really mean it, Oliver? That's wonderful to hear!" She turned around. "What do you think about getting married? It doesn't have to be right away, we can wait until the baby's born. It would be nice to be a proper family, and it's the best thing for a child. I'm from Ohio, we still believe in church weddings. You'd look so handsome in a tuxedo, and my mother has kept her wedding dress in the attic for decades. It would need some altering, but she'd be so happy if I wore it."

Oliver gulped and felt slightly dizzy. Did he want to marry Angela? He pictured driving away from the church in Carmel with Lily and feeling like he had pulled off an incredible heist. He'd convinced the most special girl in the world to marry him, and they were so happy.

He remembered when they brought Louisa home from the hospital, and he filled the hallway with balloons. He recalled the excitement of Lily Bristol's grand opening, and the first night they spent at the farmhouse. They had been so certain about everything and failed. How could he do it again?

He ran his hands through his hair and took a deep breath. He couldn't think about his life with Lily now. That was like a race car driver remembering a horrific crash before he climbed into the cockpit.

"Of course, I want to get married at some point. Why don't we get engaged now?" He stood up. "There's no time like the present. I'll go buy a ring."

"That's very sweet, Oliver." Angela kissed him. "Sometimes I worried if you were serious about our relationship, but I was wrong. You've made me so happy. You're going to be a wonderful husband and father."

Oliver tried not to think that he had been a husband and he was a father. Wasn't that the beauty of meeting Angela? He had the chance to do it all again and not mess it up. And she really was special. She was fun and beautiful and made him feel desirable.

"Being pregnant makes me so tired, I can hardly keep my eyes open." She stretched. "I'm going to take a nap. Would you like to join me?"

"A nap, now?" Oliver asked. The sun made patterns on her dress, and suddenly he was incredibly turned on.

"We can rub each other's backs." She turned around. "Can you help with my zipper?"

Oliver unzipped her dress and pulled her toward him. She smelled like almond lotion, and he buried his mouth in her neck.

"Come here." He moved to the sofa and unzipped his slacks. He leaned against the cushions and positioned her on top of him. God, she was gorgeous, with her creamy skin and ripe breasts.

"Let's go into the bedroom," she whispered. "The bed is much more comfortable."

He picked her up and carried her into the bedroom. She lay on her stomach, and he caressed her back. Suddenly she flipped over and pulled him on top of her.

"Do you know what else the pregnancy website says?" she asked, tightening her thighs around his buttocks.

"What?" he groaned, kissing her collarbone and the space between her breasts.

"A woman's libido increases when she's pregnant." She arched her back. "She can last for hours."

"Is that so?" he breathed.

Angela bucked underneath him, and he hung on like a cowboy at a rodeo. Her fingernails dug into his skin, and she slapped him gently on the thigh.

"Angela!" he exclaimed. Then he collapsed against her breasts and came in one exquisite thrust.

Oliver leaned over the balcony and felt like a movie star or a politician. He was gazing at one of the most glamorous coastlines in the world and had just made love to a stunning woman who was carrying his baby.

Angela was right; it would be nice to be a family. And what more could he ask for in a wife? Angela was bright and ambitious and she truly admired him. He really was lucky; he mustn't take his good fortune for granted.

"Oliver," Angela called.

"Yes?" Oliver walked to the door.

She sat against the headboard. "For some reason I can't sleep. Do you think this time you could actually rub my back?"

"I'll be right there." He slipped off his robe and climbed into bed.

Chapter Eleven

LILY SAT ON THE BALCONY of her suite and inhaled the scent of bougainvillea. It was early afternoon, and the harbor resembled a jewelry case. Yachts gleamed in the sun like alabaster pearls, and there were topaz-colored speedboats.

The opening was in two days, so she had hired a driver and driven into the hills to the town of Templo Pausania to buy a few things for the store. Old women tended stalls selling filigree jewelry and woven rugs and pine-scented candles. They insisted she accept gifts with her purchases and filled her basket with plums and oranges.

One woman even pressed a silver Sardinian wedding ring into her hand. When Lily said she was nowhere near getting married, the woman replied in broken English that it would bring Lily luck. Lily smiled and promised to wear it on a silver chain around her neck.

On the way back, the driver pointed out the secluded beaches of Baia di Sardinia and Liscia di Vacca. Lily gazed at the green hills dotted with flowers and the cobalt ocean littered with speedboats, and her heart lifted. The Emerald Coast was the most beautiful place she'd ever seen.

Now she studied the view from her suite's balcony and was quite pleased with her morning purchases. She looked down at her plate and picked up a piece of Sardinian flatbread. There was a bowl of cold tomato soup and a glass of grapefruit juice on the outdoor table.

The drapes were closed in Oliver's suite, and her shoulders relaxed. She hadn't thought about Oliver and Angela once since she and Ricky had returned from Porto Rotondo yesterday evening. It really had been a wonderful excursion, with dinner at S'Astore and Ricky's gift of the ruby pendant.

Could she and Ricky be falling in love? But spending more than a few weeks on the Emerald Coast every year was impossible. She had other stores to manage, and she hated being away from Louisa.

When she was with Ricky, she felt like the lead in a romantic movie. In the opening scene, she's hurt so badly she doesn't believe in love. But then she meets a handsome stranger and realizes she's going to get her happy ending.

She had promised herself she would try to be happy; she couldn't go back on her word. If she didn't take a chance, it would be like Louisa quitting gymnastics because she fell off the balance beam.

Her phone buzzed, and she pressed accept.

"Let me guess," Ricky began. "You're sitting outside eating risotto and ricotta and some kind of fruit. You're gazing at the boats and thinking this really is the most glorious spot on earth. You are fortunate to be here and wonder why anyone would want to be anywhere else."

"Are you spying on me?" Lily laughed, glancing around the balcony.

"That's what every visitor is doing on a beautiful day on the Emerald Coast," Ricky replied.

"I'm eating cold soup instead of risotto and mango ice cream instead of fruit, and I was thinking I must get fabric for the store that is the same color as the sea."

"Then you are a woman of many facets." Ricky paused. "That's one of the reasons I'm falling in love with you."

"Ricky . . ." Lily began.

"Check the hallway outside your suite," he cut in. "There's a present for you."

Lily ran through her suite and opened the door. There was a rectangular box wrapped in tissue paper.

She tore open the paper and discovered a turquoise chiffon dress. There was a quilted purse with a gold chain.

She picked up the phone. "It's gorgeous. But I can't accept any more presents."

"We have been invited to a dinner party on the yacht of Aga Khan III," he answered. "I wanted you to wear something special."

"I haven't even said yes. How do you know I'll come?" Lily asked playfully. "And for a serious businessman, you spend a lot of time on yachts."

"Yachts in Sardinia are like golf courses or country clubs. That's where people conduct business," Ricky explained. "And Aga Khan III is the grandson of Prince Aga Khan. He is a very influential man."

Lily remembered reading how Prince Aga Khan turned the wild stretch of Sardinia into a playground for the rich and famous in the 1960s. His consortium still owned most of the hotels and the marina.

"I suppose I could make the time." She smiled. "Thank you, for the dress, it's lovely. I'm just afraid I'll be like Cinderella at the ball, and everyone will know I'm an imposter."

"You will be the most stunning woman there," Ricky said softly. "And Lily, wear the ruby pendant. I can't wait to see it around your neck."

Lily hung up and felt like Audrey Hepburn in *Breakfast at Tiffany's*. Could she really spend her time drinking champagne and eating oysters? But there was nothing in the books about divorce that said she had to resign herself to carpools and chaperoning field trips. Ricky was handsome and charming, and she couldn't wait to be with him.

She fingered the ruby pendant and noticed one of the rubies was missing. What if it had fallen out when she'd tried it on in front of the mirror? She crouched down and searched underneath the table. She peeled back the rug and looked behind the sofa.

She could ask Enzo, but he might think she was accusing one of the maids of taking it. Someone must have vacuumed it up and not noticed.

Ricky might not mind if she misplaced a straw hat, but he would be upset if she lost a precious jewel. Suddenly, she had an idea. She scooped up the velvet case and hoped it would work.

Lily turned onto the Via Porto Vecchio and passed Cartier, with its glittering diamonds, and Prada, with its soft leather sandals. Porto Cervo resembled the villages she and Oliver had visited in Tuscany.

But instead of butchers with slabs of meat and delicatessens with sausages dangling from hooks, there were stores selling designer shoes and priceless jewels.

She entered a shop with a pink marble floor and pastel-colored walls. Jewelry cases held heart-shaped watches and rings set with amethysts and topazes.

"Welcome to Sybarite." A man stood behind the counter. "May I help you?"

"I hope so." Lily took off her sunglasses. "What a wonderful store, your collections are exquisite."

"We take great pride in our pieces." He nodded. "We just got in a selection of brooches designed for Princess Caroline of Monaco."

"I'm not here to buy anything, exactly." She handed him the velvet case. "I've done something terrible. A friend gave me a ruby pendant, and I lost one of the stones. I wonder if you could replace it."

He snapped it open and took out the ruby pendant.

"It's a beautiful piece. The rubies are imported from Burma, and the clasp is twenty-four-carat gold." He looked up. "Ricky has wonderful taste. He told me he was buying it for the lovely American who owned the new Lily Bristol."

"You know Ricky?" Lily asked.

"Of course." The man nodded. "Last year, he bought our finest engagement ring. A square sapphire surrounded by white diamonds."

Lily started, and her cheeks turned pale.

"Did you say an engagement ring?" she gasped.

"Yes, he brought in his fiancée. Her name was Poppy, and she was American. Long blond hair and wearing a striped jumpsuit," he remembered. "You almost never see a couple shopping for an engagement ring together. Ricky said Poppy had excellent taste and knew exactly what she wanted." He paused. "It was unfortunate that Ricky returned the ring a week later."

"He brought it back?"

"It happens sometimes, of course," he said. "One never asks why. A returned engagement ring is a sensitive subject."

He opened a drawer and took out a ruby. He inserted it in the pendant and handed the case to Lily.

"Oh, that's wonderful," she breathed. "I can't tell the difference. What do I owe you?"

"Business owners in Porto Cervo must help each other." He thought about it. "Wear it to the store opening and tell everyone where it's from. It will be our gift to the stunning owner of Lily Bristol."

"Thank you." She beamed. "That's exactly what I'll do."

Lily stepped onto the cobblestones and adjusted her hat. She felt slightly queasy—like when you left the doctor's office after conducting some tests, she thought. You knew it was probably nothing, and that any minute the nurse would call and say they came back all clear. But if there wasn't a chance something was wrong, why would you have taken them in the first place?

Ricky had said he was serious about love, but he'd never met the right woman. But surely, if he had been engaged, he had been in love before. And why hadn't he mentioned it?

It probably didn't mean anything at all. They had so many other things to talk about: the Emerald Coast's white sand beaches and Lily Bristol's grand opening and where to buy the best gelato.

The only thing she could do was ask Ricky. But the problem

with asking difficult questions was, sometimes you didn't like the answer. And even if he could explain why he'd hidden his engagement, what if there were other things he hadn't told her?

She shielded her eyes from the sun and remembered when Oliver had lied to her about Mirabelle. She had thought if only they could start fresh, everything would be different.

Lily plumped cushions in the farmhouse's living room and sighed. Oliver had been gone for a week, and she had rearranged the pantry and scrubbed the mudroom. She hadn't realized how much she would miss him. She missed him handing her coffee with two sugars every morning and calling during his lunch hour and arriving home with Momofuku blueberry cookies.

Perhaps the note from Mirabelle was perfectly innocent. They'd had a friendly cup of coffee or run into each other on Fifth Avenue. But if nothing had happened, Oliver would have told her. Instead, he'd hurried away like the villain in a spy novel.

They had to think about Louisa. They couldn't let their marriage dissolve like aspirin in a glass of water. But what if she asked Oliver about Mirabelle and he gave her an answer she didn't want to hear? Then she would have to call a divorce attorney and think about selling the farmhouse.

She straightened magazines on the coffee table and thought anything was better than living in limbo. It was like when she taught Louisa how to dive. You couldn't stay perched on top of a diving board; you had to work up the courage and jump into the pool.

She grabbed her purse and ran down the front steps. She opened the car door and slid into the driver's seat. She fiddled with the mirror and saw a figure ducking into the garage. She jumped out and ran to the garage door.

"Oliver! What are you doing here?" she demanded.

"You look lovely this morning," he said. "You should always wear that shade of lipstick, it suits you."

"It's eight o clock in the morning! Why are you in the garage?"

"I bought Danishes and wondered if I could use the microwave. The one in my room at the Comfort Inn isn't working. There's nothing worse than a cold Danish, it tastes like cardboard."

"But why are you prowling around our house? I could have thought you were a burglar and called the police."

"I hope you recognize your own husband, I've only been gone a week." He paused. "Though you look different. You've done something with your hair."

"You haven't answered my question," she said. "And you're getting pastry flakes on the garage floor."

"I brought you one too." He handed her the bag. "I come here every morning. I watched you polish the dining room table and dust the bookshelves," he admitted. "But today you walked outside, and I got scared."

"So you hid in the garage?"

"We don't have any bushes," he explained awkwardly. "It was the closest thing."

"You've been spying on me all week?" she asked, and didn't know whether to be furious or slightly happy. Oliver hadn't been having trysts with Mirabelle; he had been peering through their window.

"Well, yes." He nodded. "We really should hire someone to clean the drapes. I don't like you climbing on that ladder."

"Why didn't you knock on the door?"

He rubbed his forehead, and she noticed his cheeks were pale, and there were circles under his eyes.

"I was afraid you would tell me to go away."

"I probably would have." She fiddled with her earrings.

"Are you going to tell me to leave now?" he asked.

"No, Oliver." She shook her head. "I want to hear what you have to say."

"I had dinner at Mirabelle. I shouldn't have, but I was so miserable," he began. "She offered to show me the kitchen, and things got out of hand. It was a terrible mistake. You're the only woman I ever wanted, and I'd do anything to keep you."

"Something did happen between you and Mirabelle?" She clutched the paper bag.

"Yes, but it's not as bad as you think." He touched Lily's hand. "I promise it will never happen again."

"That's what you said when you kissed her." Lily pulled away.

"But I had a reason to kiss her, you kissed Roger," he reminded her. "This is different, it's entirely my fault."

"How you could see her again when we were trying to work things out?" she asked, and her voice rose.

"Not talking to you was the worst thing in the world. I needed to end the pain," he explained. "But I realized right away it was a mistake. I should have begged you to take me back."

"I don't think that's possible, Oliver," she said slowly. "It's better if we separate before we cause each other more pain."

"We love each other! We can't throw away our marriage like cold pizza," he protested. "We have to start over."

"What do you mean?" she looked up.

"Do you remember when we met at the train station in Naples?"

he asked eagerly. "Let's have our first date all over again. We'll be together just because we love each other's company."

"You want to go on a first date?" She laughed.

"That's exactly what I want to do," he insisted. "And I know where. Meet me at Grand Central Station at six PM."

"Where are we going?" she asked.

"It's a surprise." He handed her his pastry. "You can have my Danish too. I have to catch a train."

Lily stood under the clock at Grand Central and glanced at the revolving glass doors. It was almost six thirty and Oliver hadn't shown up. Maybe he'd gotten delayed at work or forgotten he had an evening function. She would have a bowl of corn chowder and take the train home.

She turned and saw Oliver hurrying toward her. He wore a blue blazer and carried a paper sack.

"It's impossible to get fresh peaches in New York in November." He handed her the bag. "I finally found a market on the Upper West Side that imports them from Argentina, and charges fifteen dollars a peach."

"You brought me peaches?" She looked inside.

"Don't you remember when we met?" he asked. "Your sandwich fell on the floor, and you lost your credit cards. I offered you a peach because you were starving."

"Thank you." She nodded. "They smell delicious."

"You can't eat them yet. You'll spoil your appetite." He took her hand. "Come with me."

They walked a few blocks to East 44th Street and entered a brick building. The interior had polished wood floors and red wallpaper and pinpoint lighting. Tables were set with checkered tablecloths, and it smelled of garlic and tomatoes.

"Piccolo Fiore is the finest Italian restaurant in Midtown." Oliver led her to a table by the window. "Their gnocchi Genovese is better than you'll find in Rome, and the pastas are made fresh in the kitchen."

"That's very nice, Oliver." She sat down. "But why did you drag me into the city? We have Italian restaurants in Wilton. And I'm not in the mood to have the chef come to the table and thank you for your review."

"That's not possible," Oliver said and smiled. "The restaurant is closed."

"What did you say?" She looked up.

"The restaurant is closed on Tuesdays," he explained. "We have the place to ourselves."

Lily noticed the water glasses weren't filled and the breadbaskets were empty.

"How will we eat?" she asked.

"Wait here," Oliver replied. "I'll be right back."

The kitchen doors opened, and Oliver carried plates of buffalo mozzarella and stuffed olives. There was spaghetti with meatballs and grilled asparagus. He poured two glasses of Chianti and handed one to Lily.

"Where did all this come from?" She took a bite of melon wrapped in prosciutto and had never tasted anything so delicious.

"Daniel, the chef, owed me a favor." Oliver sipped his wine. "Do you remember our first meal at Umberto's? The door was locked, and you thought we were breaking into a restaurant. I went into the kitchen and brought out eggplant parmigana and bowls of minestrone.

"I asked what you wanted to be when you weren't getting stranded in train stations, and you said you wanted to open a furnishings store." He paused. "Then you suggested I become a food critic."

"Of course I remember," Lily said, and a chill ran down her spine.

"Look what we've achieved." Oliver sat forward. "Lily Bristol is an international brand, and I'm the restaurant critic for the *New York Times*, and we have a wonderful daughter. We can't throw it away because of a few missteps. Think of what we'll miss."

Oliver's blue eyes sparkled, and Lily remembered everything she loved about him. But then she imagined him kissing Mirabelle, and her stomach clenched.

"Too much has happened." Lily fiddled with her glass. "I don't know if we can look at each other in the same way."

"I'm looking at you now, and I see a woman in a yellow dress who is more beautiful than the day we met." He took her hand. "Of all the airports and bus terminals and train stations in Italy, you ended up in Naples. Don't you think if we had the good fortune to find ourselves on the same platform, we have to keep trying?"

"It doesn't mean anything if we don't make each other happy." Lily's eyes glistened. "Every marriage is built on trust, and we broke it."

"They rebuilt San Francisco after the earthquake and New Orleans after Hurricane Katrina," he urged. "We have to make it work."

Oliver kissed her, and her heart melted. He was everything she wanted, and she couldn't imagine life without him.

"All right," she whispered. "We'll give it another chance."

"Good," Oliver said and smiled. "Because I just got spaghetti sauce on my tie, and you're better at getting the stains out."

They ate flourless chocolate cake and talked about spending a week on Lake Michigan the following summer. Oliver suggested having an aperitif, and they took a cab to the St. Regis.

Lily sipped a Casanova with Campari and orange juice and thought she never tired of the King Cole Bar. The Maxfield Parrish mural was stunning, the inlaid gold ceiling was spectacular, and the walnut booths made you feel like were in an English library. And the people! Men wore wool overcoats, and women were dressed in cashmere suits, and they all looked impossibly sophisticated.

Lily went to the powder room to refresh her makeup and returned to the bar. Oliver drummed his fingers on the wood. His fists were clenched, and he looked like he was going to explode.

"What happened?" She sat next to him. "I was only gone a minute."

"You left your phone and you got a text," he offered. "I shouldn't have looked, but I thought it might be the babysitter. It was from Roger. He's going to be in New York next week and wanted to know if you'd like to have lunch."

"Roger!" Lily gasped, and ice filled her veins. "I have no idea why he would text me. I haven't spoken to him since that night in San Francisco."

"Why does he have your number at all?" Oliver asked.

"I've had the same number for years." Lily's eyes blazed. "I thought we were going to trust each other."

"That was before Roger's name showed up on your phone." He

stood up. "I don't feel like drinking a Bloody Mary and listening to jazz. I'm going home."

Lily fumbled with her key and opened the door of the farmhouse. Oliver hadn't said a word on the train. Now he entered the living room and poured a glass of scotch.

"Don't you think it's odd that Roger would text you out of the blue and try make a date?" He filled the glass with ice and took a long gulp. "Usually when people are in New York on business, they're too busy to have lunch."

"I would never make plans to see Roger. And I told you, I have no idea why he contacted me," Lily said. "If you don't believe me, you can call and ask him if we've been in touch."

"The last person I want to talk to is the man who keeps trying to ruin my marriage." He bristled.

"No one can ruin our marriage except us, Oliver." She walked to the hallway.

"And don't tell me to sleep in the guest room." He followed her. "I paid for our down comforter, and I'm going to sleep under it."

"You're welcome to the bedroom," Lily said and smoothed her skirt. "I'll sleep in the guest room."

Lily clutched her champagne glass and glanced around the room. Colored lights dangled from the ceiling, and a Christmas tree was decorated with glass ornaments. Waiters carried trays of profiteroles, and Lily inhaled the scent of nutmeg and cinnamon.

For the first time in weeks, Lily felt slightly hopeful. She and Oliver had finally made up and were sleeping in the same bed.

They'd taken Louisa Christmas shopping on Fifth Avenue and spent a romantic weekend at an inn in Vermont.

Now they were at the Spotted Pig's annual Christmas party. Manhattan's hottest restaurateurs gathered in the Spotted Pig's private dining room to nibble scallops and drink Brandy Alexanders. Oliver flitted from group to group, and Lily felt a surge of pride. Oliver was just a boy from Michigan, and now he was the most sought-after food critic in New York.

"If we stand under the mistletoe, you have to kiss me." Oliver appeared at her side. He held a plate of fruit tarts, and she inhaled the scent of his cologne.

"As I recall, we did quite a lot of that on the train into the city." She smiled.

"I can't wait until we leave so we can repeat the performance." He kissed her. "I might even ask Ken if we can take a bottle of champagne. It's making me appreciate your beauty."

"Oliver, you don't need to flirt with me." She laughed. "It's lovely to be here. The room looks so festive, and everyone is enjoying themselves."

"I don't care about any of it. I just want to be with you," Oliver said, and his eyes were serious. "Let's never fight again. I can't bear it."

"Why should we fight if there's nothing to fight about?" she agreed. "Now go mingle. Everyone wants to say Merry Christmas to Oliver Bristol, *New York Times* restaurant critic."

Oliver drifted across the room, and Lily went to the powder room to reapply her lipstick. She walked out and saw a couple standing under the mistletoe. The woman had blond hair and wore a red dress. She stood on tiptoe and had one hand in the man's pocket.

Lily blinked and realized the man was Oliver. His hand was around Mirabelle's waist, and his eyes were slightly closed.

"Oliver!" Lily exclaimed. Her cheeks flushed and she ran down the steps.

"Lily!" Oliver jumped and raced after her. "Where are you going?"

"I'm leaving, Oliver." She gave her claim to the coat-check girl.

"We can't leave without saying good-bye to our hosts," he hissed. "It's not polite."

"You can do anything you like." She slipped on her coat. "I'm going home."

Lily hurried down West 11th Street and tried to stop shaking. Slush covered the sidewalk, but she was too upset to flag a cab.

"Where are you going?" Oliver caught up with her. "And you're not even wearing boots. You're going to freeze to death."

"I'm not your concern," she said. "Go back to the party."

"Of course you're my concern, you're my wife." He touched her arm. "Lily, stop. It didn't mean anything. Mirabelle walked by, and I was standing under the mistletoe. I shouldn't have let her kiss me. She was just being friendly. But it was a stupid thing to do, and I apologize."

"You had your eyes half-closed like a swooning teenager," she retorted. "And her hand was in your pocket."

"She gave me a Christmas present." He took a flat box out of his pocket. He tore it open and held up a silver pen. "I receive a dozen pens at Christmas. That's hardly a romantic overture."

"Keep it," Lily snapped. "You can use it to sign the divorce papers."

"I'll give it back, if you prefer," he pleaded. "I promise I'll never see her again."

Snow dusted Lily's cheeks, and she took a deep breath.

"It's no use, Oliver," she sighed. "This isn't working."

"What do you mean?" he protested. "We had the best sex we've had in months in Vermont. And we had so much fun Christmas shopping with Louisa. She's positive Santa Claus is going to bring her everything on her list."

"It's not hard to have great sex, we've been doing it for years. And we're both good parents." She twisted her hands. "But there will always be a Mirabelle or a Roger between us. We're not a team anymore."

"We'll become a team," he insisted. "We'll take up couples yoga or learn to play bridge."

"I watch you looking at me sometimes, and it's as if you're seeing someone else. And every time you get a text, I wonder if it's from Mirabelle."

"Sometimes I wonder if you wished you married Roger. But I know I'm being silly." He paused. "And I swear I haven't had any communication with Mirabelle."

"The problem is I don't believe you, even when you're telling the truth," she said, and her eyes were huge. "We can't live like this. Any moment there can be a flare-up."

"What do you want to do?" he asked.

"One of us has to leave," she said quietly.

"Leave for how long?" he gasped.

She walked to the curb and raised her arm. She waited for a cab to pull up and turned around. "Leave for however long it takes us to be happy."

―――――

Lily adjusted her sunglasses and entered the lobby of Hotel Cervo. She thought of what the jewelry store owner had said about Ricky's excellent taste in jewelry and gulped. She had to ask Ricky why he hadn't mentioned his engagement. They couldn't have secrets in their relationship.

Sofas were scattered with sea foam cushions, and vases were filled with yellow orchids, and Lily had never been anywhere more beautiful. She climbed the steps to her room and hoped Ricky had the right answer. If he didn't, she didn't know what she would do.

Lily stood in front of the mirror and zipped up her red chiffon dress. She slipped on gold sandals and dabbed her wrists with perfume. There was a bouquet of roses on the glass coffee table, and she felt a shiver of excitement.

After she'd returned from the jewelry store, she took a swim in the hotel pool. Then she came up to the suite and discovered the flowers with a note. Ricky couldn't wait to see her, and they were going to have a wonderful evening.

She fastened the ruby pendant around her neck, and there was a knock at the door. Perhaps Enzo was bringing a platter of fruit and soft cheeses. She would tell him she was going out to dinner with Ricky; she didn't need anything at all.

"Oliver!" She opened the door. "What do you want?"

"That's not a polite greeting. I would have thought after four days on the Emerald Coast you'd be more relaxed." He entered the suite. "It smells like a florist in here. Where did the roses come from?"

"They were a gift." She followed him into the living room. "I don't mean to be rude, but I'm busy."

"You really should slow down and enjoy yourself." He poured a glass of scotch. "Don't you remember when we booked our holiday, we were so excited about exploring the Emerald Coast? We even thought of renting a Ducati motorcycle and driving up into the hills."

"You suggested it. It was part of an early midlife crisis." She fixed her hair in front of the mirror. "I would never get on the back of a motorcycle."

"You could have worn a scarf and oversized sunglasses. We could have looked like a modern-day Bonnie and Clyde." He perched on the sofa. "The sun would have stretched over the horizon, and the sea would have been a dappled carpet."

"That's quite poetic, but I have a date." She fastened her earrings. "Why are you here?"

"There's something I have to tell you," he said. "But you better sit down."

Lily turned and felt a small tremor.

"Did something happen to Louisa?" she asked.

"Louisa is fine. The last time I talked to her she was baking chocolate-chip cookies." He paused. "I thought about what you said, that a relationship has to move forward. I think you're right."

"Is that all? I have to get ready." She fastened the ruby pendant around her neck. "I'm supposed to be at the harbor in thirty minutes."

"Good god, where did you get that pendant?" Oliver jumped up. "Don't tell me you're dating some Eurotrash. They buy you expensive jewels, and then they get stolen. You file an insurance claim and give them the money. It's only when you discover a

'Dear Jane' letter on your pillow that you realize the jewelry was fake. It's worse than those scams claiming you inherited ten million dollars from a dead relative in Africa."

"Ricky gave it to me," she said. "He bought it at a jewelry store in Porto Cervo."

"Ricky gave it to you?"

"If you say one word about him moving too fast, I will ask you to leave," she warned him. "It's just a pendant, and it's lovely."

"I don't think you're moving too fast at all."

"You don't?" She looked up.

"That's what I want to talk to you about." He took a deep breath. "I'm going to ask Angela to marry me."

"You're what?" Lily started, and her hairbrush fell on the floor.

"I'm not good at living alone. I end up watching *Gilmore Girls* because it's the only thing I can find on Netflix." He sipped his drink. "I always run out of toothpaste because I forget to stock up on toiletries at Grand Union."

"I don't mind if you get married, I want you to be happy." She bit her lip. "But you have to do it for the right reasons."

Oliver opened his mouth as if he were about to say something. He swallowed the scotch and ran his hands through his hair.

"What are the right reasons? That Angela and I love each other?" he inquired. "You and I loved each other, and that didn't count for anything."

"It counted for everything. We had ten wonderful years and created a beautiful daughter. Why are you telling me before you ask Angela?"

"I thought you should know," he answered. "She'll be Louisa's stepmother."

"You wouldn't ask Angela to marry you if you didn't think she would be good with Louisa," she replied. "Honestly, Oliver. I appreciate the sentiment, but you don't need my permission."

"So you won't tell me if you're going to get married again?" he asked. "I don't want Louisa raised by some hedge type who believes you need an Ivy League education and your own helicopter pad to be worth something."

"What's wrong with wanting to attend an Ivy League school?" She laughed. "But I'm not marrying anyone. I have to concentrate on Louisa and running Lily Bristol."

"Well, I am getting married and I thought I should tell you," he said stiffly. "Unless you prefer to communicate across the barbed wire fence at the playground like other divorced couples."

"I'm glad we're getting along." She flushed. "But I don't need to know the flavor of the wedding cake or the first dance song."

"Do you remember when Louisa was little, and we dreamed about her wedding?" He sighed. "Whoever thought there would be any weddings in the family besides hers."

"I'm sure your wedding will be gorgeous. You are marrying a florist." She coated her lips with lipstick. "I really have to go. I'll see you later."

"Did you mean what you said about not getting married?" he asked.

"If the right man came along, I'd consider it." Lily hesitated. "But right now, I'm much too busy."

Oliver put his glass on the side table and walked to the door.

"That pendant suits you." He turned around. "Whoever you choose will be a lucky man."

Lily walked to the marina and tried to stop her heart from racing. Why was Oliver getting married? There was something he wasn't telling her. Maybe he was just lonely. Oliver was never good at being alone. He slept with Louisa's stuffed animals when she traveled and texted the minute she landed.

Oliver could do whatever he liked. And it would be good for Louisa. She would return from her weekends with Oliver with freshly washed hair and matching socks.

After all, she was seeing Ricky. But why hadn't he told her he was engaged before? Maybe Ricky just wanted a summer romance, and she was going to get her heart broken.

She would tell Ricky she had a cold and curl up in her suite with a bowl of tomato soup and an old Meg Ryan movie. Tomorrow she'd spend all day at Lily Bristol, preparing for the grand opening. That's why she was in Sardinia after all; she wasn't looking for love.

"Lily, wait!" a male voice called.

She turned and saw Ricky striding toward her. His dark hair touched his collar, and he looked like an ad in a fashion magazine.

"I was so worried." He caught up with her. "I went to your suite and you weren't there."

"You told me to meet you at the harbor," she reminded him.

"I completely forgot." He took her arm. "I was afraid you weren't coming."

"And you were worried?"

"Of course, I was worried. I waited all day to be with you." He kissed her. "But you're here. And that's all that matters."

Lily kissed him back, and he smelled of musk aftershave. The sea looked as calm as a bath, and suddenly she felt happy. Why should she eat a bowl of soup in her room when she could have dinner on a glamorous yacht?

"I can't wait." Lily tipped her face up to his. "I haven't eaten since lunchtime and I'm starving."

Lily leaned against the yacht's railing and gazed at the harbor. The sky was black velvet, and Porto Cervo was an impossibly beautiful painting. Couples mingled on the deck, and she heard the sounds of laughter and tinkling ice cubes.

It had been a wonderful evening. The Aga Khan's yacht was even bigger and more elaborate than Christoff's. There was a ballroom with Carrara marble floors and Murano glass chandeliers, a gallery filled with Impressionist paintings, and a music room with a gold harpsichord and a Steinway grand piano. Staterooms were decorated in pastel silks and had canopied beds and oriental rugs like the inside of an Arabian palace.

The lower deck held a hothouse with beds of English roses and orchids imported from India. There was a deck where Afghan hounds lounged around, and an aviary filled with tropical birds. One room was devoted entirely to Ming vases and Fabergé eggs.

And the food! Platters of smoked salmon and Russian caviar and exotic vegetables. A chef from the Hôtel de Crillon in Paris made crepe suzettes, and a sushi chef prepared trays of dragon rolls. There was a selection of aged cognacs and two-hundred-year-old bottles of French wine.

One table displayed desserts from all over the world. Lily sampled shaved ice with mango pudding from Taiwan and vanilla lamington cakes dusted with coconut from Australia. She and Ricky shared phyllo and sweet cheese from Jerusalem and marsala custard gelato that was transported in portable freezers from a *gelateria* in Rome.

Lily tried to find a few minutes alone with Ricky, but they played in a shuffleboard tournament, and the Aga Khan insisted on taking them to his library and showing them his collection of rare manuscripts. Finally they were alone, and Lily took a deep breath.

"I've never seen anything like it." Lily leaned against the railing. "The ballrooms resemble a palazzo in Venice, and the staterooms are like the palaces described in a Rudyard Kipling book. I half expected to see a tiger or some impossibly sleek cheetah."

"The Aga Khan does have exquisite taste," Ricky agreed, standing beside her.

"And the food!" Lily sighed. "It's as if Michelin-starred chefs from all over the world gathered in one place. The Scottish salmon with wilted spinach was superb, and the caramel *croquembouche* could have been served at the finest restaurant in Paris."

"This suits you," Ricky mused. "Standing on the deck of a super-yacht with a champagne flute in your hand."

"Who wouldn't look good with the breeze blowing her hair and a ruby pendant around her neck." Lily laughed. "It's like when I attended the fashion shows in Milan. You think you must have the organza dress that resembles a birthday cake or the sheath that leaves you half naked until you picture wearing it on the street. Some things are best left as a fantasy."

"This isn't a fantasy at all." Ricky waved his hand. "Do you remember when I said I want to help you be happy? You're happy here. Your eyes sparkle, and you are radiant as a girl."

"I'm having a wonderful time. The yacht is spectacular, and the food is delicious, and the air smells of the finest cologne," Lily agreed. "But tomorrow I'll worry whether we received enough RSVPs for the grand opening and if I made Louisa's dentist appointment. "

"This doesn't have to end." He touched her hand. "I'm not going to let you go just because you have to get on a plane."

"I have to live close to Oliver because of Louisa, and I work fifty-hour weeks," she explained. "I can't flit off to Sardinia for the weekend."

"I'm falling in love with you, and I think you feel the same." He kissed her. "We need to give ourselves a chance."

Lily stepped back and fiddled with her earrings.

"I do have feelings for you. But there is something we haven't talked about," she began. "We can't keep secrets from each other."

"What kind of secrets?" he asked.

"Any kind." She shrugged. "We need to be able to tell each other everything."

"There is something I haven't told you," he admitted. "Do you remember when you came into my store, and I gave you my card? Then you called and invited me to lunch." He paused. "I had already rung all the hotels in Porto Cervo looking for you. I couldn't let you disappear."

"Is that the only thing you haven't told me?" she breathed.

"Of course it's the only thing," Ricky said and took her hand. "Let's go inside. The Aga Khan asked us to play dominos, and we shouldn't keep him waiting."

Lily swallowed and tears pricked her eyes. If Ricky was capable of lying, they didn't have anything at all.

"All this champagne gave me a headache," she said. "Please give the Aga Khan my regrets. I'm going back to the hotel."

"Did I say something wrong?" he asked.

"It's nothing." She hurried down the stairs and stepped onto the dock.

"Lily, wait!" He ran after her. "Something changed. You have to tell me what I did."

Her heart thudded and she looked at Ricky. His dark eyes shone in the moonlight, and he had never looked so handsome.

"I lost a ruby from the pendant. I felt terrible, I thought you'd be disappointed," she began. "I went to the jewelry store to replace it, and the salesman said you bought an engagement ring last year. You brought your fiancée, she was American, and her name was Poppy.

"How could you have been engaged and never have been in love before?" She looked up, and her eyes were huge. "And why didn't you tell me?"

"In Sardinia, men are not supposed to show their weaknesses," he began saying. "Poppy arrived on a yacht last summer. She was very pretty, and we swam and went horseback riding.

"She was on the Emerald Coast because she had just broken off an engagement. Everything had been arranged: the ceremony at St. James Church and the reception at the Pierre. She was afraid if she returned to America, she would be convinced to go through with it.

"Somehow I thought the best solution was to marry her. You couldn't help but be dazzled by Poppy, she was like bubbles in champagne. We went shopping for a ring and planned to elope." He paused. "A week later, her fiancé, Grant, appeared. Poppy hadn't told me the correct story. Grant had gotten cold feet and called off the engagement.

"Poppy wanted to make him jealous. She sent him photos of the engagement ring, and Grant arrived on the next plane. Poppy returned my ring and said she hoped we could still be friends.

"I was too proud to tell you," he finished. "What woman would want a man who has been discarded by someone else?"

"I wouldn't have cared," she said. "You should have told me the truth."

"There are many things I have to learn about love, but I would never hurt you," he pleaded. "Will you forgive me?"

Ricky pulled her close and kissed her. She kissed him back, and the dock seemed to spin. If she let him go, would she ever feel this way again?

"I forgive you," she whispered and felt like her heart would explode.

Ricky grabbed her hand, and his face broke into a smile. He opened the door of the red convertible, and she slid into the passenger seat.

"Where are we going?" she asked.

"Somewhere completely private." He jumped in beside her.

They drove into the hills and stopped in front of a stone villa. There was a fountain, and there were green trellises.

"It's a little sparse inside." He opened her car door. "My sister offered to furnish it, but I want to do it myself. "

Lily followed him into a tile entryway. The living room had rounded plaster walls and a patterned rug. There was a low white sofa with scattered cushions.

"The villa belonged to an American artist. At first, he couldn't convince me to buy it. The bathroom doesn't have a tub, and the stove only works if you blow in it. But then he brought me out here." He led her to the patio. "I was like all the visitors who arrive on the Emerald Coast and never want to leave. I told him he could have every penny in my bank account, as long as he sold me this house."

Lily inhaled the scent of myrtle and gasped. The view was of the whole coastline, and the sky was filled with a thousand stars. Yachts gleamed in the harbor, and she could see the lights of Porto Cervo.

"It's the most beautiful place I've ever seen." She nodded.

"Before it was beautiful." He touched her cheek. "With you, it is a slice of heaven."

Ricky's hand fumbled under her dress, and she wondered if they were rushing into things. But if she asked to go home, they might not get another chance. She was a divorced woman on the brink of a love affair; she couldn't stop now.

"I'm terribly thirsty." She hesitated. "I'd give anything for another glass of champagne."

Ricky found a bottle of champagne and two glasses and brought them into the living room. They sat on the sofa and talked about the Aga Khan's yacht and Ricky's store.

"When Louisa was born, Oliver smuggled champagne into the hospital. I wasn't supposed to drink, but he said one glass wouldn't hurt. And it was perfect! I wasn't nervous about being a new mother." She stopped and flushed. "I shouldn't be talking about Oliver. I would understand if you wanted to take me home."

"On the contrary, I think you and I feel the same," he said.

"The same?" She looked up.

"We're both nervous about what's going to happen next. But we don't want to miss out."

Ricky gathered her in his arms and carried her into the bedroom. There was a king-sized bed and a dresser with a vase of sunflowers.

He unzipped her dress, and it fell to the floor. Lily turned and unbuttoned his shirt.

"I'm falling in love with you," Ricky whispered and drew her onto the bed.

"I'm falling in love with you too," Lily murmured.

His fingers made circles around the small of her back and her body tightened. She pulled him on top of her, and he gasped. She'd forgotten what it was like to be with a new man. The sheets were crisp against her skin, and she felt almost electric. He pushed inside her, and she savored his weight and then the exquisite opening.

He moved faster, and she dug her fingers into his back. Her body shuddered, and all she could feel was the deep throbbing and the warmth exploding inside her

"Love is a very good thing," Ricky moaned and pulled her close.

"I agree," Lily breathed and tucked herself against his chest.

Lily stood at the window and smoothed her hair. Ricky was asleep, but suddenly she was thirsty. She padded into the kitchen and poured a glass of sparkling water.

She moved through the living room and noticed a wooden coffee table. There was a stack of envelopes on it and a bowl of fruit.

She picked up a peach and remembered when Oliver had given her a peach at the train station. She had been certain they would be in love forever. Now she was standing in a strange man's living room on the Emerald Coast.

She waited to become anxious, but all she felt was a giddy excitement. She climbed into the bed beside Ricky and closed her eyes.

Chapter Twelve

OLIVER STRAIGHTENED HIS COLLAR AND sighed. It was ridiculous to worry about what to wear to visit a jewelry store. But if he wore his usual T-shirt and shorts, the salesgirl would think he wasn't worth her time. If he put on his Tom Ford blazer, she'd lead him to the biggest diamonds. He finally settled on a Brooks Brothers shirt and a pair of slacks. His hair was freshly washed, and his cheeks were clean shaven.

He had spent the morning deciding how to propose to Angela. At first he thought he'd litter the suite with rose petals and have a candlelit dinner. But Angela was a florist; she saw engagements like that all the time. And he never understood why couples got engaged at expensive restaurants. The other diners cheered, and it was like being at a children's birthday party.

The concierge suggested he rent a catamaran and sail around the bay. There would be a basket of scampi and strawberries with fresh cream. Oliver pictured Angela in a striped bikini and thought nothing could be more perfect.

Now he entered Floris Coroneo and glanced around the space.

A woman wearing a linen dress sat behind a mahogany desk. There was a yellow orchid in a crystal vase and a silver vault.

"May I help you?" The saleswoman looked up. Her hair was pulled into a chignon and she had long eyelashes.

"I'm looking for an engagement ring." He approached the desk.

"What did you have in mind?" she asked.

"My fiancée is a florist in Manhattan," he began. "She's quite stunning. I want something she'd be proud to wear."

"I have the perfect ring." The woman stood up and opened the vault.

Oliver's eyes adjusted to the dark, and he gasped. Glass cases were filled with diamonds the size of small birds. There was a row of sapphires and a pink stone that deserved its own armed guard.

"The right ring reflects not only the woman wearing it but the man who gave it to her." She handed him a baguette-cut diamond flanked by emeralds. "This is from our Extremely Piaget collection. The stones are chosen for their vibrant color and ability to catch the light."

Oliver glanced at the price tag. "I don't need Extremely Piaget. Simple Piaget will do."

"The ring is the most important purchase in a marriage." She pursed her lips. "Price shouldn't be a concern."

"That's fine unless you live in a Manhattan apartment that costs more than those villages in France they try to sell you over the Internet." He sighed. "I can spend two thousand euros."

"We have key chains for that price." She raised her eyebrow.

"I know the brochures say the marriage is only as good as the ring. But you can buy a piece of tin, and the marriage can last forever. Or you can splurge on a five-carat diamond and have it end up at a pawn shop in Las Vegas," Oliver said. "I want something elegant that won't empty my bank account."

The woman opened a drawer and pulled out a velvet pouch. She handed Oliver a platinum band set with an oval diamond. "This is from our friendship ring collection. I suppose it could be an engagement ring."

"I'll take it," he said after checking the price tag and handing her his credit card. "If I pay extra, could you put it an Extremely Piaget box?"

Oliver stepped onto the cobblestones and wiped his brow. Getting married was exhausting. First you had to propose and then you had to plan the wedding. By the time you slipped into the back of a Bentley, you felt as if you'd completed an obstacle course.

It had been worth it with Lily, of course. They'd had so many good years: their first apartment in San Francisco where they hung the laundry on the fire escape; buying a dining room table so they could give proper dinner parties. But you'd think if you went to so much trouble to get married, it would be harder to undo. All it took was a visit to an attorney, and it unraveled like a stray thread on his shirt.

He thought about the first time he had returned to the farmhouse after he moved out. Suddenly, somewhere that was so familiar had seemed brand-new.

Oliver perched on a sofa in the farmhouse's living room and fiddled with his glass. He had only been gone a month, but he didn't recognize the silk cushions or the ceramic vase filled with tulips. Lily had replaced their wedding photo with a picture of Louisa at summer camp, and there was an unopened bottle of sherry on the side table.

"I'm sorry I kept you waiting." Lily stood in the hallway. She wore slacks and a wool sweater. "I was showing the new handyman around the barn."

"You shouldn't be home alone with a strange man," Oliver said.

"George is a retired war veteran." She smiled. "He's perfectly harmless."

"How harmless can he be if he held an M16 for a living?" he grumbled. "And we didn't need a handyman when I lived here."

"Well, now I do," she answered. "He's already replaced the furnace filters and caulked the windows."

"I see you're entertaining." He pointed to the bottle of sherry.

"That's cooking sherry. Even if I was dating, I wouldn't dream of bringing a man to the house." She paused. "Honestly, Oliver, I thought it was a good idea to divide the furniture together. If you're going to behave like a home inspector, we can have the attorney do it."

"I didn't think everything would look so . . . changed," he said. Even Lily looked different. Her lipstick was a new color, and her hair was brushed in a different style.

"I brought in a few accessories from the store to freshen things up." She shrugged. "I'd like to keep the floral sofa, but you're welcome to whatever you like."

"I'd like to move my things out of that overpriced West Village apartment and back into my closet."

"We both wanted a divorce," she reminded him. "It was the only solution."

"You suggested it, and I couldn't think of a reason not to." He looked at Lily. "But if you give me some time, I will."

"We tried for months, and it only got worse." She shook her head. "And it wasn't fair to Louisa. She never knew if her parents would be sharing a slice of cheesecake or throwing darts at each other."

"We never threw anything," Oliver said. "Except the surprise thirtieth birthday party you threw for me at Per Se. It was one of the best nights of my life."

She picked up a pen and a pad of paper. "Would you like our bedroom set or the daybed in the guest room?"

"I don't want to sleep in a bed we shared." He shuddered. "And you need the daybed for Louisa's friends. I would like the desk in the library. We bought it because we thought I might turn my reviews into a book," he mused. "We imagined it hitting number one on the *New York Times* Best Seller List. We even made an invitation list for the launch party: Gordon Ramsay and Rachael Ray and Anthony Bourdain."

"We had been drinking too much champagne." She laughed. "We didn't think those people would come."

"I thought so." His eyes flickered. "Together we could accomplish anything."

"I have to pick Louisa up from ballet. Make a list of everything you want, and I'll check it when I return." She slipped a ring off her finger. "I want you to have my engagement ring."

"You can't give back the ring!" he protested. "It's been on your finger for ten years. That's like cutting off an arm or a leg."

"You don't expect me to wear it?" she asked. "You should keep it, in case you get married again."

"You can at least save it for Louisa," he suggested.

"She'll inherit my mother's ring." She pressed it into his hand. "I remember when you bought it. I told you not to spend any money, but you gave Guido's cousin everything under your mattress."

"I don't want it," Oliver snapped. "And I'm never getting married again. I have my career and Louisa. Maybe I'll travel. We never made it to Greece."

"Of course you'll get married," she countered. "You're young and handsome and successful."

"If I'm so eligible, why don't we stay married?" he demanded.

"Because if someone mentions Roger's name, you go through the roof. And if I see Mirabelle in the street, I'll run in the other direction." She paused. "We can't look at each other without causing ourselves pain. And we've stopped making each other happy."

"Maybe a little pain is better than nothing at all," he murmured.

"It's not, Oliver, trust me." She gathered her purse. "I have to go. I'll see you later."

Lily's car drove away, and Oliver glanced around the room. The only thing he wanted was to have everything back the way it was: he would arrive home from the train, and Lily would greet him with a martini and a bowl of pistachio nuts. But she was right; it hadn't been like that for months.

He dropped the engagement ring on the table and finished his drink. He grabbed the bowl of nuts and walked out the door.

Oliver strolled along the marina and stuffed his hands into his pockets. Lily had predicted he would get married again; she knew him better than he knew himself. He was glad he'd told her he was going to propose to Angela. He didn't want her finding out when Louisa announced there was a new woman in Daddy's bed.

He had considered telling her Angela was pregnant and changed his mind. He didn't want Lily to think it was a shotgun wedding. No one was forcing him to marry Angela; he'd made the decision himself.

A familiar woman stood inside a boutique, and he froze. Her bronze hair was hidden by a wide hat, and she wore a knit dress. She was talking to a man with dark hair and tan cheeks.

He looked closer and realized it was Angela. And the man she was talking to was Ricky! What on earth was she doing in Ricky's store? He remembered when they'd all eaten dinner at the Yacht Club. Surely Angela and Ricky hadn't formed a friendship?

He was being ridiculous. Angela visited every clothing store in Porto Cervo. They were probably discussing a line of swimsuits or whether she could wear red with her hair.

He could walk in and say hello, but the engagement ring was in his pocket. What if Angela asked where he had been? He was a terrible liar and he didn't want to ruin the surprise. He would go back to the suite and make sure the champagne bottle was chilled.

The horizon was a brilliant green, and Oliver adjusted his sunglasses. The jewelry box jiggled in his pocket, and he couldn't believe his good fortune. He was gazing at the most spectacular coastline in the world and about to propose to a beautiful woman.

Oliver paced around the suite and tossed a piece of paper into the garbage. He wanted to propose with a poem, but he couldn't find the right words. He clicked through photos of Angela for inspiration. There were pictures of Angela jogging and doing yoga. He studied a photo he'd taken at the hotel pool and a warmth spread through his chest. God, she was stunning, with her flaming hair and high breasts.

Marrying Angela really was a good idea; they would have fabulous-looking children. And she was so ambitious. Last night, she'd disappeared for hours because a celebrity-wedding planner was interested in her designs. She returned at midnight with stories of Eva Longoria's wedding to José Bastón in Mexico and John Legend and Chrissy Teigen's three-day event on Lake Como.

He retrieved the paper and thought he was being too hard on himself. It didn't have to be Shakespeare; it was about the sentiment. The garbage can fell over, and a wad of tissue paper fell out. He bent down to pick it up and noticed a purple stick.

Angela's pregnancy test! He remembered when Lily had come flying out of the bathroom in their San Francisco apartment, waving the stick in her hand. Her pregnancy had been a surprise, and they'd both felt like they'd won at blackjack without putting money on the table.

Lily kept the stick in her drawer for a week to make sure the two lines were still there. It was only when she got morning sickness and couldn't get out of bed without eating saltines that she tossed it in the garbage.

Now he picked up the stick and frowned. Why was there only one line? He'd seen enough commercials to know that a positive result always had two pink lines.

Angela wouldn't lie about her pregnancy; it didn't make sense. She hadn't even insisted they get married; she was content to raise the baby herself. But why did she wrap the stick in tissue paper unless she didn't want him to see it?

He would have to find out before he proposed. His head throbbed, and there was a pain in his neck. If he was going to ask her a difficult question, he needed a stiff drink. He grabbed his key and walked out the door. He hurried down the staircase and entered the Piano Bar.

Oliver signaled the bartender to refill his glass. He wasn't sure how long he had been sitting in the booth. It was long enough to finish two Bellinis and watch an older man wearing a gold watch pick up a young woman in a spandex dress.

He remembered when he and Lily were first together. They spent hours in restaurants observing other couples. Lily laughed and made him promise he would never leave her for a younger woman. Oliver assured her that couldn't happen if they were married for fifty years.

How could they have been so sure about everything and let it slip away? And what if he got things wrong again? But Angela said she was falling in love with him. Maybe it was an old pregnancy test, and she took it again. How reliable could something that came with a two-for-one sticker at the local pharmacy be?

"Oliver, there you are." Angela entered the bar. She wore over-sized sunglasses and carried a shopping bag. "Why did you want to meet here? I thought we were going out on a boat."

"I needed a drink first," he stated.

Her mouth was painted red, and she'd never looked more stunning. Maybe he should forget the whole thing and board the catamaran. They would drink champagne and marvel at the turquoise ocean. After he proposed, they would make love on a round bed in the cabin. It would be like an adult version of the Rose Ceremony on *The Bachelor*.

But there couldn't be secrets in their relationship. Look what had happened to him and Lily. He had to find out if Angela was hiding something.

"I'm going to order an Orange Cervo," Angela said. "I had it at Cala di Volpe last night: mint leaves and orange juice and sugar. It was the most delicious drink I ever tasted."

They waiter disappeared, and Angela looked at Oliver. "You shouldn't be sitting in a bar in the afternoon, you're quite pale. We're on the Emerald Coast, you need to spend more time in the sun."

"I was writing you a poem and found something," he began.

"A poem?" She raised her eyebrow.

"I was going to propose on the catamaran. I bought a ring this morning from the Extremely Piaget collection. But I knocked over the garbage can in our suite and discovered your pregnancy test," he said and stopped. "It only had one pink line."

The waiter arrived with Angela's drink, and she took a long sip. She fiddled with her earring, and Oliver thought it was the longest moment of his life.

"That's because I'm not pregnant," she said.

"I don't understand," he stuttered. "You were pregnant yesterday. You insisted I marry you."

"I would never make you do anything," she corrected. "It was your choice."

"Were you ever pregnant?" he gasped.

"I guess not," she said slowly. "It was Ricky's idea."

"Ricky?" Oliver looked around for a paramedic; he was certain he was having a heart attack.

"I ran into him at the pharmacist while I was buying a pregnancy test. I thought I was pregnant, but it turned out to be indigestion; the clams at the Yacht Club were a bit off.

"Ricky was standing in line, and we exchanged greetings. A few hours later I ran into him on the dock. He said he wanted to talk about something and suggested we get a cup of coffee. He said he happened to notice I was buying a pregnancy test and wondered if I was pregnant. I told him it was a false alarm, and he asked if I could do him a favor." She paused. "He saw the way you behaved at the Yacht Club and thought you still had feelings for Lily. He wanted me to pretend I was pregnant. He's quite taken with Lily and doesn't want to lose her. He thought if you were committed to me, Lily would allow herself to fall in love with him."

"At first I thought it was a ridiculous idea. But you got so upset when I mentioned I wanted a family. I didn't want to keep dating you and miss my best childbearing years.

"Don't worry, I was going to invent a miscarriage before our wedding. You would have had time to bow out if you were only marrying me because I was pregnant." She sipped her drink. "Now that it's out in the open, we can forget the whole thing. Ricky doesn't have anything to worry about because we're getting married. And Lily would be crazy not to fall for him. He looks like an Italian film star."

"What do you mean we're getting married!" Oliver exclaimed. "You lied to me."

"Please, Oliver." She sighed. "I don't expect our marriage to be an open book. I'm sure I'll keep a secret bank account, and you don't have to tell me about every office flirtation, as long as they don't get out of hand."

"Honesty is the most important part of a relationship," he declared. "Without it, you have nothing at all."

"That's interesting, coming from you," she said. "The whole reason you got divorced was because you lied to Lily."

"It was the greatest mistake of my life. I'm not going to repeat it," he insisted. "I can't marry someone who isn't truthful."

"We're not even married yet. Think of it as an exercise they do in premarital counseling. You see how each member of the couple reacts to an unplanned pregnancy. You get an A +." She looked at Oliver. "We don't want one little setback to ruin our future. You're handsome and dynamic and caring. I really think I'm falling in love with you."

"We're not going to have any future," he seethed. "I want you to leave."

"You want me to leave?" she repeated.

"Get out of my room. Go back to New York." He waved his hand. "I don't care what you do. I don't want to see you again."

"You really want me to leave?" She wet her lips. "I suppose I could join Gaston in Mykonos. He's the celebrity-wedding planner I told you about. He's doing a wedding next week, and the florist dropped out. It's very hush-hush, he couldn't tell me who's getting married. I'm sure you'll read about it in *Us* magazine."

"That's an excellent plan." He nodded. "Your passport is in the hotel safe."

"Are you sure you're not overreacting?" she offered. "Why don't we go out on the catamaran, and you can calm down. I bought ceviche and Sardinian flatbread. It's excellent with a cold chardonnay."

Oliver studied her plump mouth and realized he would never kiss her again. And those breasts! How could anything bring him so much pleasure just by existing? For a moment, he was tempted to help her pack. They could have one more frolic in bed or interlude in the shower. But he was too old to have sex without a relationship. It was like when he'd become a teenager and grown out of comic books.

"Why don't you collect your things?" He handed her the key. "I'll sit here until you leave."

"I think you're being a little heartless. I put a lot of effort into our relationship. Everyone makes mistakes; you know that better than anyone. I really think we had something special." Angela stood up. "But I'm not going to beg. I'll pack and be gone before you go on up." She grabbed her bag. "It's too bad. We could have had a wonderful life if you had given us a chance."

"Angela, wait." Oliver stopped her.

She turned and rubbed her lips. Her dress clung to her hips, and he noticed the mole on her cheek.

"Yes, Oliver?" she asked.

"I am grateful for the time we spent together. It couldn't have been easy dating a newly divorced man," he answered. "You helped me find my old spark again. Good luck with your business."

"Good-bye, Oliver." She tossed her hair over her shoulders. "I'm sure we'll run into each other in New York."

————

Oliver stood on the balcony of his suite and watched speedboats skim over the waves. Yachts gleamed in the harbor, and the sea was the color of topaz.

A few hours ago, he'd imagined he could steer a Jet Ski while shoving a Russian villain into shark-infested waters like James Bond. Now he felt as ineffectual as the purple dinosaur on Louisa's television show. How dare Ricky interfere with his life?

But he couldn't blame Ricky. Angela only had to say no. What kind of woman agreed to pretend to be pregnant as a favor? Ricky hadn't asked to borrow a cup of sugar.

Of course it was better that he'd found out what Angela was capable of now. And he really wasn't ready for marriage. But he had gotten used to her. Angela had a way of making him feel important and successful.

He entered the living room and thought of everything he had to do: cancel the catamaran and return the engagement ring and tell Lily.

Lily! Would Lily think this was his fault? If he hadn't tried to save her from eating the tiramisu, Ricky never would have asked Angela to lie. It didn't matter if Lily was angry with him. She had to know what Ricky had done.

Angela had left her shopping bag on the coffee table. He opened the bag and took out a gold maillot. His fingers touched the fabric, and he sighed. First he would take a cold shower, then he would worry about everything else.

Chapter Thirteen

LILY ARRANGED CUSHIONS ON A striped love seat and wiped her hands on her dress. It was mid afternoon, and she had been working at Lily Bristol all day. Tomorrow was the grand opening, and she was so excited.

The showroom had a beamed ceiling and rounded plaster walls. There were linens she'd discovered at an outdoor market in San Pantaleo and woven rugs from Olbia. And the colors! Turquoise towels were stacked on an antique dresser, and magenta cushions were strewn over a daybed.

She noticed a new text on her phone and smiled. Ricky had dropped her off at Hotel Cervo this morning. He'd already sent a dozen texts, and a bouquet of tulips had arrived with a note asking her to dinner.

They still had so much to work out: how they would keep in touch, and when they would see each other. But they could Skype and send messages. And it only took eight hours to fly from Sardinia to New York.

She caught her reflection in the window and laughed. Her eyes sparkled, and a smile lit up her face. She wanted to bottle the feeling and sell it at the cash register next to the tins of almonds.

A bell tinkled over the door, and Lily looked up. Oliver stood at the entrance, clutching a shopping bag.

"What are you doing here?" she asked.

"I brought you a gift for the grand opening." He handed her the bag. "It's a statue of Vesta, the Roman goddess of the home."

"You didn't have to do that." She took out the statue. "Thank you, it's lovely."

"I always bring you a gift when you open a new store." He glanced around the space. "Everything looks fantastic."

"I'm terrified the caterer will run out of ravioli or I didn't buy enough champagne." She paused. "But I do like it. I'm so glad I decided to open a store on the Emerald Coast."

"Do you remember when you opened Lily Bristol San Francisco?" he asked. "You were worried that no one would come because there was a Forty-niners playoff game. But we couldn't fit all the people in the store and ran out of mimosas in the first hour."

"Grand openings are always exhilarating." She sighed. "So much can go wrong, and then I'm relieved when everything turns out."

"This is going to be your most successful store yet," he declared.

Lily glanced at her watch and remembered she was meeting Ricky in a few hours. "I still have a lot to do. Thank you for the gift, but I have to go."

"That's not the only reason I came," Oliver began. "I want to talk to you about something."

"If you want more advice on your wedding, now isn't the time." She moved through the store. "You and Angela can come to the opening."

"It's not about Angela and me." He paused. "It's about Ricky."

"Don't tell me you were spying when Ricky dropped me off at the hotel this morning!" Her eyes flashed. "Honestly, Oliver, I can sleep wherever I like. I'd appreciate it if you stay out of my love life."

"You spent the night at Ricky's?" he gasped.

"Yes, Oliver. I'm not a postdivorce virgin anymore." She flushed. "Now can I get back to work? I'm sure Angela is waiting for you to work on the guest list."

"Angela and I aren't getting married," he said.

Lily stopped and turned back in surprise.

"But you were so excited about proposing to her."

"I was going to marry her because she was pregnant," he began. "That wasn't the only reason; she didn't force me to do it. I admire her and thought I was falling in love with her." He shuffled his feet. "But she wasn't pregnant. She lied to me."

"Oh, Oliver, that's awful. I don't understand." Lily perched on a stool. "Angela is so focused on her career. She's not the type of woman who would fake a pregnancy to get a man."

"She didn't do it for herself." He looked up. "Ricky asked her to."

"What did you say?" Lily gasped.

"Ricky and Angela ran into each other at the pharmacist. She thought she was pregnant but it turned out to be a stomachache. Ricky said he needed a favor. He was afraid I still have feelings for you. He was worried that you might not let yourself fall in love with him. He asked Angela to pretend to be pregnant so he wouldn't lose you."

"That's absurd." Lily jumped up. "Why would Ricky think you still have feelings for me?"

"We all had dinner at the Yacht Club, and I saved you from

eating the tiramisu," he explained. "He thought I was still in love with you."

"That was hardly a declaration of love. If someone's choking and you perform the Heimlich maneuver, it doesn't mean you want to marry them."

"Ricky thought so." He shrugged. "He didn't want the competition."

"That's a charming fantasy, but I don't believe a word of it." She straightened a pile of napkins.

"You have to believe it," he insisted. "Why would Angela make it up?"

"Angela lied about being pregnant," she reminded him. "She could lie about anything. That's the problem with online dating. People make up so many things, they forget how to tell the truth."

"Angela and I didn't meet online, we met at a restaurant opening." He fumed. "And you just said she didn't need a man. I'm hardly some marketing genius who can help her career. And I might be good-looking, but I'm no Brad Pitt."

Lily studied Oliver's dark hair and blue eyes and smiled. There were new lines on his forehead, but he still looked like the boy she'd met at the train station in Naples.

"Ricky would never do such a thing. We're having dinner tonight and we're going to talk about our future. He's hardworking and sincere and . . ."

She suddenly thought about Ricky hiding his proposal to Poppy and felt slightly dizzy.

"Are you all right?" Oliver asked.

"I've been working too hard. I just need a glass of water."

"I know that look." He poured a glass of water from a pitcher.

"It's like when they killed off your favorite character on *Scandal*. There's something you're not telling me about Ricky."

"Ricky did shade the truth about something, but it's not important."

"The truth is always important," he urged. "What happened?"

"He said he's never been in love before," she said. "But then I found out he had been engaged and didn't tell me. I asked him about it, and he said she was American. It turned out she wasn't in love with him. She only agreed to marry him to make her boyfriend jealous. He was too ashamed to mention it."

"You mean he lied to you," Oliver said.

"It was a little white lie," she said, and her eyes narrowed. "I know what you're doing! Angela jilted you, and you don't want me to be happy. You made all this up so I would break up with Ricky."

"Why would I do that?" he demanded.

"Because you can't stand the thought of me being happy," she answered. "Well, I am happy, Oliver. That's not going to change. If you'll excuse me, I have a dozen things to do."

"You've got it all wrong." He walked to the door and turned around. "But I guess you'll have to find out for yourself."

The door slammed, and Lily leaned against the glass. Would Oliver really lie to her? He had never hurt her intentionally. But he couldn't be telling the truth; it was too terrible to think about.

She tried to thread the story together, like one of Louisa's daisy chains. It was possible Angela was lying, but she couldn't see why. With Angela's brains and figure, she could have any man she wanted.

Ricky was warm and caring, and he was truly in love with her.

She had never been more certain of anything. But he had lied about Poppy. What if there was some truth to what Oliver said?

If only she could talk to Poppy, she could find out if Ricky had been telling the truth about their engagement. But she didn't even know Poppy's last name. She could hardly scroll through Ricky's contacts or search his emails.

She suddenly remembered the woman she'd met on Christoff's yacht who had known Ricky for years. All those people moved in the same circles. Their lives consisted of flitting between the Greek Islands and the South of France. Maybe Marjorie knew something about Ricky and Poppy.

Lily smoothed her hair and rubbed her lips with lipstick. She grabbed her purse and hurried out the door.

Lily leaned against the railing of Christoff's yacht and sighed. She had searched the shuffleboard court and movie theater. She'd interrupted a chess tournament, but she couldn't find Marjorie.

She was about to leave when she saw a woman in a blue bathing suit. Her eyes were closed and there was a magazine folded on her stomach.

"Do you remember me?" Lily hurried across the deck. "We met a few days ago."

Marjorie opened her eyes and sat up.

"Of course! The brunette who was with Ricky," she exclaimed. "I haven't seen him at all. You must be keeping each other busy."

"I wonder if I could talk to you." Lily glanced around at couples lounging in deck chairs. "It's quite personal."

"It sounds more interesting than the squash game I was invited to," Marjorie replied. "Why don't we go into my stateroom?"

Lily perched on a cream sofa and fiddled with her earrings. The room had a walnut desk and king-sized bed and a window seat scattered with cushions. A sideboard was set with platters of soft cheeses and slices of orange.

"Christoff's yacht is heavenly. It will be a shame when the summer is over." Marjorie handed Lily a glass of papaya juice. "Now tell me what's wrong, it must have something to do with Ricky."

"We've gotten quite serious about each other," Lily admitted. "I didn't mean for it to happen. I'm only here to open Lily Bristol. But he's falling in love with me, and I feel the same."

"Then what's the problem?" Marjorie asked. "Ricky is one of the most eligible bachelors on the Emerald Coast."

"I discovered he'd been engaged and didn't mention it," Lily said. "Her name was Poppy, and they met last summer. I wonder if you knew her."

"Of course I know Poppy!" Marjorie exclaimed. "Her home base is New York, but she spends most of her time cruising around the Aegean. I remember seeing them together, but I never imagined they were engaged."

"Then you don't know why they broke up." Lily's shoulders sagged. If Marjorie couldn't help her, she didn't know what she'd do.

"It couldn't have been too traumatic. Poppy got married in April. I attended her wedding. It was in a garden in Kent, and it rained. The whole thing had to be moved inside."

"She got married?" Lily felt a warmth spread through her chest. Ricky was telling the truth! Poppy had only gotten engaged to him to make her fiancé jealous.

"Apparently it was a whirlwind courtship," Marjorie continued.

"She met Anthony on a chairlift in Gstaad and got married three months later."

"O-oh, I-I see," Lily stammered. "Thank you for telling me. You've been a great help."

"I haven't been a help at all." Marjorie frowned. "You look like I just told you I had to put your dog to sleep."

"Ricky said Poppy only agreed to marry him to make her boyfriend jealous. As soon as Ricky's ring was on her finger, he showed up and asked her to marry him. Poppy called off the engagement and went back to her boyfriend."

"That is a different story," Marjorie agreed. "Why don't you ask Poppy? I have her number in my contacts."

"I can't call a woman I've never met." Lily shook her head.

"Of course you can," Marjorie said. "When you're in love, you have to fight for what you want. And if you're going to get hurt, it's best to know now."

Lily remembered driving up to Ricky's villa with the wind blowing her hair. He'd squeezed her hand and said he was falling in love with her.

"I suppose you're right." She nodded.

"I'll send Poppy a message and tell her you'll call." Marjorie ate a slice of orange and tossed the peel on the plate. "You think love gets easier when you're cruising the Mediterranean, but it never does. Women have to help each other. Who else do we have?"

Lily stood in front of her dresser and brushed her cheeks with powder. She smoothed her hair and wished Oliver had never entered Lily Bristol. She had been so looking forward to eating suckling pig with eggplant. Now there was a knot in her stomach, and she could barely swallow.

What if she didn't call Poppy? They'd sip a gold liqueur and discuss when Ricky could come to New York. He would touch her cheek, and she would feel so happy.

But Marjorie was right; if Ricky had lied, she had to know now. She punched Poppy's number into her phone and pressed send.

"Hello." A female voice came over the line. "Who's calling?"

"This is Lily Bristol." Lily suddenly felt like a teenager making a prank call at a slumber party.

"Marjorie said you would call, but she didn't tell me what it was about," Poppy answered. "I'm on a yacht in Ibiza, and reception is terrible. I hope you can hear me."

"I can hear you perfectly," Lily said. "I'm calling about Ricky Pirelli."

"That's a name I didn't expect to hear again." Poppy laughed.

"Ricky and I are involved, and I discovered he was engaged to you last summer. I wondered if you could tell me why it didn't work out."

"You mean why Ricky and I didn't get married?" Poppy asked.

"Yes." Lily flushed. "I hope I'm not being too personal."

"If you'd called a few months ago, I would have hung up," Poppy said. "I was so hurt, I thought I'd never recover. But I met Anthony, and now I feel so lucky."

"Recover from what?" Lily asked.

"From Ricky dumping me on our wedding day."

"What did you say?" Lily sunk onto the sofa and stared out the window. The sun melted over the horizon, and the sea was a muted purple.

"I met Ricky at a party on the yacht. God, he was gorgeous,

with those dark eyes and chiseled cheeks." She paused. "We played tennis and swam and went horseback riding. Then all of a sudden, he got serious. We took a day trip to the village of Arzachena. We were browsing in the outdoor market, and he stopped in front of a jewelry stall. He bought a glass ring and said he couldn't bear to be apart. Then he got down on his knee and asked me to marry him.

"I thought he was joking, but he said he had never been more serious. The whole scene was so exotic: pastel-colored villas and hills bursting with wildflowers. I never wanted to leave. I said yes, and everyone cheered, and he slipped the ring on my finger.

"We realized I couldn't wear a glass ring; it would never fly in our circles. Ricky insisted we pick out an engagement ring together; he didn't want to get it wrong. And it was gorgeous! A square sapphire flanked by diamonds.

"I suggested we fly to Manhattan to meet my parents and hold the wedding the following summer. Everyone would have been so disappointed if there wasn't a reception with an orchestra and a twelve-tier wedding cake.

"But he couldn't leave his store. And he was afraid if I went back to New York alone, the whole thing would fizzle. He wanted to have a civil ceremony and host a party next spring.

"I thought that was thrilling. What could be more romantic than a secret ceremony performed by a justice of the peace? I bought a short white dress, and he wore a white suit, and we met at an office off the *piazzetta*. Then I had to show him my passport, and Ricky called the whole thing off."

"Your passport?" Lily repeated.

"I'm based in New York, but my father is British and my mother is from Venezuela. I don't have an American passport."

"I don't understand," Lily replied. "What does that have to do with anything?"

"Ricky always dreamed of opening a clothing store on Fifth Avenue. He needed a green card," she explained. "He had to marry someone with an American passport."

Lily remembered Marjorie saying Ricky adored everything about America, and felt a pain in her chest. She clutched the phone and gasped.

"He just said he didn't want to marry you?"

"He was more diplomatic than that." Poppy paused. "He said he realized how important my family was and he had gone about it all wrong. He suggested he visit New York at Christmas and meet my parents. I might have believed him, but the next day he left for Rome. He said his uncle was ill, and he had to take care of him."

"And after that?" Lily whispered.

"I never heard from him again." Poppy sighed. "I was so angry, I wished I'd kept the ring. It was my idea for him to hold on to it. I didn't want to show up at my parents' apartment wearing an engagement ring from a man they hadn't met." She stopped. "But Anthony is perfect, and we're going to spend part of the year in England. Not the summers, of course, it rains so much, it would be like living in India."

"I'm glad everything turned out," Lily said, and clutched the side of the dresser. "You've been very helpful."

"Ricky is a lot of fun and a wonderful kisser. I hope you'll be happy," Poppy replied. "You're everything he dreamed of."

"What do you mean?" Lily asked.

"Marjorie said you're from New York," she said. "You're exactly what he wanted."

Lily hung up and walked to the dresser. She took the ruby

pendant out of the box and snapped it around her neck. Then she
sank onto the sofa and burst into tears.

Lily sat at an outdoor table at Il Pescatore and moved peaches with
vanilla ice cream around her plate. The sky was thick with stars,
and the air smelled of hibiscus and juniper.

She had wanted to talk to Ricky before dinner, but he was
already seated at the table. Then the maître d' brought a compli-
mentary bottle of pinot noir, and the chef came out to greet them,
and she had to join him.

Ricky ordered scorpion fish and *fregola* pasta, and they talked
about his store and Lily Bristol's grand opening. Lily ate sautéed
cockerel, and her chest tightened. It was all so perfect, with the
boats lapping against the shore and the sound of tinkling glasses.

"You're very quiet." Ricky ate pears with white chocolate. "You
must be tired from preparing for the grand opening. We should
have an early night."

"Oliver came into the store this morning." Lily fiddled with her
spoon.

"Your ex-husband came to see you?" Ricky asked.

"He wanted to see the store." She paused. "He told me yesterday he was going to propose to Angela."

"Does he always share such intimate details about his life?"
Ricky inquired.

"Well, she would be Louisa's stepmother. He was very excited,"
she answered. "But this morning, he said they're not getting married after all. Angela said she was pregnant, but he discovered she
lied to him."

"That's shocking! But it's better he find out now." Ricky

concentrated on his dessert. "That would be a terrible way to start a marriage."

"He asked Angela why she lied, and she said you put her up to it." Lily looked up, and her eyes were huge. "You were afraid Oliver was still in love with me and didn't want the competition."

"That's absurd!" Ricky frowned. "I haven't wanted to say anything, but Oliver seems a little unbalanced. Obviously, Angela jilted him, and he was trying to come between us."

"That's what I thought. I told him he just didn't want me to be happy . . ."

"You see, we agree on everything." Ricky beamed. "I hope he didn't upset you. Let's take our glasses of Mirto and walk along the beach. There is nothing more soothing than the sand between your toes."

"But then I remembered about your engagement to Poppy." Lily kept talking. "I thought if I could find out if you told the truth, I'd be more confident that Oliver was lying.

"So I went to Christoff's yacht and saw a woman I met a few days ago, Marjorie. Marjorie said she attended Poppy's wedding in April."

"Poppy got married?" Ricky looked confused. "That's wonderful news. I'm glad she and her fiancé worked it out."

"Except it didn't match what you told me. Marjorie said it was a whirlwind courtship; Poppy and her husband met in Gstaad and got married three months later. She suggested I call Poppy and find out the truth."

"Lily," Ricky stopped her. "You don't have to go to such measures. I should have told you I was engaged to Poppy, but I was embarrassed. In Sardinia, males are taught to hide their failures."

"It wasn't any trouble getting hold of Poppy. She was on a

yacht in Ibiza. She said you suggested having a civil ceremony because you didn't want her to go back to America without you." She paused. "But when she presented her passport, you stopped the wedding. You wanted to marry her for the same reason you said you are in love with me. All you wanted was a green card."

"Everyone makes up stories after a relationship ends," he implored. "You haven't even met Poppy. How can you believe her? Perhaps she was angry at her new husband and wanted to cause trouble."

"All I wanted was someone to explore the Emerald Coast with. You didn't even have to kiss me." Her eyes glistened. "Then you said you were falling in love with me, and I started to feel the same. How could you lie to me? It's the cruelest thing in the world."

Ricky swallowed the Mirto and placed his glass on the tablecloth. He leaned forward and took her hand.

"You have it all wrong, I am in love with you. You are bright and beautiful, and we share the same goals," he began. "I ran into Angela at the pharmacist and noticed she was buying a pregnancy test. I merely suggested that it would be a pleasant surprise if she were pregnant. I was worried that Oliver still had feelings for you. At the Yacht Club, he behaved like a lovesick figure in a Shakespeare play. But I would never tell Angela to lie about a pregnancy.

"And what happened with Poppy last summer was completely different. You don't understand what it's like growing up on the Emerald Coast. I own a designer boutique, but I'm no different from Petro the newsagent, who sells the *Sunday Times* and Violet Crumble bars. I might get invited on fancy yachts, but they never leave the port. And I could as easily afford one of the Bentleys parked outside my store as a trip to the moon.

"At night, I would read American newspapers and watch American television. You could be successful doing anything: becoming an athlete or a hairdresser or owning a chain of stores. Americans don't care what village you come from, or how many languages you speak, or what schools you attended.

"When I finally got the chance to go to New York, it was better than I dreamed: boulevards wider than Porto Cervo and every kind of shop! I took the escalator to the top of Ralph Lauren, Fifth Avenue, and thought I could have that. Four floors of exclusive fashions on the most important street in the world.

"I came back to the Emerald Coast and met Poppy by accident. We had fun, and she was very pretty, why shouldn't I marry her?" He paused. "Then I found out she didn't have an American passport and got cold feet. I wouldn't even be able to work in New York.

"I stopped the wedding because I needed time to think. Poppy left, and the affair just fizzled." His eyes dimmed. "You have to believe me. I don't care where we live or what we do, I just want to be with you."

"I don't understand." Lily frowned. "Enzo said you were educated abroad and well-traveled."

"I went to a Catholic boys' school in Sicily," Ricky admitted. "And before last summer, I'd never been farther than Rome. But we'll explore the world together. And you can show me San Francisco. I've always wanted to see the Golden Gate Bridge."

"Please stop." Her head ached, and she'd never felt so tired. "Oliver and I met when we were twenty-two, and we were so in love. All we wanted was to be happy. Then he told one small lie, and it was like a tapeworm we couldn't get rid of. I could never be with someone who didn't tell the truth. I've had a lovely time, but

I should go." She pushed back her chair. "I'll return the pendant in the morning."

"Keep the pendant." He walked around the table. His fingers caressed her neck, and she shivered. "Maybe after you sleep on it, you'll change your mind."

"I won't change my mind." She gathered her purse. "Good-bye, Ricky. Thank you for showing me the Emerald Coast."

Lily left the restaurant and hurried along the rocks. How could Ricky lie to her about everything? She'd let herself fall in love and now her heart was breaking.

She took off her sandals and walked along the shore. She remembered running on the beach in Portugal with Oliver on their honeymoon. She pictured building sand castles in Connecticut with Louisa. Ricky said the sand was soothing between your toes, but tonight he was wrong. She perched on a pile of driftwood and let the tears roll down her cheeks.

Lily spread preserves on whole-wheat toast and dusted her omelet with salt. It was the morning after her date with Ricky, and today was the grand opening of Lily Bristol. She stirred sugar into a cup of coffee and walked to the balcony. The sea was like a tapestry, and it was going to be a spectacular day.

After dinner with Ricky, she'd come back to the suite and taken a long bath. She told herself she had one night to cry, and she curled up with a box of tissues and a book she'd bought at the hotel gift shop.

She had been wrong to date so quickly; she had only just gotten divorced. But you couldn't predict or prevent falling in love. The most she could do was concentrate on something else: the grand opening of Lily Bristol and going home to Louisa tomorrow.

There was a knock on the door, and she hoped it was Enzo. She couldn't deliver the pendant to Ricky; she would have Enzo do it. After all, he was her butler.

She opened the door, and Oliver stood in the hallway. He wore khakis, and his arms were folded over his chest.

"You took my breakfast. I can smell the cheese omelet from the hall." He entered her suite.

"What are you talking about?" she asked. "Room service left the tray outside my door half an hour ago."

"I ordered an omelet an hour ago, and it never arrived." He glanced at the tray. "And you hate grilled tomatoes."

Lily noticed the side plate of grilled tomatoes and frowned. Had she forgotten to hang the room service menu on the door last night?

"The tray may have been closer to your suite, but I thought they made a mistake," she conceded. "I always order a cheese omelet when I travel."

"So do I," he reminded her. "I'm the one who told you it's hard to ruin eggs and cheese. It's the safest thing on the menu."

"I guess you're right." She handed him the plate. "Here, you can have it."

Oliver put it back on the table. "You look a little peaked. Why don't we share it?"

"There's only one plate. How will you take it to your room?"

"I'll eat it here." He pulled out a chair and placed a napkin in his lap. "Do you mind pouring me a cup of coffee? And I'd like a piece of toast with butter."

"Help yourself." Lily walked to the dresser. "I need to get ready. I have to be at Lily Bristol in an hour."

"You were just about to have breakfast," he urged. "And it's not healthy to eat standing up. You tell Louisa that all the time."

"All right, Oliver, I'll have breakfast with you." Lily sat at the table. "I don't want any pepper on my side of the omelet."

Oliver cut the omelet in half and pushed hers to the side of the plate.

"We're both out of sorts." He ate a bite of eggs. "If Louisa behaved like this in the morning, we'd tell her to go back upstairs."

"You know how I get before an opening." She smoothed her hair. "I can never sleep."

"Then you shouldn't be drinking coffee," he insisted. "Call room service and order chamomile tea."

"I don't need you telling me what to do." She pushed back her chair. "I'm not hungry after all. You can finish the omelet."

"Lily, wait," Oliver pleaded. "I'm in a terrible mood, and I'm taking it out on you. Angela left last night."

"I'm sorry." Lily sat back down. "But that must be what you wanted."

"What I wanted was for her not to lie to me in the first place," he sighed. "I can't complain. She settled her half of the bill and left me a coupon for a dozen free roses. I'll never use them. I'm done with dating."

"Of course you're going to date." She laughed. "You don't like being alone."

"I'll take a class at the New School and work on a book of restaurant reviews."

"Why don't you take Louisa to Vermont for a week," she suggested. "You can see the leaves change and buy fresh maple syrup."

"You just want the house to yourself so Ricky can stay over." He eyed her carefully. "I don't mind if you introduce him to Louisa, but I'd prefer that he doesn't spend the night. We don't want to set a bad example."

"Ricky isn't coming to America." She brushed crumbs from her dress. "I told him I don't want to see him again."

"That is news." He looked up. "I hope I didn't have anything to do with it."

"Of course you had something to do with it!" Her cheeks flamed. "I decided I had to find out whether Ricky told the truth about his engagement. It turns out he wanted to marry Poppy for the same reason he said he was in love with me." She traced the rim of her cup. "He dreamed of owning a clothing store on Fifth Avenue."

"I don't understand." He frowned.

"He needed to marry someone with an American passport so he could get a green card," she explained. "Of course, he said I got it all wrong, and he was in love with me. But how could I believe him?"

"I'm terribly sorry. I was certain Angela was telling the truth about Ricky," Oliver said. "I had to tell you. I didn't want you to get hurt."

"I can't think about it now," she said quickly. "I have so much to do. Ricky said he was going to help at the grand opening, and I gave Dolores the day off. It's exhausting doing everything myself. But tonight I'm going to curl up with a bowl of soup, and tomorrow I'll get on the plane. I've never been so excited about folding Louisa's laundry."

Oliver put down his cup. "I'll help you at Lily Bristol, if you do something for me."

"Do what for you, Oliver?" she asked.

"Come to the opening of Nero's tonight," he urged. "I hate reviewing restaurants by myself. I get full before the entrée. And it's supposed to be the sexiest restaurant on the Emerald Coast. I don't want to be the only man without a date."

"I'm not going to be your date." She shook her head.

"I didn't mean it like that," he said. "It's just awkward to eat alone. Please, we've come all this way. We don't want to spend our last day on the Emerald Coast by ourselves."

It would be fun to go to the opening of Nero's. And why should she spend her last night on the Emerald Coast alone? She would have plenty of nights by herself when she returned to Connecticut.

"All right, Oliver." She stood up. "I'll go with you. Now I really have to hurry. I'll meet you at Lily Bristol in an hour."

Oliver ate the last bite of omelet and stood up. He walked to the door and turned around.

"Wear that dress you wore at the Yacht Club," he said. "You looked like Audrey Hepburn in *Breakfast at Tiffany's.*"

"You watch too many classic movies." She laughed. "I'll see you later."

Lily slipped on her pumps and glanced at her phone. There was a text from her store manager in San Francisco, wishing her good luck. Even her mother had sent an email saying she was proud of her.

She put on a wide-brimmed hat and grabbed her purse. She would think about Ricky later. She was on her way to the opening of Lily Bristol Sardinia, and it was going to be a great success.

Chapter Fourteen

OLIVER HURRIED ALONG THE COBBLESTONES and smoothed his collar. It was evening, and the *piazzetta* was filled with couples browsing in boutique windows. Sports cars idled on the pavement, and the air smelled of imported cigars.

Lily Bristol's grand opening had been a huge success. Lily flitted around the space, filling champagne flutes and making sure no one ran out of canapés. The cash register rang all afternoon, and by the time she turned the sign to *Chiuso*, they were both exhausted.

Now he approached the entrance of Nero's and searched the sidewalk. Lily said she would meet him there, but he couldn't see her. There was a line out the door, and a valet juggled keys to Lamborghinis.

Perhaps Lily had decided to stay in the suite and go to bed early. He checked his phone and wondered why he felt nervous. It wasn't a date; they were just going to sit across from each other at dinner.

The line parted, and Oliver noticed a woman wearing a silver taffeta gown. Her dark hair was tucked behind her ears and she carried a velvet clutch.

"There you are." Oliver bounded up the steps. "I thought you weren't coming."

"I'm not sure this was a good idea." Lily patted her hair. "Everyone is under thirty, and I've never seen so many sequins."

Oliver glanced at the crowd and noticed women with straight blond hair and bronze skin. The men wore linen blazers and held gold cigarette cases.

"You're the most beautiful woman here." He took her arm. "And we came for the food. The chef is famous for his lobster risotto, and the pistachio sorbet is the best in Sardinia."

Oliver opened the double glass doors and led Lily inside. The restaurant had a pink marble floor and upholstered chairs. Tables were set with bone-white china, and floor-to-ceiling windows opened onto a garden.

"It's lovely," Lily breathed. "It's like eating in someone's private mansion."

"No wonder it's called Nero's." Oliver consulted the menu. "Thirty euros for ham and cheese antipasto! The owners are making a fortune."

"It does seem expensive." Lily glanced at the prices. "Maybe we should split an entrée."

"Don't be silly, that's why I have an expense account." He signaled the waiter. "We're going to order their finest champagne. We have a lot to celebrate."

"I don't know what we're celebrating." She took a sip of water. "Your fiancée lied about being pregnant. And the man I was falling in love with was only interested in immigration."

"Angela wasn't my fiancée. I didn't formally propose." He winced. "And I never trusted Ricky; he was much too good-looking."

"There's nothing wrong with being attractive." She laughed.

"You're right." He paused. "You look beautiful tonight. In some ways, you're exactly the same as when we met in Naples. And in other ways, you're completely different."

"In what ways?" she asked.

"You're poised and successful, but most importantly, you're comfortable with yourself," he mused. "I hope Louisa turns out to be just like you."

"All I want to do is go home and make peanut butter and jelly sandwiches." She sighed. "I love the Emerald Coast, but the gleaming yachts and glamorous people get exhausting."

"Do you remember when we stayed at the Hotel Baglioni for Lily Brisol Milan's grand opening?" he asked. "I was so upset that your parents paid for our suite, I couldn't enjoy it. Your mother thought I would never amount to anything, and all I could see was what was wrong.

"If only I knew how good we had it. Eating dinner at a Michelin-starred restaurant and visiting Milan Cathedral. Going back to our suite and making love on linen sheets."

"You worried about everything, and none of it was important." Lily looked up, and her eyes were liquid gold. "Did I tell you Roger is getting married? My mother wrote to me. His fiancée is from Houston, and they're having a reception at the Fairmont."

"Mirabelle is selling her restaurant and moving to Chicago," he commented. "She's opening a fusion restaurant with several partners."

"That sounds exciting," she said stiffly. "Tell her congratulations."

"I haven't seen her." He shrugged. "I read about it in the *New Yorker*."

The waiter poured glasses of champagne, and Oliver watched bubbles float to the rim. Suddenly, he stood up and held out his hand.

"Will you dance with me?" he asked.

"I'm much too tired, and there's no room to dance." She glanced around the cramped space.

"We'll dance in the garden," he insisted. "It's good to get fresh air before a meal. It improves the palate."

"I could use some air," Lily conceded, sipping her champagne. "All right, one dance."

He led her into the garden and put his arm around her. She rested her head on his shoulder, and the air smelled of citrus. Lights twinkled in orange trees, and Oliver did what he'd thought he would never get to do again.

He tipped her face up to his and kissed her.

They ate braised goat and sorbet with berries for dessert. After dinner, they strolled along the harbor and admired the yachts. Oliver took Lily's hand, and she didn't tell him to let it go.

Now they stood in the hotel hallway, and Lily took out her key.

"I'm so tired. I'm afraid I'll sleep in and miss my flight," she said. "I can never set my alarm with a twenty-four-hour clock. I always mix up the AM and PM."

"Ask the concierge to send you a wake-up call," he suggested.

"That doesn't help, I stuff the phone under my pillow." She laughed. "I need something buzzing in my ear."

"I'll set it for you." Oliver took her key and opened the door. "It will only take a minute."

He entered the suite's bedroom and perched on the bed. He fiddled with the clock and placed it on the bedside table.

"You're all set." He stood up.

Lily dropped her earring on the dresser and walked over to Oliver.

"Thank you for dinner, I had a lovely time." She reached up and kissed him.

Her mouth was warm, and he kissed her back. He drew her close and ran his hands down her back. She smelled exactly as he remembered, of lavender shampoo and some kind of floral perfume.

"I've never wanted anything more than to take off that taffeta gown and kiss your bare shoulders," he said. "But I couldn't forgive myself if I took advantage of you when you drank too much champagne."

Lily dropped her other earring on the bedside table and unzipped her dress. It fell to the floor and she unhooked her bra.

"I'm not the least bit drunk," she assured him. "And there's nothing I want more."

He kissed her collarbone and slipped his hand under her panties. Her eyes flickered, and she let out a small moan.

"I love you and promise I'll never hurt you," he whispered.

"I love you too, Oliver," she murmured and pulled him down on the bed.

Everything was sweet and familiar: the curve of her stomach and the mole on her thigh and the way she whispered his name.

Their bodies rocked together, and he had to hold himself back. Then she wrapped her arms around him, and they moved faster, and he came with an incredible force.

Oliver slipped on a robe and poured a glass of water. Lily had fallen asleep, but he was suddenly thirsty. Child-sized pink sandals sat in a box, and he thought they would look lovely on Louisa. He sipped the water and climbed back into bed. For one moment, he had everything he wanted.

Chapter Fifteen

LILY ZIPPED UP HER SUITCASE and checked her purse for her passport. Oliver was gone when she woke up, and now she had to hurry. Her plane left in two hours, and she still had to call a taxi and drive to Olbia Airport.

There was a knock at the door, and Lily answered it.

"Oh, Enzo! It's wonderful to see you. I wanted to show you photos of the grand opening, but now I don't have time." She ushered him inside. "And I forgot to ask the concierge to call a taxi. Would you mind calling them and taking down my suitcase? I overslept and I'm afraid I'll miss my plane."

"A taxi is already waiting downstairs. I checked your flight information, and your flight has been delayed an hour," Enzo said. "You have plenty of time. I also delivered the jewelry box to Ricky." He handed her an envelope. "He sent you a note."

"I'll read it later." She dropped it into her purse. "I'm sorry I'm so rushed. I'll send you a text and tell you everything that happened when I board the plane. The opening of Lily Bristol was a huge success. I wish you had been there, you would have been pleased." She paused, and her eyes glistened. "I don't know what

I would have done without you. You listened and never judged me. That's the trait of a real friend."

"I have enjoyed our time together very much." He beamed. "You are a beautiful young American divorcée. Any man on the Emerald Coast is lucky to be in your company."

"I'll come back next year with Louisa, and you should bring your wife and daughters to New York," she urged. "Louisa would love to show them Coney Island and the Museum of Natural History and Dylan's Candy Bar."

"It would be our pleasure." He picked up the suitcase. "Carmella has always wanted to see the Statue of Liberty."

"There's one thing you have to promise to do if you come," she said.

"What's that?" he asked.

A smile spread across her face and she chuckled. "You have to promise to call me Lily."

There was another knock on the door, and Lily opened it. Oliver stood in the hallway. His cheeks were lathered with shaving cream, and he clutched a razor.

"I was standing on the balcony and saw your suitcases being loaded into a taxi." He entered the suite. "You weren't going to leave without telling me!"

"Put the razor down, Oliver. You're making me nervous." She followed him. "And I was about to leave. I overslept and don't want to miss my flight."

"That was one of the best nights of my life," he protested. "You can't get on a plane without saying good-bye."

"We'll see each other when you pick up Louisa next Saturday." She shrugged.

"I don't want to see you every other weekend," he spluttered. "I'm still in love with you and thought we'd be together."

"We can't be together," she reminded him. "We're divorced."

"We'll get un-divorced or live in sin." He waved his hand. "I don't care what we do, as long as we share a room."

"We can't jump back into a relationship, it's not fair to Louisa," she answered. "We don't want her to think marriage is like the revolving door at Bloomingdale's. And just because we had a wonderful night, doesn't mean we've learned to trust each other." She looked at Oliver. "I don't know if I can go through all that again."

"But you're the one who said you only want to be happy," he pleaded. "You were happy last night."

"We're adults now. Being happy isn't enough. We have to feel secure and think about our future."

"At least, let's talk about it," he insisted. "People spend their whole lives searching for that kind of chemistry. We've had it since the moment I saw you at the train station in Naples. We've been given another chance. It would be criminal to throw it away."

"I can't talk about it now." She looked at Oliver. "We hurt each other so much. We tried so hard, and it only got worse. It would be the same thing all over again."

"Let's see a counselor or go on a couples retreat," he urged. "One of those places where they don't let you bring cell phones, and you learn to appreciate the taste of a mango."

"We've been to a therapist, and we don't need anyone to tell us how fruit tastes." She took a deep breath. "I'm very sorry. But I don't think it's going to work."

"Are you sure?" He looked like a boy who traded his last *Star Wars* card. "At least think about it."

"All right, I'll think about it." She touched his cheek. "Enjoy your last day on the Emerald Coast. I'll see you soon."

Lily stepped into the taxi and slipped on her sunglasses. There was a spot of shaving cream on her finger, and she rubbed it on her palm.

Last night had been wonderful, and she did have feelings for Oliver. But she was a career woman and a single mother; she had to be responsible. She couldn't change her direction because her heart fluttered and there was a warmth in her chest.

Someone knocked on the car window, and Lily looked up. Oliver stood on the curb. His feet were bare, and he held something in his hand.

She rolled down the window and wondered if he was going to ask to come with her.

"What is it, Oliver?" she asked, and for some reason her heart raced.

"You forgot your credit cards." He handed her a leather wallet.

"Thank you," she answered and burst out laughing.

"What's so funny?" he demanded. "You wouldn't be laughing if you arrived at the airport without your credit cards."

"You still have shaving cream on your cheeks." She giggled. "You look like Santa Claus."

"Is that better?" He wiped his cheeks. "Will you have lunch with me on Friday? I'll drive up to Connecticut, and we'll go to that inn on Main Street."

"I'd like that." She nodded. "I'll see you then. Have a safe trip."

The taxi pulled away, and the bay spread out before her. The sea was the color of emeralds, and the air smelled of the sweetest perfume. She leaned back on the seat and was so happy.

Acknowledgments

This is a special book to me, and I want to thank my wonderful agent, Melissa Flashman, and my fabulous editor, Lauren Jablonski, for making it all possible. Thank you to my amazing team at St. Martin's Press: my publicist, Brittani Hilles; my marketing person, Karen Masnica; Brant Janeway; Jennifer Enderlin; and Jennifer Weis.

Sometimes it's not enough to thank individual friends; it's important to thank a whole community. A huge thank-you to the educators and parents at St. Margaret's Episcopal School, particularly Tony Jordan, Phoebe Larson, and Will Mosley for taking such great care of my children. Thank you to Jessica Parr, Sara Sullivan, and Cathie Lawler for really being there. And thank you to my children, Alex, Andrew, Heather, Madeleine, and Thomas, for being everything in the world to me.

1. How do you feel about Lily asking Enzo to find her a man because Oliver is staying in the next room with his new girlfriend? Would you do the same thing in Lily's situation or would you try to be happy alone?

2. Do you think Lily and Oliver tried to keep their marriage together for too long or not long enough? If the same things happened in your marriage, would you try to keep it going or end it?

3. Do you believe there is a real connection between Lily and Ricky or do you think Lily is being swept up in a holiday romance? Give examples to support your position.

4. Oliver obviously loves Lily, but he's made some bad mistakes. How do you feel about Oliver? Do you find him to be a sympathetic character? Why or why not?

5. Do you think Lily's mother should take some of the blame for Lily and Oliver's problems? Have you encountered someone like that in your romantic relationships, and how did you handle him or her?

6. Angela is an interesting blend of a focused career woman and someone who wants a husband and family. What are your thoughts on Angela? Do you think Oliver overreacted to what she did?

7. The Emerald Coast of Sardinia is a dream destination with gorgeous beaches and glamorous yachts. What is your idea of the perfect destination, and what do you look for when you are planning a trip?

St. Martin's
Griffin

8. Ricky is handsome and charismatic, and it is easy to see why Lily fell for him. Do you think he really had feelings for Lily? Why or why not?

9. What are your thoughts about the ending? Could you picture a different ending, and if so what would it be?

10. Imagine the story picking up six months later. Where would Lily and Oliver be and what would be happening?